Martini Mystery

Marci Darling

HOUSE OF MARTINI

Martini Mystery

Martini Mystery
A House of Martini Paperback Book
House of Martini edition/September 2016

Cover Design
Cover Art 2015 © Paul Dexter Inigo
Formatting by Rik: Wild Seas Formatting
(http://WildSeasFormatting.com)

ISBN 978-0-9981362-0-2
Ebook ISBN 978-0-9981362-1-9

Library of Congress Control Number: 2016917723

Table of Contents

To George, Annabelle, and Henry
and our magical years in New Orleans

Prologue

Something smashes to the floor and I hear a skitter. Please don't let that be a rodent. Please oh please! If a rat comes near me I will not be able to stay in hiding, I don't care how many murderers there are running around this attic. Fucking footsteps! And not just regular footsteps but the scariest kind: limp-drag footsteps. Maybe I injured him with my stomp.

I realize the sharp heels of my Louboutins make an excellent weapon and I silently slide them off. They catch a moonbeam and sparkle, like the most beautiful north star. I make a quick silent wish: 'please let me get out of here alive'. I re-adjust them in both hands for full-force. Wouldn't that be cool if there were little daggers in these heels? Or tiny derringers in the heels? And everyone said I was a fool for buying $5,000 shoes! Ha! My heart is pounding right out of my ribcage, no easy feat in this tight-ass corset. Breathe, Ellington.

These bastards have no idea who they are dealing with. They think I'm some soft cream puff they can easily squash but they have another thing coming. I hear footsteps getting closer and closer. I take a deep breath. OK I admit it – I'm scared. But no fear! I feel my strength gathering as I picture myself stepping out from behind this cabinet in full sparkling, nunchuck glory. My spinning shoes would blind the villains with their dazzle. I'm like that crouched golden panther from Cartier stalking its prey.

Damn I wish I had a swirling cape I could disappear into right now. But I don't. So here goes.

Chapter 1

Jazz Martini

Vodka, Lemon-coated Glass

Perpetuating illusions is one of my specialties, which you would know if you could see my costume closet. It's full of my exquisite collection from my showgirl days, and since moving to New Orleans, I've added all sorts of new ensembles. My current favorites are my ladybug costume complete with wings and a polka dotted tutu; my steampunk Victorian ghost costume with a corset, bustle and goggles; my peacock tutu with massive feathered fans; and of course my ever-expanding collection of top hats. I even have a few unitards from my days in the circus, but honestly, unitards were never a good look on my juicy hourglass figure. Come to think of it, I'm not exactly sure who a unitard looks good on—not only does it leave little to the imagination regarding the nooks and crannies of the human body, but it highlights areas of the body that are better left…how shall I say…to the imagination.

I'm sitting at my antique mahogany vanity listening to "Horn Man Blues" by Dr. Micheal White. I'm letting it work its alchemical wonder, making me feel slinky and I slowly lower one side of my silk robe to reveal one bare shoulder. I pretend

I'm onstage dancing, climbing the steps into a giant champagne glass for a bubble bath

. For years I was highly paid to be half of a contortionist burlesque duet. We called ourselves the Daring Duo of Delight and we were flown around the world to perform and yet, I am not, nor have I ever been, a contortionist. I called myself a 'contortionist illusionist', and I would balance my partner on my foot while she twisted herself into a pretzel. People loved our act but it was never clear exactly what I did. "You're the straight man!" Lady Lola said. She was the Oyster Girl and the director of our burlesque show. In her act, she emerged out of a giant oyster and played with a beach-ball-sized pearl—dreamy! She'd say, "You're Dean Martin and she's Jerry Lewis." Okay, I guess in that equation I'd rather be Deano. Although I would never want to be a man with all that boring clothing and those scratchy whiskers. Unless of course they were cat whiskers—now those, I would like. Although my Grandmother had a few cat whiskers and they weren't cute so maybe, nix the whiskers. Although I have always wanted a fluffy tail.

I turn sideways in my mirror to see what I'd look like with a waving fluffy tail when I notice the time. I have been messing with my hair for the better part of an hour, but finally, even with the intoxicating music, it becomes clear to me that my hair is choosing its own disagreeable path today, a path called 'there's too much humidity so I shall deceive the world into thinking you have stuck your finger into an electric socket today.'

I sigh and pull it back, clipping a luscious blonde ponytail up high on my head, long waves cascading around my bare shoulders. I don a Trashy Diva dress, my black and ivory silk-velvet Garbo coat, and then I carefully take down a velvet bag from a high shelf and slowly unwrap the crème de la crème of all accessories: my vintage Hermes Kelly Handbag in rouge. It's so beautiful I want to climb inside and roll around like a panda in a bamboo forest. The red leather gleams as I admire the handmade artisanal craftsmanship of the stitching. I don't usually like Hermes — it's too stifling and something about it makes me feel like tap dancing on their stuffy glass cases. But vintage Hermes, with its exquisite hand-sewn saddle stitches — I'll take it. Especially the Kelly, and not just because I adore its namesake, Grace. I saunter back and forth in front of my mirror to see how it looks hanging on my arm. It's stunning and makes me look like an older, wiser, curvier, trashier Grace Kelly. Perfect.

I walk outside to meet my lover, who is picking me up after a day of teaching at the University. He's my husband too, but that sounds so mundane: *husband*. I prefer lover. My lover is a sexy cliché, tall, dark, and handsome as they come. He's smart, funny, with messy dark hair and thick black glasses — exactly what I would order if I visited an ice cream shop where you could order up your dream fantasy. He is a bit of a curmudgeon, but I just ignore the grouchy parts and focus on the nice parts. He walks up the brick steps to our porch and smiles at me, my favorite kind of smile, the one that is a mixture of adoration, and awe.

"You look beautiful," he says. "I love your hair."

I smile back and say, "Thank you." But I'm a little worried. Does he think this hairpiece is my real hair? He is a bit absent-minded, yes, he's a professor, but honestly, we've been together for nearly ten years, married for five of them. He sees me every day. Hasn't he noticed that my normal hair is not long and curly but swings in a sassy bob around my chin? In any case, I'm not going to burst his bubble. I have a firm rule about never pointing out my flaws to my lover. When he guesses I'm a size two when I'm really a size ten, I don't correct him. I just smile and pat his hand and move the conversation onto other things.

He smiles when he sees my handbag. "You're wearing it." I parade back and forth so he can really see it's magnificent color shimmering in the light. Winston *loves* Hermes. It appeals to his stuffy side. But for me, the Kelly bag transports me straight into the glamour of *To Catch a Thief, Rear Window,* and *Pillow Talk.*

We are off to date night at my favorite restaurant, Crepe Nanou. Dark, red, and dripping with romance, Crepe Nanou is an ex-showgirl's dream place. Instead of paintings on the wall, they have frames that look like tiny theaters complete with velvet curtains and tassel cords. Inside the frames are vintage photos of dancers. The red wine flows freely and Edith Piaf plays over the din of people talking. It is the perfect place for Bohemian Night with drunken poetry and gasping epiphanies and intellectual debate peppered with laughter.

But tonight is Date Night and not Bohemian Night, which means there will be drunken declarations of undying love, maybe a little footsie under the table, and that sparkly sense of falling head over Chanel heels in love over and over again. Winston is gazing at me with tears in his eyes. He softly sings a couple of lines from a song he wrote for me, "When I first saw you there, starlight all around. And you, you brighten the corners."

I love it when he sings to me in his deep sonorous voice. This is my favorite part of our wine-filled dinners together—his drunken rhapsodies of love. I have ordered my favorite entrée, Crepe Oignon Fromage—a crepe with carmelized onions covered in melted swiss cheese, with little roasted potatoes that melt in your mouth. Every bite is a little taste of ecstasy. I'm just pondering the true meaning of ecstasy when our dandelion-puff-of-a-waitress comes over to refill our wine glasses. She looks so transparent and thin and gentle, she might fall apart if I blow in her direction. But then I see her arm as she leans over to pour my red wine.

She has the word "CALAMITY" tattooed in large capital letters down her forearm. She smiles shyly at me and floats away. I have to wonder what has occurred in this girls' life that would make her want to tattoo CALAMITY on her forearm?

But then Winston pulls me out of my reverie by dropping

the bomb, the big one, the one that will reset the course of our lives forever.

"Oh, I forgot. I found this on our porch today," he says, fumbling in his pocket with one hand while holding a glass of wine in the other hand. He finally pulls the mystery object out of his pocket and lays it on the table. It is an envelope, but not just any envelope. It is a *beautiful* envelope—orange and red and pink, like tongues of fire lapping at me. I pick it up, admiring the way my short red nails look against the colors of the envelope. I turn the envelope over and it has a heavy wax seal on the back. It's a golden seal, bearing one regal letter—R. I run my finger over the rough wax, wondering if it was a ring or a stamp that was pressed into the hot wax. I happen to be a connoisseur of fine letter writing, which of course involves pens with plumes, velvet smoking jackets, and hot wax. I have a gorgeous stamp to imprint the wax. It says "M" for Martini and instead of being surrounded by flowers or cherubs, the letter has a tiny martini glass in one corner. Very sophisticated if I do say so myself. Even though I'm not a sophisticated person. Too much pressure.

Even with my wandering mind, I'm awestruck. "Is this what I think it is?" I ask Winston.

Winston smiles at me like a pirate surveying his booty. He has taken off his tie and unbuttoned the top buttons of his white shirt, his beautiful neck and chest taunting me. He leans back and stretches out long legs, one arm draped across the back of his chair. He lifts his glass to me with another toast— the man loves his toasts.

"Wine goes in at the mouth, love goes in at the eye; these may be the only truths we know until we grow old and die...I lift the glass to my mouth, I look at you and sigh." He downs the rest of his wine glass and signals Calamity-Dandelion-Puff for another bottle.

I do love it when he quotes Yeats—but I'm a little preoccupied with the envelope. If I was a more careful person, I would have opened the envelope with care, but I'm not, so I tear it open. Inside is a stunning card showing flames leaping around the edges and inside are women, their heads thrown back in anguish or ecstasy—it's hard to tell which. They're either getting burned or dancing with glee amongst the flames. I gasp at the beauty and whisper, "A royal invitation, it's just like a fairy tale..." I read aloud from the golden letters, shimmering in the candlelight. "Rex invites you to its royal ball, Fables of Fire and Flame, on Mardi Gras night. Please come in proper attire—floor-length gowns with full-length evening gloves in white for the ladies and tuxedos for the gentlemen. Blahblahblah! "Oh yes!" I say. I fist-pump the air. I know it's not graceful, but I can't help myself. "I have always wanted to attend a ball! A real ball!" Visions dance in my head of a gorgeous shimmering dress—like the one Deborah Kerr wore in *The King and I* when she danced with Yul Brynner, the one that looked like liquid silver the way it shimmered under the lights. I have always dreamed about wearing a dress like that! "How did we get this?" I ask Winston breathlessly.

"You know it's all a secret," he answers, looking more like a pirate every second in the flickering candlelight. "No one knows who invited who... the invitation just appears on the porch one day."

"I have been waiting for this for years you know," I say. I can feel my cheeks getting hot with excitement, or maybe too much wine. I have always wanted to set one of my romance novels at a Mardi Gras ball, but to describe it properly I need to smell it, touch it, hear it, dance in it. I tap the invitation. "This could be my chance to really deepen my writing. Few people outside New Orleans know about the ball subculture here."

"You mean the class system that consists of rich, old, white people who all agree to create their own form of temporary royalty?"

"Winston, it is considered a great honor to be chosen as a king or queen of the "balls"."

"Yeah, a great honor by other white-bread people, but not

by anyone else. It's not like it's an actual accomplishment."

"What about Marquessa Gigi? She was anointed a title by other non-royal people."

"Gary was anointed Marquessa Gigi for his, or her, work in the LGBT community. *That is* an accomplishment."

"Yes, well it's all just make-believe, isn't it?"

"I'm just glad you're not a Count," he interrupts me, sipping his wine.

"Winston! Stop yourself." He's talking about my showgirl days when we all gave ourselves royal "performer" names and sometimes the worlds would intersect, like when I went to rent a movie on my roommate's account at the local video store. The tall, doughy clerk said "Katie's account?" and I answered, with a disbelieving smirk, "Katie's not a Count." The clerk stared at me and said, "Katie's account." I tilted my head and said, "Um, no, Katie's *not* a Count." I couldn't figure out how the clerk knew about our titles, and why on earth he was hellbent on calling Katie a Count. I sighed and explained, "Are you thinking of Valerie? Valerie is a *Countess*, Eva is an Empress, Katie is a Queen... there is no Count." At this point I was thinking this guy was a few sandwiches short of a picnic. Counts are males, not females and there were no males in my performing group.

He dropped his head in his hands and shook it slowly saying, "Please don't do this to me. I've been here since nine this morning." Now he said in slow motion with exaggerated consonants, like he was talking to my ninety-five-year old grandmother. "Katie's account." And it finally clicked.

"Oh! Katie's account! Yes! Of course!" I'm not sure I've ever blushed so deeply. Goodness. Winston loves this story and brings it up at every opportunity.

With all this talk of royalty, I suddenly feel very posh and formal and my tone becomes crisper with every word. "Remember visiting the Flemings? Remember those massive oil paintings of both of them in full royal wear? Milton was wearing a red velvet cloak trimmed in fur with a crown and a scepter, and they had a huge glass case in their entryway with their royal doodads."

"Is that the official name for royal accoutrements? Doodads?" ?

I ignore him. "And it was triple-locked, like they were afraid the pink panther might rappel down from the ceiling and steal them."

"Sad, like people who can't let go of their glory years on the high school football team."

"Sad?" I ask, raising one arched brow. "Or brilliant?"

Winston puts his elbow on the table and rests his chin in his hand. "Why are you suddenly speaking with an English accent?"

"I think it's brilliant. Everyone here agrees to suspend disbelief and cynicism to buy into this fantasy that these balls mean something, that the capes and beads are worth something, even though we all know they're not. New Orleans is like Neverland—no one ever grows up."

"You fit in perfectly."

"So do you, Mr. Poppycock. There's a rest home around the corner for hot men who choose to act like old fuddy-duddys."

"Your vocabulary is colorful tonight."

"I'm practicing inserting words from the 1920's into my daily vernacular. I'm working on a romantic story set among the speakeasies of the Prohibition era. There will be many hootenannys."

"That's a good one," he says, laughing.

Calamity Dandelion Puff interrupts us to refill our glasses and when she sees the invitation in my hand, she says, "Is that what I think it is?"

I nod gleefully.

"May I see it up close?"

I hold it up for her—no way am I going to let her hold it. She bends over to look closer, her hands on her knees.

She whistles low and soft. "It's beautiful. I collect Mardi

Gras Ball invitations, they're works of art you know. I have a couple from the 1800's."

"Have you ever been to one? What's it like?"

She laughs. "No. I wish. I've been here since I was eight years old and never got an invitation. Someday, maybe." She floats away and I raise and lower my eyebrows at Winston, "Told you so."

I hug the invitation to my chest. "This is perfect for my new article for New Orleans Magazine. They asked me to write on the best cocktails in the city, focusing on Bloody Marys and vintage cocktails. The balls always have some signature historical cocktail that is hard to find anywhere else so I'll have the scoop firsthand."

"Now *that's* an article I will help you research." Winston studies cocktail culture like a top scholar, studying the history, collecting retro martini shakers and different shaped glasses.

"Good, I'll need your expertise. New Orleans takes its cocktails as seriously as Paris takes its museums."

"True. They have raised the level of mixology. Now that's something I can drink to." He lifts his glass and we clink.

My body is humming with excitement. "This is amazing. You know I have really wanted to sink my teeth into something other than my usual romance novels, something that has the potential to surprise me, like a cream puff—that secret inner life—the rich creamy explosion in my mouth..."

He narrows his eyes at me in a smoldering way. "I have something that could explode in your mouth..."

I laugh and flick my napkin at him. "The Mardi Gras balls are so secretive. They have awesome 'secret inner life' potential."

"I've heard they can be boring and last about eight hours."

"Eight hours in a stunning ballgown, dreamy."

"Eight hours in a penguin suit, nightmare."

"I can't wait to see for myself. We need to find out what goes on at these balls. Just imagine, someday we can tell our grandchildren about it." I clap my hand to my cheek. "What will I wear? It has to be the dress to end all dresses. Shimmering or fluffy? Poufy like Deborah Kerr or silky streamlined like Jean Harlow?" Did I say that out loud? Winston is not usually privy to my fashion meanderings—I don't want him to think I'm shallow. Although if he hasn't determined my depths and shallows by now, our future looks bleak. "Oh I can't wait!" I take one last loving glance at the invitation before tenderly sliding it back into its envelope and into my Kelly. "Winston, inspiration has struck. If I set my next novel at this ball I can write off my ballgown and accoutrements." Winston glances at me sharply, breaking into my reverie with that look I hate, the look that asks, 'How much money do you intend to spend?' But I ignore his boring puritan frugality and float back into my reverie.

"Little ol' me, an imported Yankee, off to my first ball." I sigh happily. "I may be Yankee in origin, but my heart has been stolen by New Orleans."

Winston looks more and more like a hot pirate. I stand up and move behind his chair. I tilt his head back and kiss him upside down, sliding my hands down his neck, driving myself wild. He pulls my head down to kiss me even deeper. "Winston," I say, now that I'm feeling ignited, "let's take that wine home. I'm going to give you a dessert you'll never forget."

"Let's go," he says, his deep voice making my blood feel like warm honey pouring through my veins. We pay the check, grab my bag, and head out to the car.

I stop. "Winston, Winston, Winston, hold up." He stops and I dig in my handbag for the invitation. "Wait, did you ever hear that sometimes there are secret messages written on the back of the invitations in invisible ink?"

"No, why would they do that? How the hell would anyone read it?"

"Blacklight of course."

"Where in the hell does anyone find a blacklight? We

don't have a blacklight."

"Yes, but I know who does." He looks at me, waiting. "Walter at the Napoleon House."

"Why the hell would a historical bar from the 1800's have a blacklight?"

"I don't know, but the other night they marked my hand with one for the open bar. Let's go!"

"Now? Are you kidding? I thought we were heading home?" He puts his hand around my back and firmly pulls me close for another long deep kiss. I gasp because it feels damn good, and hot. I can feel my body surrendering even as my mind is off and running through the forests of secret messages.

I whisper, my lips against his ear. "The sweet, sweet torture of desire will only build as you drink a Sazerac and I uncover the secret message.

"Ellington, I am moderating an *important* panel in the morning, a huge panel that is critical to the University funding. I don't have time to go to the Napoleon."

"I'll make it worth your while." I purr, sliding my hand down his hips. There's not a snowball's chance in hell I'm not finding that secret message tonight. I march to the car.

Winston heaves a huge sigh and walks to the car with an exaggerated, slump posture. He knows there's no talking me out of it, panels be damned.

"There better be a damn good invisible message on that thing."

Chapter 2

El Diablo

Lime Juice, Tequila, Crème De Cassis, Ginger Ale

It's an unusually cool night and I push the button to turn on my seat warmer, allowing the warmth to enfold me like an enormous pair of feather burlesque fans. "Mmmmmm," I say as I sink down further and reach a hand over to massage Winston's thighs. "I'm thinking after we go to the Napoleon we can duck into a cobblestone alleyway for some wild sex. But wait, I want you to wear a top hat. Where can we find you a top hat at this hour?" I imagine Winston striding down Royal Street in riding boots, top hat, a cane, and a gorgeous cape swirling behind him. In my fantasy the Quarter is lit by flickering lanterns and it smells like flowers - not vomit or sewage as it so often does. "It sounds unbelievably erotic to make love to you in a top hat right now."

Winston laughs. "I'm not wearing a top hat, even if we could find one at this hour, and I have no doubt that you could. And before you ask, I'm not wearing a cape either."

Damn it! He knows me too well.

"Also," he continues, "The alleyway sounds a little uncomfortable and a lot dangerous."

Now it's my turn to sigh. Oh Winston, always being logical. He's right of course. The alleyways of the Quarter are known for the scoundrels who lurk there. I pull out the invitation and study every inch to see if I can make anything out. "Winston, has the thought occurred to you that the secret message on this invitation might be specific to us. What if they want us in the tableau thing? Maybe they want me to be some sort of fiery greek goddess? Or queen? You know the balls usually have a mythological theme." I gasp and grab his arm. "What if they crown me queen?"

"Ellington..." Winston says with a deep breath.

I interrupt him before he can finish, "If you don't believe in magic, it will never happen to you." I pull down the sunshade mirror to reapply my deep red lipstick, Dark Side.

Winston turns up the music and Billie Holiday's mood-spinning voice gently cups my soul in the palm of its hand and soothes me, like a baby bird in a nest. We are passing the most beautiful mansions on St. Charles with their columns and fountains and enormous front doors. One of my favorites looks like a wedding cake house, and I can't help thinking what a waste to have these mansions inhabited by one family. They would make the most beautiful schools.

I am thinking about screaming and laughing children sliding down spiral staircases on the banisters when we pull up in front of the Napoleon House on Chartres Street. New Orleans' first mayor, Nicholas Girod, lived here in 1812, and I wonder if *I* could ever run for mayor. The first thing I would do is turn a few mansions on St. Charles into schools, then I would make a ban on black umbrellas. Colors like fuchsia, tangerine, and turquoise are required to spread cheer on gray days, although I'm sure Nicholas Girod could have cared less about umbrellas back in the 1800's—he was too busy concocting schemes to rescue Napoleon from exile. I wonder how New Orleans would be different had the Little Emperor had actually made it here.

Winston and I enter the bar in all its tattered and

charming glory. The walls are dark and peeling and the brick shows under the plaster. There are several portraits and busts of the Napoleon here and there, and the bar dominates the entire front room. There are a few tables in the front but we sit at the bar. I ask the bartender if Walter, the maître'd, is here tonight.

The bartender is wearing a white shirt, plaid vest, and bowler hat over his slicked hair. He has groomed his moustache into Dali-esque points and little gold spectacles sit perched on his considerable nose. "Back there," he says, pointing over his shoulder. Winston sits at the bar while I search for Walter. I walk through the bar and into the next room. It opens up into a succulent open-air courtyard with tinkling fountains and overgrown palm trees. One fountain on the wall is Bacchus, the Greek God of wine and pleasure, spitting water out of his mouth into a little pool like he's blowing raspberries on everything somber. He's a perfect mascot for the Quarter, and for my own life.

I don't see Walter and I'm thinking I should duck under the velvet rope and head upstairs to the glamorous second floor to track him down. Bacchus seems to be encouraging me. There's a sign saying, "Do Not Enter. Reserved for Private Party." I'm tempted, I'm dying to know what's on my invitation, but I finally decide to behave and head back to the bar.

When I return to our rickety barstools, Winston has ordered us Sazeracs.

"Did you know the Sazerac was the first cocktail ever invented in America?" he asks.

"I thought that was up for debate?" I say, sliding onto a stool.

"Only by cocktail amateurs. Where else would the first American cocktail be invented? It has to be New Orleans."

"Remember the cocktail party we went to upstairs? The sweeping staircase and those ornate chandeliers?" I ask him, taking a sip followed by a nibble on his ear.

"Yeah, for the new Dean."

"Imagine if Napoleon had actually made it here. Maybe he would have slept up there. I read a book once claiming that Napoleon was slowly poisoned on Elba. They found boatloads of arsenic in his hair after he died. Did you ever hear that theory?"

Winston tilts his head. "I heard that, yes, but I thought it was *traces* of arsenic?"

I shake my head. "Nope, *boatloads*, and did you know that there is a legend that there was a jewel on the necklace of Aphrodite, and it fell into the sea and became Elba."

"Elba?"

"That's the island where the Napoleon was exiled. I went there when I was backpacking. I mean, if I ever get exiled, send me to Elba! It's gorgeous!"

Winston takes a long sip of his drink and puts his arm around me and squeezes. "Man I love this bar."

I am so happy he's getting caught up in the ambience of the Quarter, although he'll deny it. Winston does not like it down here. He sees the drunks and crazies roaming the streets and thinks it's uncivilized. He's more comfortable in the lounge at the Ritz full of clean people acting "appropriate." There's a lot of inappropriate behavior in the Quarter.

I, however, will take the wild French Quarter over civility any day. I'm very comfortable in chaos and noise, probably because of my noisy childhood—how could it be anything *but* with five brothers and sisters? I ask the bartender again, "Do you think Walter will come out soon? I'm hoping to borrow his blacklight, unless you happen to have one behind the bar?"

"I don't have one, but let me check on him."

While I'm waiting, I open my adorable Kelly and take out our Rex invitation, running my fingers over the raised golden script. "It looks like an illuminated manuscript from medieval times," I whisper, tilting the card so Winston can see the raised golden letters and admire the craftsmanship. My reverie is enhanced when the sound of bagpipes in the distance enters the bar. All heads swivel to the window to see where the sound is coming from. As it grows louder, it is accompanied by low humming. A line of flickering torches outside the door shows up, and the humming gets louder, turning into the full-blown Gregorian chants. The ambience is so thick and medieval right now, I feel submerged in an alternate reality where past and present merge into one. It's like spelunking in a time cave.

"Ooooh, what if this invitation was an actual portal and we were catapulted back in time?"

"Feels like we might be," Winston says, looking out the window. "What the hell is going on outside?"

The doors of the Napoleon House are open and from our barstools we see a line of flambeaux torchbearers parading down Chartres street. Flambeaux is a beloved Mardi Gras tradition created for the first parade to light the route. It's wonderfully eerie and primal and romantic to see these sweating men wearing leather belts holding the weight of massive torches, some bouncing and spinning them while they light up the night.

The flambeaux carriers are preceded by a beautiful young woman on a large horse wearing a white flowing robe, a crown of flowers in her hair, and carrying a very long sword.

"Ahhhh, it's the Joan of Arc parade."

Winston looks puzzled, so I say, "A few years ago a New Orleanian realized that Joan of Arc's birthday fell on the same day as the Epiphany, which is tonight, the official Mardi Gras kick-off. The Epiphany is always twelve days after Christmas so it always falls on January 6."

"The Epiphany and Twelfth Night are the same day?"

"Yes and because New Orleans is the sister city to Orleans, France, someone invented the Joan of Arc parade. It's a newer parade but still really popular."

The flambeaux carriers are followed by a large group of men and women wearing the traditional medieval robes of monks and nuns. They carry candles and have solemn faces. They are followed by another woman on a horse, this time dressed as Joan the prisoner. There are other riders dressed in armor carrying billowing medieval flags and swords. "There's something very austere and beautiful about this parade, even though it's actually a decadent indulgence of someone's historical fascination."

Winston and I walk out on the sidewalk so we can submerge ourselves in the spectacle.

A very drunk woman with stringy dishwater hair comes up to Winston and pats his arm. "Hi Love!" she slurs. She smiles and her teeth are yellow and rotted and I can smell the booze from three feet away.

Winston takes my arm and pulls me into the parade. I ignore the creepy woman, there's so much beauty around me: candles, horses, chanting monks in burlap robes. One hands me a doubloon and a candle. I LOVE getting gifts. "I love this," I tell Winston, my body ignited with the sheer creativity swirling around me. "Let's follow them down to the cathedral and watch the end reenactment of St. Catherine De Fierbois." I have to resist jumping up and down.

"What is St. Catherine Fireball? What about our blacklight?"

"Oh my god, Winston, we can get a blacklight later," I say, tugging on his arm. "We will miss the whole thing if we don't hurry."

He growls the way he does when he is not pleased but he follows me and I tell him the story as we make our way down the cobblestone street. "Joan said her "voices" told her that there was a sword hidden behind the altar in a church called St. Catherine De Fierbois, in France. No one believed her but they dug behind the altar, right where she told them and guess what they found?"

"Dirt?"

"Ha ha. They found a rusted sword with five crosses, exactly as she described. She asked the churchmen to bring it to her and they did and they made her two sheaths, one of velvet, one of gold. She, of course, being the humble warrior, had one made for herself in leather—more conducive for battle."

"How do you know these things?" Winston asks as he takes my hand and we walk briskly down Royal to Jackson Square.

"Oh my head is full of useless yet awesome historical facts, although I have to say, I would have kept the velvet and golden sheaths."

"Is this the reenactment?" Winston asks me as the woman on the horse leads the procession through Jackson Square.

"Yes, they'll go in the church and pretend to find the sword." The haunting beauty of the old majestic St. Louis cathedral combined with the chanting and women on horseback is giving me powerful chills.

The warrior Joan charges into the St. Louis cathedral in her armor and I gasp in delight at the drama and raise my arms to cheer, but just then, I am knocked to the ground by a hulking monk who grabs at me and my purse before I even know what's happening. There's *no way* someone could snatch this purse from me, except over my dead body. I am pinned to the ground and the guy is huge and heavy and grabbing at my purse with thick fingers, but I'm holding it in my arms like a baby. We are struggling. *No one* is taking this handbag.

I realize where I am. *Oh no!* I am NOT lying in the dirty street in my silk velvet Garbo coat!

Winston tries to pull him off me, but the monk clings to me, his robe scratchy, and whispers in my ear, "Stop the killing of the king." He shoves something into my hand and collapses. All I can see is his bushy brown hair and I try to push him off me but he is pinning my arms with his hefty weight.

Someone else is trying to pull him off me. Things are moving in slow motion. I've never been mugged before and it's a strange sensation. Someone is screaming and I realize it's me at the same moment that I see the monk start to convulse. In the split second before the convulsions reach his face, I see his young unlined face. White foam pours out of his mouth. Dear god, he's having a seizure! Maybe he's an epileptic! Oh shit, there is no way I'm grabbing his skanky-ass tongue and holding it! Maybe I should stick something in it? A spoon? A stick? I can't remember! I feel like I'm up to my neck in swamp mud, unable to move my feet or avert my eyes. But as I watch, the white foam turns red and it looks like rubies are spilling out of his open mouth.

In one final convulsion he rolls onto his back and looks at me. It's a moment scorched into my brain forever, those staring eyes. It seems he wants to say something more and my compassion overrides my repulsion as I try to remember my first aid training. Should I elevate his head? I push one arm under his head and his eyes open wide in a frozen stare as he takes one final breath and stops forever. Paramedics are swooping in, and Winston gently guides me backwards so they can administer CPR. I see the flashing red lights of an ambulance slowly moving closer. There's no way he could really be dead. Strangers don't just stumble into you and die in your arms. I'm pretty sure the paramedics can bring him back to life. They have to. These things don't happen.

My hands are shaking so violently, I hold them out in front of me like I'm staring at a science experiment. I wonder, in an odd detached way, if I'm going to faint. But suddenly I have fallen through a Hitchcock portal and I'm like Tippi Hedren in *The Birds*. Birds are gouging out the eyes of everyone around me and I cover my eyes to stop the vision. No, wait I must really be in shock! I would never be Tippi. I'm Grace Kelly in *To Catch a Thief*. Elegant, cool, ice queen, even surrounded by scary things. I think I need to lay down, so I do, right where I'm standing.

I can see Winston's mouth moving as he leans over me, but I can't hear him. If he combed his hair he could look like Cary Grant, and I want to park my convertible on an ocean cliff and have a picnic with him. And I think about Cary Grant jumping from roof-to-roof, and cat burglars, and how he was so acrobatic in his fight scenes since he was in the circus, and I was in the circus and I wonder if I could flip and somersault and roll right now. I want to try it but I don't want to get my coat dirty. And anyway, it's too late. But my mind is somersaulting without my consent so my circus training is happening with or without me.

Everything feels surreal and all I can feel are Winston's arms around me.

All of a sudden my ears pop and I hear his voice say, "Are you all right? Are you hurt?" The concern in his face melts me. He swoops down and picks up my purse, which was lying open at our feet. He hands me the handbag. "Did he take anything from you?" he asks.

With shaking hands, I look inside my bag: invitation, lipstick, keys, credit card, identification, cell phone. "No, everything is there." I say, shaking my head, but then I look at my hand, which is bleeding and still clutching whatever the creepy monk shoved at me. It's an antique photo of four young guys standing in front of a theater. What the heck?

I show Winston. "Nothing taken, but he slipped this in my hand."

Winston looks at my hand and says, "You're bleeding."

"Just a scratch."

He looks at the photo closely, his eyebrows bunched together in that way I love when he's focusing intently on something. He discreetly slips out his phone and snaps a picture of the front and back of the old photo, sliding the phone back in his pocket. It all happens so quickly I'm not sure it even happened.

The monk is being hauled away by the paramedics, and I feel an overwhelming need to sit down. Have I fallen into *The Big Sleep*? I think I've seen too many film noirs. I want to pretend this never happened, rewind to ten minutes ago when the world seemed so beautiful and romantic, but two uniformed police officers approach me, bursting my bubble.

"Ma'am," they say, "Are you all right? Are you hurt?"

I shake my head and hold up my bleeding hand. "No, just a scratch."

The paramedics rush over with a little suitcase in their gloved hands. The one who looks like Rock Hudson bandages my hand and asks me questions. The little one who looks like Peter Lorre wraps me in an ugly brown blanket and tells Winston I'm in shock. The police stay close by me, watching me and talking quietly to each other and on their walkie-talkies.

I don't know if they're protecting me or making sure I don't go anywhere.

After a few minutes they look at Rock Hudson and he nods. They turn to me and say, "We need to ask you a few questions."

Winston comes to my rescue. "Officers, my wife has just received a terrible shock. Can questioning wait?"

The male cop says, "We actually need her to answer a few questions right now. She can come down in the morning to make a longer official statement."

I pat his arm. "It's all right Winston."

The cops lead me to a park bench for questioning. The other cop is a stunningly beautiful woman in a police outfit and I think I must get me one! I've always wanted a cop uniform! Why are these shallow thoughts crossing my mind at a time like this? She has luxurious, thick, black curls framing her beautiful mocha face, startling green eyes, and the fullest, plumpest, pinkest lips I've ever seen. I stare at her, reveling in her beauty, but she's tough, and she doesn't even smile at me.

She introduces herself as Officer Washington. The questions are almost insultingly obvious: What happened? (I was knocked to the ground by a guy from behind.) Who was this guy? (I have no idea.) Had I ever seen him before? (No.) Did he take anything from me? (I don't think so. But he did slip this old photo into my hand.) Why would he do that? ("I have no idea.)"

I tell them about the seizure and suggest he was possibly an epileptic. They nod and take notes. There are so many witnesses that they soon deduce I just happened to be the unlucky one the monk happened to fall on.

The police take the photo from me and stare at it for a long time. "Ms. Martini, do you know who the men are in this photo?"

"No. I've never seen them before."

Detective Washington narrows her eyes at me and holds the photo up to her eyes with her gloved hands. "They're at a theater."

She holds the photo out to me and I look closely at the photo myself. My adrenaline has pumped the shock out of my system and I feel so clear-headed and focused I'm thinking my gaze might burn a hole right through the photo. "Yes, they're standing in front of the St. Charles Theater. I've spent a lot of time in old theaters doing research for my books." We both look over our shoulders at Le Petit Theater, behind us in Jackson Square. Its known for its ghost, a 23-year-old actress who fell to her death off the third floor balcony in 1927. She helps people find their missing costumes. But the St. Charles Theater is much older and has its own ghosts.

Detective Washington is holding the photo with gloves. They take out a bag and shake it before slipping the photo in. Another man strides over and both detectives straighten up. "Captain."

The man has my favorite kind of moustache, a massive handlebar moustache that makes him look like a wise old cowboy that will spit out his tobacco before saying something important to my future.

He looks right into my eyes and says in a thick southern accent, "Ellington Martini?" I nod and hold my breath, waiting for his message. I'm hoping it will be something along the line of 'Time to wake up Miss Martini. Your nightmare is over. You can get in your convertible and drive the cliffs of the

Riviera now.' But instead he says, "Ms. Martini, I'm Captain O'Reilly and my wife is a huge fan of your books." He turns to the detectives. "This is Ellington Martini, the romance novelist." They barely nod, folding their arms. He takes my arm to help me off the bench. "I think we can let Ms. Martini head home for the night. I'm sure this has been very upsetting for her." I nod, afraid if I blink my eyes I'll break down sobbing and never stop. His reassuring, growly, voice keeps talking. "We'll be sure to call on you in the morning, not too early," he says with a laugh. "I know you writers are night owls. You can fill us in on the details again after a good night's sleep." He passes my arm to Winston and says, "You take good care of our city treasure now, Mr. Martini. If this woman's writing gets interrupted I'll never hear the end of it from the Missus." He chuckles at his own joke, but his voice is getting more distant to me and everyone's faces are blurring.

Chapter 3

Heat of the Night

Muddled Jalapeño, Lemon Juice, Watermelon Juice, Citrus Vodka, Elderflower Liqueur

Before I know it, we are driving down Prytania on our way home. I lean back in my seat like a deflated balloon. Winston puts one hand gently on my neck. "Are you okay?"

I nod. "I think so. What are the chances, of all the people at that parade, that some guy would fall over on *me* while having a seizure? And if you're having a seizure, why would you hand someone an antique photo in the middle of it? And why did he say, "Stop the killing of the king?"

Winston doesn't know this part. "He said what?"

"He wheezed in my ear, 'stop the killing of the king,' in this scary raspy voice. And before you ask, I have no idea what it means or why he said it to me."

Winston says, "Do you think he randomly picked you or do you think he knows you from somewhere? Did you ever meet him, maybe while researching an article? Would he know you from your books?"

The hairs on the back of my neck stand up. "You think he recognized me from my book cover photo and came after me?

Singled me out? Winston! That is so creepy!" I shiver. "Oooooh! It's like a horror movie. No, it had to be random. I refuse to think that my books could bring something so vile into my life."

Winston takes my hand and holds it tight. He's silent for a few minutes, then says, "I wish there was something I could say to change this night."

"Me too," I answer, when I'm interrupted by the sound of a raucous brass band. "Do you hear music or a siren? Or both?" I ask. "Or have I been sucked down some sort of New Orleans vortex with brass bands and sad sirens and scary monks?" I put one hand over my Cartier Tank watch to get my bearings. It was the watch Jackie O. wore with such classic elegance, and it gives me the strength of a woman holding it together in the face of violence and ugliness.

If Jackie O. can do it, so can I.

"I hear it too," Winston says. "There must be a Second Line parade close by, probably the Funny Phorty Fellows. Some people in the office today were talking about it."

"Yup, they kick off Mardi Gras on the Epiphany every year." I release a long sigh. "I never thought these words would come out of my mouth, but I'm not sure I can handle any more parades."

The sounds of the joyous horns are drowned out as the sirens get closer and the smell of smoke becomes more pungent. When we stop on Napoleon Street, we see the flames. The Atchafalaya Jazz Club is glowing from the inside with smoke billowing out of a window and flames appearing and disappearing behind the window, like Blaze Starr the night she met Governor Long. *Come on Earl, come see what my millions of hot flaming tongues can do.* In the few moments we are watching, the building emits a deep shuddering moan that quickly turns into a roar of rage and the entire side of the building erupts nearly all at once into a massive wall of flame.

Firefighters are arriving in a frenzy, leaping out of their trucks in full gear dragging their hoses. We can't drive by and are forced to stand still in our cars and watch. It's a helpless feeling, watching a building eaten by flames. As we watch, a brass band marches up the island in the middle of Napoleon followed by a long line of wild shouting men. They are not marching but dancing with drinks in their hands, their necks covered in stacks of colorful Mardi Gras beads. The upper parts of their faces are covered with half masks. The police have arrived and stop the parade from moving closer, but the music keeps going and the revelers keep dancing and I'm starting to question the sanity of this place. I watch as one or two of the men lift the masks off their eyes and their faces become somber as they watch the Atchafalaya burn, but the rest of them keep dancing, some linking arms and turning in circles, their drinks sloshing out of the plastic cups. They seem to be cheering on the flames.

I feel sick.

The police send us on a detour down to Tchoupitoulas to get home. I look over my shoulder and watch the dancing silhouettes. It reminds me of something, and I pull out my invitation with images of dancing or writhing in the flames. Yeats rains down on my head and I whisper to myself, "Come Away, O Human Child, To the Waters and the Wilds, With a fairy, hand-in-hand, For the world's more full of weeping than you can understand."

Chapter 4

Corpse Reviver

Gin, Cointreau, Lillet Blanc, Lemon Juice, Absinthe

I'm so tired when I get home that all I want to do is collapse. But when I pass my art studio, it beckons me and I let go of his hand.

"Aren't you tired, Honey? It's pretty late."

I shake my head and whisper, "I have to..."

Winston nods and kisses me on top of my head. If there's one thing Winston understands with no questions asked, it's the need to create. I flip the light switch and the chandelier softly lights up the room. I open the windows and am immediately wrapped in a soft blanket of honeysuckle air. I can hear someone singing, and I poke my head out the window for a better look. From my second story window I can see beautiful mansions and colorful shotgun houses, all jumbled haphazardly like a handful of jacks thrown by a child. Directly behind me is an old carriage house and I can see right into the window. I should probably respect my neighbor's privacy and turn away, but I can't resist leaning even further out the window to get a better look.

I can see a pair of stocking feet sticking out of a patchwork quilt, a hand with a mug in it, and another hand waving back and forth in time to the music she is making. I can't see her face, but I know it's my elderly neighbor, Harriet. I had no idea she could sing. Just this morning she told me about her twin brother who was born three weeks after her in their shotgun cottage. I have never heard of twins being born three weeks apart, so I'm thinking this was a tall tale, but you never know around here. When I first moved here I had never heard of a shotgun cottage, and Harriet explained it to me: "Oh it's a single story house with the rooms one after another and one long hallway down the middle. If you stood at the front door and fired a shotgun out the back, it wouldn't hit anything." She laughed when she told me, with her shaking voice, protruding yellow teeth, and sparse hair. But her voice isn't shaking now. Her ringing operatic voice floats up to my window, clear and sweet.

I close my eyes and let the tears roll. It makes my heart ache to think of the monk tonight. His staring eyes keep flashing in front of my mind, his writhing, the blood filling his mouth... Harriet's voice is like cold water on a burn, soothing me, pulling me out of the darkness. Classic New Orleans — just when you think you can't take any more of the screaming brutality and violence, a parade of notes bubbles right out of the split sidewalks and weaves its rhapsodic cocoon around your soul.

My neighbor stops singing and I see her move over to an old turntable and gingerly lift the needle, placing it on a record. The horns start up with "St. James Infirmary Blues", one of my all-time favorites. I blow my nose and close my swollen eyes and let the music pour over me. The music beckons, swampy, fecund, and oh so inviting.

Did you see scary things tonight? Dark and violent and bloody things? Let the music transform it all.

I stand and stretch and my hips start moving in a golden honey way, slow, undulating, golden. "St. James Infirmary Blues" is a classic about a young man cut down in his prime.

It's played at nearly every Second Line in the city, and nothing brings me more joy than a Second Line: gold-toothed smiles, shouts of glee, feathered boas, top hats, and shiver-dancing, hoodlums, whores, and vagabonds join doctors, teachers, and senators to dance down the street, waving handkerchiefs and carrying umbrellas.

But they don't carry umbrellas because it's raining.

Oh no.

These umbrellas are decked out in feathers and glitter and beads. They *dare* the rain to come because guess what?

Nothing keeps the rain away like some sultry music and sparkles.

Which is exactly how I became a showgirl in the first place.

I rise and pull out a bin of glitter and feathers and sequins and beads and dump it on my worktable. I make anything and everything I can think of in this room: I write stories, paint canvases, make up dances, sew costumes, tutus, hats, fascinators...

At the moment, however, I'm making umbrellas.

My worktable has my latest umbrella lying in the middle with my tools: Swarovski crystals, beaded fringe, colorful ribbons, and a whole lot of glue. I plug in my hot glue gun, pick up my beads and feathers, and start to create, although it's hard to see when my eyes are filled up like a storm gutter after a downpour. I work on my latest umbrella until the night grows quiet and only the crickets are left and I can't see straight from exhaustion. The umbrella is catching the light in a way that makes it more sparkly than anything I've ever seen at Tiffany's and I gently place it on top of my hat rack so the glue can dry overnight. I walk quietly to our bedroom, slip silently into bed, and fall asleep against Winston's back.

Chapter 5

Dirty Little Secret

*Vanilla Vodka, Godiva White Chocolate Liqueur, with a
kiss*

In the morning I wake up to the phone ringing. I like old-
fashioned phones next to my bed — the kind that plug into the
wall and have curly cords. This drives my tech wizard,
Winston, crazy. He loves all the latest gadgets and gizmos, but
I prefer living in my 'old movie' world. It makes me feel
glamorous to roll over and answer the phone with a husky
"Hello?" The phone is big and curved in my hand and I'm still
living in the pink bubble of my dreams, having forgotten for a
moment the events of last night.

"Mrs. Martini?" A brusque voice says.

"Yes?" I'm so tired my voice has descended an octave so I
sound like Lauren Bacall in *Dark Passage*. And quite honestly
the man on the other end sounds like Humphrey Bogart with
a southern accent.

"This is Detective Boudreau from the NOPD. I'm calling
to ask if you could come on down to the police station to make
your official statement this morning, say ten o'clock?"

I want to let out a moan as last night comes flooding back

like a broken levee on Lake Pontchartrain. "Ten o'clock? Yes, Detective Boudreau, I can do that. Which station?"

"French Quarter. 334 Royal Street. We'll be waiting."

I roll over. Winston, my darling Winston, has already left for work. But he has left me a note on my pillow. "Let me know if you need me for anything today. I love you. Winston." I bury my face in his pillow and inhale his Hermes cologne. Oh how I wish he could stay with me all day after last night. Even the smell of his cologne makes me feel better. He's my lighthouse.

Ok, I'm getting distracted. I rise up on my elbows. Pull it together Ellington. I glance at the clock. It's nine o'clock! And if I've got to be at the station in an hour, I have about 15 minutes to get dressed so I have plenty of time to get down there and park.

I open my closet doors and see what I have that is appropriate for a police station. I'm thinking a black pencil skirt and simple black wrap top and black velvet heels, ala Sophia Loren. (And before you judge me for acting shallow and caring about what I wear after the night I had last night, just know that dressing well is an excellent defense against the ferocious chaos of the world.)

So, I need something fabulous and something that shows I'm an upstanding citizen. Do I have anything like that in my closet? I don't think I do. An outfit can look completely respectable on someone else's body, but my shape makes everything look obscene. Take, for example, my Ralph Lauren wrap dress. Now old Ralph is known for his elegant upscale clothing. It should make me look like I'm about to have lunch at "the club" followed by a visit to my polo ponies at the stables, but on me the dress says "sex." I don't have the flat chest and slim hips of those Ralph Lauren models—I fill the dress out in ways Ralph never considered. I need to focus!! Lauren wrap dress it is!! And I need power shoes. I sit on my pink velvet chaise lounge in my closet and ponder the options.

I feel vulnerable, so I need shoes that make me feel

powerful and protected.

That would mean riding boots. I stare at my riding boot collection, trying to decide which pair will make me feel the most powerful. I finally choose a tall black pair and after I jam my feet into the damn things—I forgot how tight these boots were—I strut in front of my closet mirror. They make me feel so jaunty. I trot past the mirror one way and gallop back the other. I really should take up horseback riding. I have loved horses since I was a child, and I even had a stable of gorgeous horses in my backyard that only I could see. I galloped everywhere, but my parents could never afford lessons so my stable stayed invisible.

But just because I don't own a horse doesn't mean I can't take advantage of the stunning riding attire! What's cuter than a pair of shiny riding boots and a fitted riding jacket? With a faux fur collar! Yes! Paired with a pencil skirt, nix the wrap dress... Perfect! I pass for respectable and I look exactly like the type of person who doesn't have people knocking them to the ground while foaming at the mouth.

A swooning feeling is washing over me and I wish I was heading back to bed to pull my pillow over my head and cry.

Bootstraps, Ellington! Pull it together. Sigh.

I fix myself a cappuccino, put on my Matador lipstick, and take one last look in the mirror. I almost decide to switch handbags, but I adore my vintage Kelly, even if it was traumatized last night. Plus it matches my outfit perfectly, adding a dash of grace and elegance. I smooth my skirt and head for the police station.

I drive down St. Charles listening to Louis Armstrong and let my mind dream of an older, sweeter era, with soft romantic edges. The enormous roots of the oaks erupt through the sidewalks like zombie arms. I can't think about zombies at a time like this, but if zombies existed anywhere it would probably be New Orleans with all its Haitian and voodoo cultures. I love to research Marie Laveau, the voodoo queen from the 1800's. I plan to write a book about her and the famous octoroon balls and all their fabulous outfits, which reminds me, what in the world am I going to wear to the ball?

As I cross Canal Street into the Quarter, my daydreams take a skeezy turn when I park in front of a massage parlor that has signs advertising services in Asian writing... questionable services. An Asian man stands in front, smoking a cigarette and using wild gestures to help me parallel park my car, even though I don't need the help. I'm a bit of a parallel parking savant, able to squeeze into the tiniest of spots. I wave in thanks anyway, (mannerly woman I am), and run across the street.

The French Quarter has a pungent odor that never leaves. Not necessarily a good odor either, but distinctive. The police station is a grandiose pink building built in the 1800's. It is stately with huge white columns in front of it. The front courtyard is filled with motor scooters stamped with the NOPD logo, a star over a moon — kind of a romantic logo for a police department, more fitting to a gypsy wagon. As I walk inside the building, I am awed by the lofty ceilings lit by several massive chandeliers. The building itself is fancy and screams officious and stately, but the faded rugs and vending machines place it squarely into the category of "dilapidated glamour". I walk up to the front desk and tell the very serious woman in uniform I have an appointment with Detective Boudreau. After punching buttons and speaking quietly into a flat black phone, she tells me the detective will be right out to see me.

While I'm waiting, I look in the front display cases. They are a jackpot of historical oddities: A rusted star-shaped police badge, handcuffs from 1820 (they look painful), an opium pipe from 1850 - (scared to think of the lips that might have touched that). What a scandalous display for a police station! (Actually my grandmother kept an opium pipe that eight people could smoke at once, I guess so no one would feel left out. She was very thoughtful that way.)

"Ms. Martini?"

I remove my enormous round Prada sunglasses and turn around, even though I don't want the whole world to see that I've been crying, but I'm not sure why since no one would care. Stumbling around the Quarter with swollen eyes on any given morning is an ordinary sight.

It's the beautiful woman from last night talking to me, Officer Washington. Officer? Detective? I don't know. I look at her nametag.

"Hello Detective Washington, I'm sorry I'm such a mess." I straighten my skirt and smooth my hair. Something about her makes me feel like I'm under a bright light: no shadows.

"Last night was rough and, well, I don't have to tell you what kind of night it was. You were there." I'm hoping she doesn't notice I feel nervous, although I shouldn't since I've done nothing wrong. But if she's going to stare at me with those x-ray eyes, staring into my soul in a way that makes every bad thought that has ever crossed my mind seem like cause for jail time... I shudder.

And there's no way I'm wearing one of those hideous orange jumpsuits, I'd look like a day glow teddy bear.

She doesn't smile which makes me squirm even more inside. Doesn't she know it's socially improper to not smile at someone who is smiling at you?

"Follow me please," she says, leading me back through a large room with cubicles filled with police officers on computers and talking on phones.

When I'm nervous, I can be quite loquacious. "My goodness, this is just like the movies. Your lobby, by the way, is just beautiful. Those chandeliers! They really do look like they belong in an old saloon. Did you know this building used to be a saloon? I read that on the plaque outside. Do you think that long counter-like desk in the front used to be the bar? Makes me want to dance on top of it in my petticoats, kicking over everyone's glass beer mugs like Debbie Reynolds in the *Unsinkable Molly Brown*. Did you see that movie? Debbie Reynolds was excellent, although now that I know her questionable parenting tactics with poor Carrie Fisher, I have a hard time enjoying her movies. Did you read Carrie Fisher's book, *Wishful Drinking?*"

Detective Washington peers over her shoulder at me, like the school librarian used to look at me over her glasses right before she'd tell me to quiet down. I think she's going to say "Pipe down, kid" but instead she says, "Can I get you some water?" which might be code for 'Shut the hell up Lady,' or might be her way of being polite.

Either way, I shut up and say, "Yes thank you."

She leads me to a room with a table in it and motions me to sit in the wooden chair. The chair has wheels on the bottom of it, which I find out when I sit down and it scoots across the floor, leaving me on my ass on the floor. Not a good scene in a pencil skirt, but thank goodness I'm alone. Unless there's a team of people watching me behind the mirror. God I hope not. I sit back down, fold my hands and ankles, and wait in perfect elegance for her to return.

The room is plain white and every dirty scuff can be seen. It's quite unpleasant. I'm wishing the walls were covered with something more sweepingly beautiful, like Van Gogh's sunflowers, or *Starry Night*. When I backpacked through Europe as a young girl after studying Van Gogh at school in Paris, I got separated from my friends. In the days before cell phones, there was nothing I could do but stare at the train window at the countryside and inhale Chanel No. 5. In my infinite backpacking wisdom, I had packed a large bottle of Chanel No. 5. After my shoulders went numb within hours, I decided the first thing that had to go was that heavy glass bottle. My friends couldn't bear to watch me throw it away, so we decided to pour it over our clothing, blankets and packs. And so I inhaled Chanel and wondered if I'd ever find them again. When the train passed an endless fields of sunflowers, I suddenly felt calm and knew everything would be okay. I found my friends the next day sleeping in the Brindisi train station on their way to Greece.

Detective Washington returns with my cup of water, startling me out of my sunflower Chanel reverie. She has the Detective from the previous night with her.

"Mrs. Martini, this is Detective Boudreau from last night."

"Yes, I remember. I spoke with him on the phone this morning." I stand to shake his hand. "Good morning Detective Boudreau."

"Good morning, Mrs. Martini. Thank you for coming in this morning."

"Of course."

He sets an old fashioned tape recorder on the table. "Do you mind if we record you?"

"Of course I don't mind. Wow, we're going old school. I haven't seen a tape recorder like that since I was little."

He doesn't respond and I take a sip of water and try to ignore flutters in my belly. Why in the world would I be nervous? I haven't done anything.

The detectives both sit down. Detective Boudreau leans forward on his elbows, and I'm distracted by the way his blue police shirt tightens over his bulging biceps. (I'm not attracted to him, but I do admire a bulging bicep.) He pretends not to see my admiring glance but he flexes for me. Yum.

"Thank you for coming in this morning," he says in a serious detective voice. "We just need to ask you some more details about last night. Can you give us a rundown of what happened again? No detail is irrelevant And let's start a little earlier with what brought you to the Quarter."

I take a deep breath and tell them the story of last night, leaving out the parts about the top hat and cape. But then I think, maybe I shouldn't leave any detail out, so I spill every detail, including my proclivity for top hats and capes. They scratch notes as I talk. It makes me feel better to state the facts as it they were a storyline and not actual events. Laying them out puts everything in order instead of events swimming around, taking over my mind.

I take my power back in the telling.

Officer Washington interrupts when I get to the part in Jackson Square. "Did you see anything unusual right before the monk fell on you? Even out of the corner of your eye? A color or hat or even a shoe you can remember?"

I pause for a moment, tapping my chin, which sometimes helps me remember lost thoughts. "The Joan of Arc parade is different because people don't stand and catch 'throws,' they walk with the parade and are handed things like doubloons, candles, medallions... it was crowded and everyone was screaming, so there was a lot of noise and a lot of chaos. People were bumping into each other so no, I didn't notice anything except the main event until the monk fell on me."

My momentary feeling of order about last night vaporizes when I talk about the monk. "There were so many monks in the parade they all blur together. Why did he pinpoint me? And then that insidious whisper, 'Stop the killing of the king'. What does that even mean?"

"Wait, you didn't tell us this last night." Both detectives seem to get excited by this new tidbit and start writing with vigor in their notepads. "Is that exactly what he said? Word-for-word? Did he say anything else?"

"That's it, word-for-word." The power in the room has shifted to me, and it makes me relax a little bit.

"You have no idea what it could mean?"

"No, I don't, unless he meant stop the killing of a Mardi Gras king."

"Do you know anybody named King?"

I think for a moment. "No."

"Do you know any Mardi Gras kings?"

"I know people who have been kings in the past Mardi Gras but not any current ones. Unless he meant for me to stop the killing of someone who is about to be made king."

"Did your husband recognize the victim?"

"No, neither of us had ever seen him before in our lives."

She nods quietly. "Your husband is a professor at Loyola?"

I nod.

"Because the victim was a Med student at Tulane named Duncan Pike," she continues. "We wondered if their paths had ever crossed."

What are they getting at? "No, Winston teaches Music Business at Loyola. He doesn't meet many people in the medical field." But my mind is spinning. The name Duncan Pike sounds very familiar but I can't place it.

The detectives exchange a glance. "We were a little surprised to learn that Duncan Pike had taken some music classes at Loyola a few months ago, so we thought he and Mr. Martini may have known each other or at least seen each other in passing."

"Winston might have known the victim? He would have said something last night."

Detective Washington nods. "Maybe. Maybe not. Where is he now?"

"He's moderating a panel at Loyola this morning. He would have come with me but he said the panel was critical to their funding."

"They are scribbling quickly in their notebooks. "A panel on what?"

"I'm not sure exactly."

Detective Washington reads from her notes without lifting her head. "This morning's panel at Loyola was called, "Uniting Universities to save Higher Education: Can Loyola combine forces with Tulane?" The Universities allow cross-registration and have recently decided to consider merging due to Loyola's economic troubles."

"I didn't know Loyola had economic troubles."

"Even though your husband teaches Business?"

Oh shit! They sound accusatory. Could Winston be in trouble? Of course not. He hasn't done anything.

As far as I know.

My heart goes from beating to pounding like a drum on a Sunday in Congo Square. I decide the best course of action is to close my mouth at this point until I can talk to Winston.

Detective Washington sets a manila envelope on the table and pulls out a large photo. She slides it in front of me. It's a picture in black and white of an antique cane, at least it looks antique. She finally says, "Any idea what this is?"

I take a deep breath before answering, even though it's obvious. "A cane?"

She is watching me carefully. "It's actually an archaic weapon called a *colichemarde*." She points to the tip. "It's a French cane that narrows to a point so sharp it's a lethal weapon. It isn't legal to carry one these days, but they were common in New Orleans during pre-Civil War times as a means of protection."

Detective Boudreau adds, "Men carried the canes openly around in public, but they became a problem because it was too easy to solve a fight with a duel. These days, people collect them, but I've never seen or even heard of one being used in an actual murder."

I gasp, like I'm in the billiards room with Colonel Mustard. "This was the murder weapon?"

Detective Washington says, "The end point actually broke off and lodged itself at just the wrong angle under the victim's rib cage."

I slowly sink my face behind my faux fur collar like a turtle retreating into its shell. "Wow. *Wow.* That just made a really creepy bad night even creepier." My mind starts to float away, and I deepen my breath and try to focus on my breath, trying to bring my mind back.

"Are you hearing me?"

Shit, she can tell I've checked out. I nod.

Detective Boudreau says, "We thought it was most likely a random killing last night, someone in the wrong place at the wrong time. This kid was clean – old Uptown family, resident of Tulane Medical School, top of his class, no history of drugs, not so much as a parking ticket. But the weapon puts a whole new spin on it."

Detective Washington stands up, "As you know if you read the news, catching killers in New Orleans is about as easy as wrestling an albino alligator out of a swamp. We depend on eyewitnesses to provide reliable information, so if you think of any other detail, even something that might seem irrelevant or trivial, you call us immediately. " She hands me her card.

I have been stunned into silence, in shock I think, but the writer in me is intrigued. An archaic murder weapon? How fascinating.

Both detectives walk me out of the station and as we emerge into the sunshine, a truckload of feathers pulls up. We watch an older man in a baseball cap unloading a cape of massive pink feathers out of the back of the truck. The cape is so heavily beaded with intricate patterns and colors that I can see his muscles straining as he struggles to lift it. He places it onto the shoulders of a fierce-looking young man standing next to him. There are warrior stripes drawn on the younger man's face with pink paint. His dark eyes look like he's ready to take on the world, to hold its head down if necessary and make it run in place, but because he's covered in pink feathers, his beauty overrides his combative posture.

"It's the Mardi Gras Indians," I say to Detective Washington, clasping my hands together in front of my heart. "They are my *favorite* part of New Orleans. The first time I saw one of their costumes I thought I'd died and gone to heaven. I used to be a performer and have seen my share of stunning handmade costumes but I had never seen anything like these. The colors, the feathers, the intricate hand beading — it would take years to sew a beaded cape like that."

Detective Washington nods her head and her face has softened for the first time, watching the boy put on his headdress. She folds her arms. "Yes, and every piece of costume tells a story about their lives. No two are alike."

More trucks are pulling up and Mardi Gras Indians are spilling out of them like syrup spilling out over pecan waffles.

The dirty streets are filling up with these beautiful beings. "They aren't usually in the Quarter, are they?" I ask.

Detective Washington shakes her head. "No, but you never know where they're going to show up. That's one of the things that makes them so special."

"Don't they usually parade on Dryades Street on St. Joseph's day? That's the only place I've ever seen them."

"That's my neighborhood," she says softly.

This surprises me. I hadn't imagined Detective Washington living anywhere, much less that area. It's full of crumbling houses with rusted bars on the windows and known to be one of the most dangerous neighborhoods in the city. "That's where I watch the Zulu parade on Mardi Gras Day," I say.

She smiles and I feel like we might be friends. Should I invite her out for a drink? A cocktail? Coffee? I don't know, so I say, "I'll never forget my first Zulu. I was walking down this plain street when all of a sudden the doors of the houses opened and these gorgeous beings came walking out like exotic birds who have grown too big for their cages. Their costumes were so big they had to turn sideways to get out the doors. Old people, teenagers, even babies being carried on their mothers' hips were strutting down the dirty streets, sparkling like the most beautiful jewels you could imagine. That's the moment I really fell in love with this city, the beauty emerging from the ugliness."

She laughs. "I was born and raised in a shotgun on Dryades. My whole family were Indians. That's how we kept the boys off the streets, hide the heroin needle and give them a sewing needle. Makes all the difference."

"Is it true the Indians started when the Native American tribes would hide runaway slaves?"

She shrugs. "That's what they say."

Just then the boy in pink who was glaring into the sky a few minutes earlier, sees Detective Washington and his toughness shatters into a smile.

"Tula!" he shouts.

Detective Washington smiles back. My goodness she seems too beautiful to be a cop. "Hey Mo," she says in her raspy New Orleans drawl, "You look amazing." She walks over and bumps fists with him.

I long to follow her. I watch the older man put his arm around her and squeeze her shoulders in a fatherly way. When he smiles, I can see his missing teeth. I stand behind the iron gates of the police station and watch them. Detective Washington looks over her shoulder at me as more Indians and their helpers surround her.

"You take care now Ms. Martini."

"I will." I wave in a lame white girl way as I reluctantly leave the safety of the pink building. Detective Boudreau is leaning against a column watching the whole scene as more cops come out of the building with big smiles on their faces. I look at the take-no-prisoners-face of the young boy in pink feathers, and he reminds me of someone… me. My inner soul boy would probably look just like that. And just because someone fell over dead on me under suspicious circumstances and the cops might suspect Winston doesn't mean I have to crumble. I can be a fierce warrior in pink feathers, just like that boy. I hold my head a little higher and saunter away from the station. When I glance behind me Detective Boudreau is watching me.

Chapter 6

SoMuchtoDrinkSoLittleTime

Muddled Lemons, Mango Puree, Mango Vodka

I'm walking to my car when I realize I'm starving.

How I wish I was one of those people who lose their appetite when they are under stress. Unfortunately, I am just the opposite, I'm like a great white shark swimming with my mouth open, eating everything in my path. I am suddenly ravenous for a plate of beignets piled in powdered sugar. I feel the pull of Café Du Monde and their mountains of sugar and I head in that direction as my phone rings. It's my best friend, Bellamy Banjeau. I know, her name makes her sound like a Lady of the Night in a Storyville brothel, but she's not—she's an eye doctor with a cushy job that pays her six figures to work two days a week. "Bellamy! I'm so glad to hear your voice!"

Bellamy has a Greta Garbo voice. It's deep and elegant and slides over you like an ivory silk slip trimmed with black lace. "I'm here having coffee with Miss Ava," she purrs. "I just finished a grueling lecture on eyes at Tulane Medical School and I'm in desperate need of a drink. Hoping you are free to meet for lunch and some 25-cent martinis at Commander's

Palace?"

"Oh thank goodness you saved me! I'm in the Quarter and I was having a snack attack and headed to Café Du Monde for beignets."

"Well, by all means, do not let us interrupt a woman and her quest for a beignet!"

"No, no, I'm much better off with actual food. How soon? It will take me about twenty minutes to get back to my car and drive to the Garden District."

"Perfect," she says. "We'll meet you there."

I hop in my car and make my way to Washington and Prytania where I am immediately cheered by the restaurant's turquoise and white striped awnings. Commanders is the Grande Dame of New Orleans restaurants. I have an allegiance to old stalwart places, especially ones that send their servers around in crisp black and white uniforms with a bottle of vodka to top off my Bloody Mary every time it gets a little low. Bring it on, my little penguin friend, bring it on! The owners, the Brennans, had a moment of sheer brilliance when they created the concept of 25-cent martinis to increase their lunch business. Boy, did it work.

One surefire way of making money in New Orleans is offering cheap liquor.

Bellamy and Ava pull up in Ava's old white Cadillac. Bellamy is wearing a Nanette Lepore tweed suit and Ava is wearing a hot pink shift dress that accentuates her beautiful olive skin and black curls. Ava dresses astoundingly well for an eighth grade history teacher. If I taught eighth grade every day I think sweats would be the best I could do. Except that would corrupt my motto that nothing keeps the wolf from the door like a good pair of shoes. Ava always manages to look amazing, even if she just rolled out of bed. Bitch. Maybe it's all the years she spent in NYC wrangling Rockettes. And yes you heard me correctly. Ava lived in Manhattan and wrangled Rockettes for her job, getting them to their PR events with lipstick in place. That could be why she makes teaching seem so graceful and effortless: if you can wrangle the Rockettes I guess you can wrangle eighth graders.

I rush into both of their open arms. "I'm so glad you're free today!" I gush as we are led to our table. "Last night, well, last night..." I surprise myself by bursting into tears. Each of them takes one of my arms and gives me a squeeze.

"Shhhh, there, there, Honey," Bellamy says. "You're all right now. You just let it all out, Darlin'. You're safe. You're with us now."

"That's right," says Ava. "We're here." She pats my back as I pull myself together.

Bellamy says, "Look at me, Sugar."

I raise my brimming eyes to her and she uses a wadded lipstick-stained tissue she has found floating in the bottom of her purse to blot my eyes.

"You couldn't even find a clean tissue for me?" I ask.

"And she's back, folks!" she says, motioning Ava to hunt down a clean tissue in the restaurant. Bellamy is a take-charge person. She summons the waiter and asks for three dirty martinis, up, with extra olives.

"Wait!" I say. "I need a Bloody Mary! I'm researching my article on the Best Bloody Mary in New Orleans!"

"Of course, Honey," said Bellamy, patting my arm. She changes the order and Ava returns with a stack of tissues for me.

I say, "I'm so sorry for making such a spectacle of myself. Last night... just threw me for a loop."

Ava says, "Don't think twice about crying in this restaurant. They've seen it all."

I take a long sip of my cold water, and proceed to tell them all about the Joan of Arc parade. Their eyes are as big as bayou moons as they listen to my story, interrupted only by Ava softly whispering 'shitake mushrooms' after every few sentences. Since she is always surrounded by children, this is as close as Ava gets to cursing. By the time I finish, our drinks arrive. I take a long sip of my Bloody Mary, and even though my mouth is on fire from the Tabasco, I take a bite of the spicy green pepper garnish and it ignites my mouth further. I start waving my hands in front of my face and guzzling water as the tears start rolling again. This time it's tears of spiciness.

"My Goodness Hon, you *are* a mess today," Bellamy says, handing me her water since mine is empty. A hush has fallen over the table.

"Well?" I ask when I recover, discreetly fanning my tongue. "What do you think?"

"My god, Sugar!" says Bellamy. "I don't know what to think after that story! My Darlin', this is all very dramatic. I mean, my god, having a strange man keel over on you? I've had my fair share of men fall on me, but this is just... I don't know what to say, I truly don't. This is traumatic for you, bless your little heart. I think I'd need therapy for a year if this happened to me!"

"I think if that happened to me, I'd end up in the nuthouse!" Ava says.

I look at her over my tall celery garnish. "You didn't end up in the nuthouse when you were carjacked at gunpoint in your own driveway last year."

"True. I didn't end up in the nuthouse but I *felt* like I was in one. But this is just, an even worse violation. I mean having someone stabbed and falling over on you. Did he get blood on you?"

"No, but I saw it spilling out of his mouth." I lean forward to whisper. "You know how people get that trickle of blood when they die out of their lips. It is truly gruesome, and heartbreaking. But it's strange," I pause and pull my riding jacket collar closer around my neck, "I feel disconnected. It all happened so fast, and I was so caught up in the parade and the night."

"Yes," Ava says, "We know you have a tendency to get carried away."

I nod. "You know how those parades are—it's like being dipped into the collective unconscious of the entire city.

Fecund creative debauchery at its wildest. I always feel, I don't know, separated from reality, when I go to the parades.

"Me, too," they both say, nodding, encouraging.

"Usually it's a joyful separation like I've been whisked away in someone's beautiful fantasy, but sometimes, I feel separated in a scary way. Like the Chaos parade right after the Storm with its dancing skeletons and tattered floats. Life and death marching hand-in-hand."

"I know exactly what you mean," Bellamy nods. "It's a New Orleans gumbo is what it is." She starts shaking invisible spices into an imaginary pot while she says, "Throw in some breathtaking beauty, a little horror and mayhem, a dash of murder, a pinch of sadness and sprinkle it all with bouncing joie de vivre and there you have it—a New Orleans gumbo."

Ava shivers as she says in a hushed tone, "Remember those guys in the bloody skeleton outfits that were screaming and cursing at us at the St. Joseph's Mardi Gras Indian thing?"

"Skull and Bones?" Bellamy responds? "I just read about them. I've lived here all my life and never knew a thing about them. Apparently it's a two-hundred-year-old Creole tradition that they run through Treme and diffferent neighborhoods on Mardi Gras morning to wake everyone up. That would scare the daylights out of me, but the neighborhoods love it. Can you imagine?" She giggles. "Remember Ellington wore that bubblegum pink sundress with her big sunhat and that pink marabou backpack to the nastiest street in the city. She stuck out like a sore thumb with all those screaming cursing bloody skeletons."

Ava laughs and says, "They say the skeleton costumes are a warning to kids to stay away from the dark side? I don't get it and they are scary, but it's still a cool experience to see them live."

I shake my head, "I don't know what to think of those guys. I mean, my gawd, how many people are murdered in this city every day? Maybe it's like dressing in gory costumes for Halloween—if you make light of your worst nightmare it's not so scary anymore. I guess the monk just seemed like one of those New Orleans moments where fact and fiction meet. Maybe I do need therapy. Nothing is making sense. Oh, I'm feeling hot." I fan myself with my hand and peel off my jacket.

Bellamy moves my drink away from me. "It's all those spicy drinks, Honey. Slow down. You need something cooling. A Mojito should do the trick. Mint is cooling to the body." Bellamy is a master of creating cockamamie recommendations she makes up on the spot. She may have actually heard this somewhere, or she may have made it up, but usually people believe her because of her medical degree, although I can say with certainty that she made up this particular prescription about mojitos being cooling. "Here, have my olive till the server comes back. Olives are cooling too." I swear she thinks if she says something with authority, people will believe her and just their belief will heal them. I open my mouth to answer and she quickly stuffs an olive in. "You need to slow down, Honey, you've had a terrible shock."

"Stop babying me! You're going to make me cry again," I whisper, trying to stop the tears from falling by tilting back my head, which only makes them pool until they spill over and slide down the side of my face to land in my ears.

Just then our dear friend and pilates teacher, Jimmy Tate, stops by our table.

"Ellington! My darling, how are you?" He leans towards me and whispers, "I just finished cocktails upstairs with this super cute French artist. If I'd known y'all were here, we could have..." He stops as his eyes focus in on my face and his tone of voice changes. "What's the matter Darlin'? You look traumatized."

Bellamy shushes him as Ava whispers, "She is *not* doing well. She just told us the mother of all horror stories about her night last night."

Jimmy Tate gasps in horrified delight. "Oh do tell. Dish and Swish immediately. What happened?" Faster than you can say Daiquiri he has dragged a chair over from a neighboring table and is leaning in to hear the story.

"Do you want me to tell him?" Bellamy asks in her no-nonsense voice, the one reserved for difficult subjects that leaves no room for argument.

"I suppose," I say, not eager to relive the drama yet again. And yet, it makes the entire event less surreal and less crazy the more it's talked about. I keep thinking I'm waking up in a bad dream.

Bellamy tells them the entire story nearly word-for-word with a whole lot of dramatic flair. I have to give her credit for her steel-trap memory. She seems to be remembering more details than I did, and she wasn't even there.

Jimmy Tate lives next door to me. Besides being voted New Orleans Best Pilates teacher, he is one of the most well-known costume collectors in the country. He is one of those people who does costume reenactments; like getting dressed up and re-enacting the Battle of Gettysburg. He is eating up the drama of the story like it's a hot beignet that's been dipped in a chicory latte—it falls apart so fast you have to stuff it in your mouth as fast as you can. We all have wild and dangerous New Orleans stories of course, but this one takes the cake. I have seen cops with their weapons drawn crawling over my car at a stoplight; Jimmy Tate has been mugged at knifepoint more than once; Ava was carjacked in her own driveway, and Bellamy's house was looted after the storm... twice... but no one has *ever* had a man fall over dead on them, much less a monk in the middle of a parade.

Ava is munching on a green bean garnish from her drink. "Do you have any idea why this guy singled you out?"

"No," I answer, thinking back to the night before.

"You did nothing out of the ordinary?"

"Well, the whole parade was out of the ordinary of course. But no, not that I can think of. I mean, we went to the Napoleon first... Wait... there was something extraordinary last night." All of them lean in even closer. "We got an invitation to the Rex Ball." There is a collective gasp as I continue. "I opened it at Crepe Nanou, but I pulled it out at the Napoleon and looked at it. That was the only thing extraordinary last night. Do you think that could be why he pinpointed me in the first place? Maybe the old photo has something to do with the Rex Ball?"

All of them start talking at once.

"How the *hell* did you get an invitation to Rex?" Jimmy Tate nearly shouts. "I've lived here my whole life and never been invited to Rex."

"What did the invitation look like?"

"When is the ball?"

"Where is the ball?"

"Who do you think sent you the invitation?"

"What do you think you're going to wear?"

"Ladies!" I say fiercely. (This includes Jimmy Tate since he is the biggest princess of us all.) "I haven't even thought about the ball! I'm still trying to figure out what happened last night."

They pat my shoulders, hands, elbows. "You're right, Sugar," says Bellamy. "You have enough to think about right now. Maybe we should brainstorm together on why this... monk... would focus on you because of your invitation. Do you think he had a message for you. Maybe something about the invitation itself, or the ball, or something in the invitation?"

"Well, he stuck the photo into my hand and whispered 'stop the killing of the king' in my ear."

"He what?" Ava is stunned. "You didn't say he actually spoke to you! What the heck does that mean, 'stop the killing of the king?' Ooooh, do you think someone is plotting to kill the King of Rex this year and you're supposed to stop it?"

"Why would anyone want to kill the king of Rex?" asks Jimmy Tate. "The kings and queens of balls are nobodies. It's not like it's an assassination of someone critically important." We all know Jimmy Tate feels snubbed because he's never been asked to be royalty.

"Wait, who *is* the king this year?"

"I don't know. I don't follow this stuff." Bellamy says. "The only thing I do know, is that they usually choose someone important to NOLA society." She leans in even closer and whispers, "My Uncle Beau always goes. He was King about thirty years ago and *still* tells us about it every chance he gets. He said last year the fucking prime minister of England came and bowed to the King of Rex. I mean, *what is going on in these balls?*"

We all look at Ava. She teaches mythology and history and she is well-versed in New Orleans history and traditions. There isn't a conspiracy theory around that hasn't been evaluated by Ava. She loves them. She taps the table with her finger. "That is true. The first krewe, Comus is considered the most powerful, and Rex is nearly as powerful. In the old days the krewes would roll a red carpet down Canal Street and meet in the middle with a bunch of pomp and circumstance and the Rex king would bow to the Comus king, establishing Comus' power."

Jimmy Tate sighs. "And how does wearing tights and getting falling-down-drunk show power?"

She continues, "The krewes started out as a way for powerful people to meet in secret and make their plans. It's always been this way. Before phones and emails, they needed a 'front' that wouldn't raise suspicion. They met in taverns and bars, but in New Orleans, they created krewes, which were like clubs, but even more exclusive. They had the money and the power and they wanted to keep it that way."

"But it seems Mardi Gras would work against the rich and powerful staying that way." Bellamy says. "The whole reason for Mardi Gras is to turn the world upside down for a while — the rich trade places with the poor, the powerful with the weak — everyone is on equal footing because of the masks, and everyone is pretend-rich with all the beads."

"Festivals like Mardi Gras are no threat to the rich and

powerful, if anything it allows them to stay entrenched," Ava says. "Who do you think is pulling the strings behind the scenes?"

"But that's one of my favorite things about Mardi Gras," I say, "No corporate sponsorship. No one is trying to get you to buy anything or make them money. It's just communities pooling their resources to create a beautiful creative explosion of fun."

Ava raises one skeptical eyebrow—she has great arched brows like Bette Davis in *Dangerous*. "Just like the games at the Coliseum in ancient Rome. They distracted the public with shallow entertainment, gave them something to talk about that meant nothing so the people in power could stay that way and the public was kept too busy to ask too many questions, like why local schools are such poor quality."

Jimmy Tate takes a swig of my Bloody Mary and is immediately distracted. "Oh Girl! That Bloody Mary is delicious with a capital D!"

"I know," I smile, happy to think of something else other than last night for a moment.

He drops his voice. "When I was little my cousin told me if I stood in front of a mirror and said 'Bloody Mary' three times, a bloody woman would appear behind me and kill me with a butcher knife. Even now I don't dare try it."

It's such a relief to think about something other than last night I leap on the subject like a frog's tongue catching a fly. "I just researched this. No one knows the origin of the name, although they say Queen Mary was called that because of all the murders she ordered. I probably shouldn't tell you this, I don't want to spook you…"

I look around the table at their faces, all eyes morbidly fascinated by what I might say.

"I'm not sure I can take anymore spooky stories," Bellamy rumbles, "but you hooked us now."

We all lean our heads closer together and my eyes grow wide as I whisper loudly, "I read research the other day that it's scientifically proven, that if you look into a mirror in the dark, your facial recognition cues misfire and you will start seeing other things in the mirror besides yourself."

Jimmy Tate gasps and his eyes are even bigger than mine. "Ha! That explains why people see Bloody Mary in the mirror."

"Exactly."

"But it doesn't explain how they get stabbed," Jimmy Tate says as he takes a swig so strong his drink goes down by at least three inches.

"Honey, have you ever known a single person in the history of the world who got stabbed by Bloody Mary in the mirror?" I ask, sitting back in the tufted booth.

I can see him thinking about this, racking his brain for even one murder.

"Wait, can we get back to Rex?" Ava is like an alligator who has caught a deer—she's having trouble swallowing but come hell or high water, she is not letting go.

Bellamy interrupts, "Do any of y'all know if *this* is true? I heard a story a few years ago about Rex. One of the Bush dynasty clan, Laura I think, came as a special guest to pay homage to Rex royalty."

I'm still hot so I lift my hair off my neck. "Well, she's not exactly powerful. She is *married* to power, but does that count?"

"That *is* true." Ava says over me. "And you know Comus quit parading in the 90's when they passed an anti-discrimination law saying all krewes had to reveal the names of their members."

"I wonder what secrets they are hiding?" Bellamy says as she cuts into her fried green tomatoes lathered in the white foamy remoulade sauce. She points her fork at us like a villager with a pitchfork. "And before any of you say anything about my diet, fried green tomatoes count as an excellent source of vegetables, or fruits, or whatever the hell a tomato is."

"Even though they are probably about a thousand calories a bite?" Jimmy Tate says, nibbling on his olive nonchalantly.

Bellamy shoots him a glare.

I interject. "I've always wondered why the date of Fat Tuesday changes every year? I know they count forty days back from Easter for Mardi Gras, but why does Easter change every year? Just because it's the first Sunday in April?"

"Easter's date is determined by the first Sunday after the first full moon after the Spring Equinox," Ava answers.

Jimmy Tate laughs. "How pagan of those Catholics to plan their big holiday around the Spring Equinox."

"They are celebrating the same thing the pagans celebrated—death brought back to life, just like Winter turns into Spring and the dead earth erupts in flowers."

"And bunnies come hopping out with Easter eggs?" Jimmy Tate asks.

"Bunnies and eggs represent fertility and rebirth, and they are the emblems of the pagan spring goddess, Eostre."

"Seriously? That's just blatant plagiarism."

"Yes well, that's what happens when you want to take something over and make it your own. The Comus founders did the same thing. They were inspired by a mystic society in Mobile, Alabama called the Cowbellion de Rakin Society."

"Cowbellion?" asks Jimmy Tate, swiping the hot pepper garnish off my drink. "I like that word. It sounds like a group of cows wearing bells around their necks are forming a rebellion."

"Wasn't it Comus who first created the flambeaux?" I ask, leaning my swimming head on Jimmy Tate's shoulder. "I love those torches, although I feel kind of bad for the guys carrying them, they look so hot and sweaty and people throwing coins at them. I mean, really people? You can't hand them a dollar bill?"

"Oh I agree," Ava nods. "They should change that tradition after almost two hundred years. The poor things have to bend down and grab coins off the ground *while*

54

carrying a massive heavy torch. Ridiculous."

Jimmy Tate says, "It's good exercise, all those squats with the extra weight. And they could use it too. Where do they find those guys? Under a freeway overpass? I haven't seen that many missing teeth since I carved jack-o-lanterns last year."

"Jimmy Tate!" Ava stops him. "That is so rude. Those poor guys probably need the money, and every coin counts."

Jimmy Tate has his dander up now. "Well, let's hope they head straight to the dentist and not to the corner liquor store."

"*Jimmy Tate!*"

"Just sayin... you might be singing a different tune if one came into your precious school and pissed all over your library books."

I giggle silently into my straw. Jimmy Tate had a high hobo wander into his pilates studio and relieve himself on the bucket of eucalyptus-scented ice towels. It was two years ago but he's still mad about it.

Bellamy reads from her phone. "It says here that Comus created the first night parade with rolling floats and torches, and it was so popular that the next year thousands of people came from out of town to see the revels."

Ava is looking at Bellamy's screen. Her eyes grow big and she whispers, "Oh dear."

"What?" the entire table says at once.

She looks at us and bites her lip. "The first parade was torches and a float of the devil."

"So?" Jimmy Tate says. "Hell is a common theme for parades."

Ava exhales, "Those are also the symbols for the Illuminati." We all read *The DaVinci Code* a while back for our book club and are well-versed in illuminati symbology at the moment.

"There's no such thing as the devil, Darlin'," Jimmy Tate says.

Ava hushes her voice and looks around. "I just read about

a neighborhood where all the pets started disappearing. They finally found the guy and he had black eyes and had shaved his teeth into points like a wolf. It's not the devil you have to worry about, it's the people who believe in him."

Bellamy reads from her phone in her professor voice, "Comus dressed as demons at their first parade because they based their entire krewe on John Milton's Masque about the Greek God, Comus and temptation." She turns her phone to face us. "Look at their old invitations, demons and devils, illuminati symbology."

"From the beginning, the invitations were works of art," Ava says. "They had them created by artists and they were so beautiful people collected them and framed them. They still do."

Jimmy Tate moves his arms like a conductor silencing the percussion section. All eyes turn to me as Jimmy Tate whispers, "Do you have your Rex invitation with you? Can we see it?"

"No! I mean, yes, I have it with me, but no, I'm not pulling it out here. What if there's another looney toon in here looking for someone to drop dead on?"

There is silence for a moment before Bellamy says, "Powder room conference. *Now.*"

"Wait!" says Jimmy Tate. "What about me? I can't go in the ladies room."

Bellamy points towards the hallway. "There's a large single powder room down here. We can all fit. But we must be discreet. Ellington, pretend you're sick and we'll help you in there."

"*What?* That's not discreet!" I whisper back.

"Can you pretend to choke?" asks Jimmy.

"No, that's even less discreet. Ava, can you go flutter those big brown eyes at the maître d while we all slink in, then you join us? Dear god, what are we? Sixteen? We're adults. Why can't we all go in the same restroom for god's sake?"

"I'll do it," Ava says cheerfully. She loves anything

clandestine.

And so, one at a time, we all head for the powder room.

Chapter 7

The Black Key Cocktail

(A dark, rich experience)

Black Barrel Rum, Pure Maple Syrup, Angostura Bitters, Orange Bitters

Once all four of us are squeezed into the super-luxe powder room, I brace my back against the door, open my bag, and slowly pull out the swirling red and gold envelope. The room is quiet like everyone is holding their breath. It seems illicit, more like a drug deal than the unveiling of an invitation, but there's a reason these are my closest friends: their minds are ignited by beautiful things just like mine. I let them revel in the envelope, turning it in slow circles like a Chanel model on a runway. They ooh and aah, gushing about the lush colors and swirling shapes. If you stare at it long enough it feels like you are dissolving into swirls yourself, which I guess is the point.

"Is the paper handmade?" Ava asks. "Look at that nubbly texture."

"I'm not sure," I answer, but it feels deliciously rough under my fingertips.

I slowly pull out the actual invitation with a little teasing, like Gypsy Rose Lee emerging from her dress, and there's a collective gasp.

"Can we touch it?"

"Of course! My goodness, it's not a Picasso."

They all reach out hesitant but hungry fingers to touch the gold embossed lettering. The whole group is giddy with delight when our reverie is interrupted by the clatter of everything inside my purse as I drop the damn thing.

Bellamy is counting my lipsticks as she picks them up for me. "Ellington Martini, why do you carry around so many lipsticks in your handbag? I've only seen you wear one color since I've known you — bright, deep red."

"Bellamy, I'm sure you know there are as many shades of bright deep red as there are birds in the sky. Some have blue undertones, some pink, some are matte, some gloss... depends how I feel."

She starts reading the colors as she puts them back in my purse. "Let's see, we have Matador, Rebel, Diva, Smoke and Mirrors, True, Ruby, Burgundy, and Dark Side." She opens Dark Side and twists the bottom to make the deep red color appear. "Lawdy, if this lipstick could walk, it would swagger."

Jimmy Tate is holding something that fell out of my purse and turning it over in his hand. "What the hell is this?"

We all look. He's holding what looks like a heavy rusty skeleton key about the size of an index finger.

"Where did you find that?" I ask.

"In your purse."

"*In my purse*? Not possible. I have never seen it before in my life."

Bellamy mutters, "Honey, a squirrel could be living in your handbag and you wouldn't notice with all those lipsticks."

I would glare at her but I'm too intrigued by this key. "How in the world would I carry a thing this size in my own handbag and not notice? The weight alone would tip me off that something wasn't right."

Ava's eyes are huge. "What if that monk slipped this into your bag?"

This horrifies me. "How in the world would he have done that without me noticing? And why?"

"Well you got knocked to the ground right? Did your purse open or anything spill out?"

I nod. "Actually my purse did open when it dropped to the ground."

Jimmy Tate is whispering loudly. "What if it was open before it hit the ground?"

I suck in my breath and am feeling suddenly panicked. I close my eyes and a full body shiver courses through me. When I open my eyes I have six eyes staring at me. I breathe deeply, straighten my spine to make myself taller, spread my feet apart, and put my hands on my hips like Wonder Woman.

Bellamy says carefully, "Sugar, what are you doing? Why are you standing like that?"

"This, my dear Bellamy, is a power pose. I recently read it is scientifically proven that if you stand in a "power pose" for two minutes, it raises your power hormones and lowers your stress hormones." All three of them immediately mimic my pose.

"Is it working?" I ask.

Jimmy Tate looks down at his body and adjusts his feet even wider. "I can't tell yet, but I do kind of feel a teensy bit stronger."

I exhale with my eyes closed, and when I open them, I say, "I have made a decision. I'm going to solve this crime."

Jimmy Tate stifles a snort, "Honey, leave this matter to the police. This is dangerous, with a capital D."

Bellamy nods. "He's right. This is not the job for you."

I shake my head. "No, listen, I didn't say anything before because it's so preposterous, but the detectives seemed to imply that Winston may have known the victim. What if they suspect him? I will clear him before he even knows their suspicions." I am feeling more and more like a superhero. "Also, this is perfect for my next novel. I'm going to write the ultimate mystery. 'A monk falls over dead on a novelist and she solves the crime'."

"Um, no. A big fat no, Ellington." Ava is firm. "This is crazy. You are a writer, a performer, a Bon Vivant. You have no experience in crime. This is the real deal, not Nancy Drew and the Case of the Missing Eyeglasses."

Jimmy Tate nods his head in agreement with Bellamy. "I know for a fact you've seen too many James Bond movies, all those spy-themed slumber parties we had. But those are *movies*, not real life."

I feel gleeful. I'm taking back control. "Listen, all of you, this is my chance to protect Winston *and* to live out one of my stories, blur the lines between fiction and non-fiction. I could create a whole new genre: Creative Nonfiction Mysteries."

Bellamy sighs and takes my hand. "I think this is a bad idea but I sure as tarnation am not going to let you gallivant around playing Sherlock Holmes by yourself. We'll look into this together."

Jimmy Tate sighs. "I just want it to go on record that I don't think this is a good idea at all, but I will not abandon my friend in her time of need. Should we tell the real detectives, the professional ones?"

"No," I say a little too robustly. "I mean they are very nice, but they will definitely not approve of this."

Jimmy Tate rubs his hands together. "So, what's our first move?"

"Well, I guess the first move should be gathering information. First, I will text Winston and ask him if he knew the victim last night, just to verify what I already know, then I will have him send me the photo from last night." I text him.

"Wait, how did Winston get the photo? Didn't the police take it?"

"Yes, but he took a picture of it before they even got there."

"Damn that man is a quick thinker."

"I know. All *I* could think of was Grace Kelly and Cary Grant. Then, I will go to the Locksmyth on Magazine Street and see what I can find out about this key."

"Wait, shouldn't we give the key to the police?" Bellamy says.

"I suppose we should. But it won't hurt if we check it out first. Then, we'll find out everything we can about the weapon and try to figure out what the 'killing of the king' means."

Bellamy raises her hand. "I'll do that. I have time to do a little research this afternoon." She is trying out one of my lipsticks in the mirror.

"And we should find out more about the victim. The detective said his name was Pike."

Bellamy's head whips around to look at me. "Wait, Pike? What was the first name?" she asks.

"Duncan," I answer, and when I see her face I know I've made a mistake. Her face turns pale and she hunches over like she's been punched in the stomach. She fumbles for her phone, dialing her mother with shaking hands.

"Bellamy?" I rub her back like she's a child with the stomach flu. "What is the matter?"

She starts speaking to her mother's voicemail. "Mother? Call me as soon as you can." She hangs up and texts the same phrase. Finally she looks up, her blonde hair staying in perfect place even when her face looks like a hurricane is passing through it. "Duncan Pike is my Yankee cousin. I mean, he's part Yankee, part New Orleanian."

"What?" We all gasp at the same time.

Bellamy nods. Her doctor manner is kicking in and she's talking in a bizarrely calm manner. "I haven't seen him in several years. He was at Yale for years and now goes to Tulane Medical School. We were really close when we were little, but not anymore. My mother and his father are brother and sister." Her voice is calm but I can see the tremors underneath. Being a doctor, it takes a lot to rattle her. Once we were in the reptile room when a snake was eating a mouse. Bellamy kept her eyes wide open when the snake unhinged its jaws to grab the mouse — while I ran screaming covering my eyes. Then I heard her shout a word I have never heard her use in all her well-brought-up elegance. "COOL!"

But I guess it's different when you're related to the mouse.

A tear escapes and we all crowd around her to comfort her. She waves us away and starts to freshen her face in the mirror. "I don't even know why I'm crying. We weren't close. I just can't believe, that little freckle-faced boy died in such a brutal way. We used to open our gifts together on Christmas morning." She puts on her lipstick perfectly, even with a shaking hand. She tosses that silky blonde curtain of hair, dabs her nose with a tissue and says, "I have to go to my mother."

Ava says, "I'm driving you."

"We will come too," says Jimmy Tate.

"No, Ava can take me. Let me see how my mother is doing and I'll let you know when you can come by."

Ava and Bellamy leave arm-in-arm as Jimmy Tate and I head back to the table to gather our things, pay the bill, and head outside.

Chapter 8

Death in the Afternoon

(Invented by Papa Hemingway himself)

Champagne, Absinthe

We step outside Commander's Palace and I take a deep breath of the honeysuckle air. "Damn, that was a dramatic lunch. I feel terrible for Bellamy. My goodness, if I had known she was possibly related to the murder victim I would never have mentioned his name.

"Are you really thinking of doing detective work?"

"More than ever! We can't keep letting these thugs take over our beautiful city. If the police can't contain the crime here, then it's up to citizens like us."

"Is this you or the Bloody Marys talking?"

I laugh. "The Bloody Marys of course! And they're awfully bold, aren't they? Damn those drinks were good and damn if I didn't drink one too many."

Jimmy Tate laughs. "I'm feeling a bit woozy myself." He suddenly puts his arm across me like a seat belt on a roller coaster. "Hold up: skeleton key, secret society, Booyah!" He does his victory dance which involves moving his arms like the side rods on a high speed train and shuffling his feet in fast motion.

"Booyah what?"

"Ellington, the Quarto! Don't you know about the Quarto?" he says, still chugging like a train but now turning in circles too.

"The secret society in the cemetery?"

"Yes. In *this* cemetery." He points at the cemetery gates across the street, then toots while tugging his arm down twice like he's yanking the pull cord on a train whistle. "Lafayette No. 1."

"I know they were a secret society, but what does this have to do with a key?"

"Oh Darlin', you didn't pay attention on our ghost tour last week, did you?"

"I did, of course I did, but I don't remember anything about keys."

"The Quarto was a group of four friends who supposedly guarded some very important secret. Legend says they burned all their papers before they died, but they did leave a key and passed it on to their children. They asked to be buried together here and supposedly the key opens some part of their tomb."

"Well, why hasn't anyone ever opened it."

"Maybe they didn't have the right key."

I gasp. "Oh my. Let's do it."

We link arms and run across the street. "Serendipity," I squeal but immediately feel woozy. I sigh. "I so wish I could hold my alcohol better. How in the world do Bellamy and Ava drink so much and remain stone cold sober?"

"It's their Irish blood."

"Ava is Hispanic and Bellamy is French."

"Honey, don't be so literal. Consider yourself lucky you can't hold your liquor. You'd make a terrible alcoholic."

"True."

We are walking briskly to the tomb of the Quarto and

everything seems magnified. I listen to the twigs and fallen leaves crunch under our feet. The air smells like wet earth and looking at the jumble of tombs is somehow comforting. New Orleans has never buried their dead underground, but above ground in tall stone vaults called 'ovens'. "Don't you think the cemeteries here look like stone villages built by Dr. Suess."

He laughs. "If Dr. Seuss had been a mad scientist, yes."

The 'ovens' tilt this way and that, overgrown with moss and weeds. "It's fecund here, don't you think?"

"You just like saying that word: fecund."

"True, it sounds so dirty. Fecund." We both giggle. Fecund with decay, the endless juxtaposition that is New Orleans—fertile life teeming with death. But how clever that it is the dying plants that make the soil so much richer for the new tender growth.

The cemetery seems unusually quiet and still. I am wary. Cemeteries in NOLA are notoriously dangerous. Big stone tombs make excellent hiding places for people of ill repute. Every guidebook will tell you to stay away unless you're with a tour group. And Jimmy Tate is not exactly a macho muscleman. I'll put it this way, in a streetfight, I'd put my money on me.

But Lafayette #1 is small and usually busy with people walking off their martinis after lunch—safety in numbers as my mother used to say. Today I see no people, and my heart is pounding harder and harder. Probably finding it hard to pump all that vodka around my body.

We find the Quarto. "You keep watch while I look for the keyhole."

"No, Girl. *You* keep watch. I'm used to spending more time on my knees than you."

"Well that's true."

He drops to his knees, running his hands all around the stone, even down at the overgrown bottom. "Give me a boost so I can reach the top."

I clasp my hands like my cheerleading sister taught me

when we practiced lifts. He puts his foot in it and heave-ho's himself up. "Ow! Take off your shoe."

"Oh, alright." He slides off his shoe and stands in my hands again.

My phone pings and Jimmy Tate's shoes are digging into my hands. "Hop down for a second, you're killing me." He does. I check my phone. "Oh, Winston sent the photo and he says he did not know the victim, although he looked familiar. He looked familiar to me too, although in the heat of the moment, the whole world looked familiar and totally unfamiliar at the same time."

We stop to look at it closely. The photo is of the four young men in antique clothing standing in front of the St. Charles Theater. Jimmy Tate looks closely at the clothing, scanning up and down. "Their clothing looks like mid-1800's." He scans up to the faces. "Holy fuck, Ellington!"

"What?"

"That's John Wilkes Booth."

"Who? Lincoln's assassin?"

"Yup. The devil incarnate. Ava was right, the devil *was* in New Orleans."

"Are you sure?"

"Damn sure!" he shouts, then whispers in a thick southern drawl, "How could I ever forget those cold-blooded eyes. Reptilian. Scary." He shivers.

"Why in the world did the monk hand me a picture of John Wilkes Booth?"

"I have no idea. I've seen a lot of pictures of him but I don't know much about him. He gives me the creeps. All I *do* know is that he was an actor."

"I remember that too, probably the only fact I know about him."

"He's standing in front of the St. Charles Theater."

"Do you think he ever performed here?"

Jimmy Tate pulls out his phone. "Googling, googling... Yup, he performed as an actor in many cities, New Orleans being one of them."

"Does it say what year?"

"1860."

I feel a buzz of excitement running through me. I take the notes on my phone. "Those are excellent clues: Booth, St. Charles Theater, 1860. And the police said that colichemarde weapon was common in pre-civil war times so the dates connect. Does it say what play he did?"

"Does it matter?"

"Of course it does. Maybe the other men are actors and we can find out who *they* were."

We are startled when we hear a twig snap loudly nearby and a crunch.

"Hello?" I call, quickly putting my phone into my handbag. The photo seems dangerous all of a sudden.

The crunching footsteps are getting closer and I look around for a weapon to defend us. But then a stooped old man with thick white hair to his shoulders and tanned wrinkled skin steps out from a nearby tomb. He smells strongly of alcohol, which I'm surprised I can smell since I probably smell strongly of alcohol myself. His black shirt is partially unbuttoned and I can see leather straps around his neck holding a medallion and what looks like a vial of something. He is wearing a big sunhat and baggy jeans, but most striking of all is his walking stick. It is tall and the wood is twisted and weather-beaten and perfectly swirled like the ringlet of a victorian doll. It is ornately carved and topped off with a strap he has looped around his wrist, along with several other leather bracelets and a big silver watch.

I quickly grab a tissue out of my bag and pat my face. "Hi!" I say. "You scared us. I thought you were a burglar."

He laughs gleefully and his teeth are so white and straight I wonder if they're real.

"Taking a walk in the cemetery?" he asks.

I glance at Jimmy Tate. Probably best if we don't tell anyone we are looking for the secret lock. I decide to distract him. "Your walking stick is just amazing! I've never seen one like it. Where did you get it?"

He holds it up. "You like Havashana? Ain't she purdy?"

"Havashana?"

"That's her name." He runs one gnarled hand over the carvings. "Named her after the Goddess of the Seven Sisters. She's very special."

I move closer so I can see the details. "My Dad would love a walking stick like this. Did you get it around here?"

He laughs. "Sure did. Made her myself."

"You carved this yourself? You must be a master woodcarver." I look closely at him now. "You know, you actually look exactly like Gepetto.

"Well, the story of how Havashana came to be is pretty interestin'." He caresses her while he talks. "One day I was walking over by the hobo camp, over there by the Mississippi. I was surrounded on all sides by trees twisting this way and that. Now I like a crooked tree, better than straight trees even — people leave the crooked trees alone. I was looking at those branches twisting up to that white sky when I tripped and rolled. Scraped up my face, almost lost an eye, but when I stopped rolling and opened my eyes, I was lying on my back and Havashana was on top of me." He leans forward with a whisper. "She likes to be on top."

Jimmy Tate who had been unnaturally quiet clears his throat, our secret signal that whomever we are talking to just might be off their rocker.

The old man continues in his slow syrup voice, "Of course, I can't refuse a lady, so I took her home. That night I dreamed I was fighting a medieval battle for a queen, so I carved a medieval sword here," he points to a sword carved into the stick, "And I carved a crown and scepter here, for the Queen." He points out the crown and scepter. He holds the stick out to me. "Go ahead, you can touch it."

I run my finger over the gorgeous, intricate carvings. There's a series of shapes intertwined together like snowflakes layered on each other.

He speaks softly, "That's Voodoo Lace. It's my specialty."

"I've never heard of Voodoo Lace. It's beautiful."

"Well, you never heard of it because I made it up," he laughs. "It's my signature."

Jimmy Tate steps closer and peers at the stick. "Look at that, is that a coin?"

"Yup. A Medieval Coin from Spain. I put amulets into all my sticks."

Jimmy Tate reaches a finger out and lightly touches the coin. "Looks really old."

The man smiles. "1100's." He takes the strap off his wrist and hands me the stick. "Go ahead, hold her. She feels real good in your hand."

I put my hand over the well-worn handle and it fits. "I feel like I've been transported into a storybook."

The old man says, "That's because Havashana is my axis aundi."

"Axis mundi?"

"My connection between Heaven and Earth."

"Ooh I like that, axis mundi. Dancing is *my* axis mundi. Oh my goodness, how rude of us. We got so excited about Havashana we didn't even properly introduce ourselves. This is Jimmy Tate and I'm Ellington Martini."

I reach out my hand to shake his. His hands are rough and tan. The Bloody Marys have loosened my lips so I say, "Your hands remind me of the turquoise-sellers in Arizona."

"I been to Arizona when I was young. Superstition Mountain."

"I was born at the foot of Superstition Mountain! Boy did I long for that turquoise, but we could never afford it. My Nana always said, 'Who needs to buy turquoise when we can look at the turquoise sky for free?' Of course she practiced black magic and had her feet amputated, so she's not *totally* reliable."

Jimmy Tate folds his arms. "Boy your Nana sounds a lot

more interesting than mine. Mine had blue hair, wore dowdy pioneer dresses and aprons and spent all day cooking."

The woodcarver laughs and holds out his hand to shake Jimmy Tate's. "I'm Ed, but most people call me Grandpa Boogie."

"Grandpa Boogie?" Jimmy Tate smiles. "I like that."

Ed nods. "I'm a dancer."

"Me too!" I cut in. "What kind of dance do you do?"

"Oh all kinds, but mostly the boogie woogie. I work over at Jacque-Imo's. I'm their dancer."

"What do you mean? I didn't know Jacques-Imo's had dancers."

At the mention of Jacques-Imo's, Jimmy Tate's interest perks up. "Jacque-Imo's has the best Shrimp Etoufee in New Orleans."

Ed nods. "And their Alligator Cheesecake."

"Yes. Wait, have I seen you there? Do you dance in the bar area in front?"

Ed smiles. "Not exactly *in* the bar. I dance *on* the bar, and on the tabletops, and sometimes out on the sidewalks."

I look at his bowed legs and his hunched posture and I can't picture how he climbs on top of tables. "Do you take Havashana with you?"

"Of course. Jacque helps me up on a table or on the bar and I just stay up there dancing. It entertains their customers while they're waiting for tables, and since most people are waiting for hours, they *need* the entertainment. ... and I need the drinks. I get paid in cocktails... best job I ever had.

"What is the boogie woogie like? I'm dying to see!"

"I'll show you." He pulls an ipod out of his pocket and fiddles with it. He sticks earbuds in his ears and starts to bounce. Jimmy Tate and I can't help ourselves. We start clapping and cheering him on as his bouncing morphs into shoulder rolls, even though we can't hear the music. Then he builds up momentum to start moving his hips in circles. He shakes his head happily while he dances, his hair moving like freshly picked cotton in a wind storm. For his finale, he turns in a circle. His body moves slowly into each movement, but once its there, he moves like he's twenty-five years younger, and with so much joy. At the end he raises one arm in the air with a huge smile and shouts, "Welcome to Vieux Carre!"

Jimmy Tate and I are hoarse from screaming and our stomachs hurt from laughing so hard. Damn it feels good to laugh.

"That was *awesome!*"

Grandpa Boogie leans against a rock, panting, with his big smile. "Buy me a drink?"

"After that performance you deserve one!" Jimmy Tate and I look at each other. The Quarto investigation will have to wait for now. "We are heading down to the Locksmyths on Magazine, but we can get a drink afterward?"

"How are you getting to the Locksmyths?"

"Streetcar. We just had a few cocktails so we'll have to come back for the car. Why?"

He smiles slyly. "I have a very dear friend who works at Locksmyth's. Haven't seen her in a while. Mind if join you?"

I don't dare glance at Jimmy Tate since I know he'll be shaking his head at me. We have enough to worry about without an elderly tag-along, but I don't want to be rude, plus I adore old people. Fabulous stories to tell and I don't mind hearing them over and over. I link my arm in his. "Not at all. We'd love the company."

We start walking towards the entrance as Ed tells us about the cemetery. "Did you know this cemetery was once part of the Livaudais plantation? Would have been mine if they'd kept it in the family."

"You're kidding? You're part of the original Livaudais family?"

He nods. "I wonder what they would have done with the bodies if we hadn't sold the plantation."

I press my lips together. "Bodies?"

"Thousands of Yellow Fever victims were dumped at

these gates, and every other plague that blew through the city. They say when the moon is full you can still hear the screaming and moaning of the dying, and the ones they left behind."

"That's creepy," I rub my arms which are erupting in goosebumps.

"Are you sure it's the voices of ghosts and not the good people of the Garden District having a good time?" says Jimmy Tate, tugging on his seersucker blazer.

Ed laughs so hard he slaps his knee. "Well I never thought of that. Could be."

Chapter 9

Bourbon and Peach Smash

Peach, Mint, Ginger, Simple Syrup, Fine Bourbon, Punt e Mes, Ginger Ale

I'm thanking my lucky stars it isn't July as we walk from St. Charles down to Magazine Street—the sidewalks steam in July. We turn onto Magazine and there's the Locksmyth shop. It doubles as a leather and shoe repair and it looks like all kinds of crazy from the outside (and the inside, for that matter). It's painted black and someone has written all over the front in white paint little phrases like: 'There's a little blue jay wearing red shoes on a sad night' and written in tiny letters: 'But you'll never be forgiven for whatever you've done with the keys.' And written extra-large under a childlike painting of a boat and anchor: 'You can ask any sailor for the keys from the jailer.' And my favorite quote is written in a spiral so I have to turn my head to read it: 'And I'm sick of pretending, I'm broken from bending, I've lived too long on my knees.'

This place is crazy, but I like it. There are old shoes hanging on the front of the shop as well as pieces of iron in various shapes: horseshoes, leather bridles with iron rings, and my least favorite: an open leg trap, it's jagged teeth dirty, stained, and rusty. There's something about traps that turns my stomach. I turn my face away and open the door for Jimmy Tate and Ed.

Inside the shop the smell of leather and chemicals is so overpowering, I'm wondering how anyone could possibly work here and not suffocate. I hold the door open for as long as possible just to let some clean air in. The shop is stacked floor to ceiling with shelves of all different types of shoes, from steel-toed work boots to tiny shiny pink ballet slippers. And behind the counter is a large wall of different sizes of keys: car keys, house keys, lock box keys, and skeleton keys. Some are smaller than my eyeball and some are bigger than my arm, fingertip to elbow. And I have to wonder what in the world the giant keys open — some locked rusty old gate belonging to a giant somewhere in the clouds?

There is no one behind the counter but there are a lot of loud buzzing noises coming from the back. Whomever is back there is trying to drown out the noise of the drills and saw with Tom Waits. "Invitation to the Blues" is playing loudly, and as always when I listen to Tom Waits, his rough voice speaks to me on a level I don't understand with my mind but I fully understand with my soul.

And it's a battered old suitcase to a hotel someplace
And a wound that will never heal.
No prima donna, the perfume is on,
An old shirt that is stained with blood and whiskey…

How apropos for me this afternoon… oh how I long to be the primadonna I was yesterday at this time, before it was all ruined with blood and wounds and battered souls.

I tap the silver bell in front of me on the counter that's used to call the counterperson, but the ring is so light there's no way anyone will hear it. Then I see the sign next to it. It reads 'Do you really think this tiny bell can make anything happen, Stupid? Use the Big Guns. They always get the job done.' I follow the arrow and see a large dismantled shotgun hanging on a thick rope that is attached to an extra-large cowbell up on the ceiling.

Ed and Jimmy Tate are watching me.

Jimmy Tate folds his arms and says, "Yeah, Stupid. Use the big guns."

I reach up and tug on the shotgun. I like guns even less than I like traps, and the feel of the metal in my hand gives me the heebie jeebies. Jimmy Tate is looking around his feet on the floor with a face like he's just bitten into a lemon. I realize this is the kind of place where a rat might run over your toe, and I know Jimmy Tate has folded his arms so he doesn't actually touch anything in the shop. I start looking at the floor myself, but try to blur my vision so I don't see any of the pony-sized cockroaches or rats that populate New Orleans.

But then the counter person appears and she's quite beautiful in a wicked queen sort of way. Her hair is black in choppy lines above her shoulder, the front held back with a pair of goggles worn like a preppy hairband. She has a chain of flowers tattooed across her neck like a choker and both of her delicate white arms are tattooed from wrist to shoulder with vines and moonflowers. There is a tear tattooed on her cheekbone that looks like a beauty mark. Her eyes are bright green and she's wearing an old slip covered by a butcher apron and tall brown boots. Think a rough and dirty Elizabeth Taylor in *Butterfield 8*. I feel oddly attracted to her, but not like I want to do her, more like I want to take her home and make her cookies while she tells me all her troubles. She sees Ed and leans forward to shake his hand. "Grandpa Boogie," she says in a deep voice that sounds well-acquainted with cigarettes. "How the hell are ya?" She shakes his hand.

He smiles back. "Hunter. Haven't seen you in a while. Just met these little nippers at the cemetery." He points at us with his thumb. "Said they were coming to the locksmyth shop and I decided to tag along to see you."

She looks at me and Jimmy Tate. "You must be the little… nippers." The word sounds obscene when she says it, and I cover my breasts with my arms as she turns to Ed.

"Still dancing at Jacques-Imo's?"

"Sure… when they'll have me."

That's when I spot the tall twisting walking stick leaning against the wall of keys behind her. "Are you a woodcarver too, or did Ed make that stick?"

She glances behind her shoulder. "Ed of course." She picks up the stick, runs her fingers over it, and mutters, "Such a beauty." It looks like another unusual twisting root, the kind that grows up out of the swamps. It's carved with things I wouldn't expect, like alligators and swamp trees, I can't help but notice her fingers as they caress the stick. They are tattooed with things I also wouldn't expect: one set of knuckles reads "FUCK" in crudely drawn letters, and the other reads "OFF", The fourth knuckle has a smiley face. I have to wonder if that was done to her one drunken night and now she's stuck with it, or if she did it herself on a bad day. I'm going to guess the latter. In any case, I introduce us.

"I'm Ellington and this is Jimmy Tate."

She nods her head as a greeting. "Hunter."

I point to a coin inlaid on her stick, what looks like an old coin of some sort. "What's that?"

"That's an antique coin. First century Rome. Emperor Nero. I'm a collector."

"Of coins?"

She stares at me. "No, of taxes."

I snort with laughter. "That's cool." Where did that come from? Something about Hunter is making me use words I haven't used since sixth grade. Oh I hate it when people make me blush and stumble, but there's something about her that is very appealing in an 'I want to see the Coney Island Freak Show even though it will make me sad and sick' kind of way. I redirect my attention. "So, is it Nero stuff you collect or antique coins?"

She doesn't answer but rubs the coin with a cloth to make it shine even more.

I fumble to connect, "Isn't Nero the one who fiddled while Rome burned?"

"He was misunderstood," Hunter says, looking at me through her long thick lashes.

Jimmy Tate now snorts. "Yeah, Nero was a psycho, about as misunderstood as Frankenstein." He breaks into an imitation, "But he didn't *mean* to strangle her, he was trying to give her a hug."

Hunter stares at him and I don't know if she wants to slug him or throw him out. Instead she laughs in a bawdy way, like Mae West. She points at Jimmy Tate. "I like you."

What about me? Why didn't she say she liked me?

Jimmy Tate points at another case on the wall behind the counter. "You collect butterflies too?"

Hunter looks over her shoulder. "I like pretty things."

I'm feeling quite sad for all those beautiful butterflies pinned to a board, and it must be showing on my face because she looks at me and says, "Don't worry princess, I don't kill them. I find them."

"You find them? With their wings intact?" Jimmy Tate is leaning over the counter to get a better look at an electric blue butterfly.

"Yup. I have a knack for finding perfect butterflies." She looks at me like she'd like to eat me for lunch. "And I know how to handle the most delicate of wings so they don't break."

Now Jimmy Tate is scrunching his eyebrows together as he looks from her to me. Ed is laughing, apparently delighted by Hunter's behavior.

She shrugs and lays the stick back in its place against the wall.

I can't stop trying to read all her tattoos. My head turns sideways trying to read the words interlaced with oleander up her arms. "I like your tattoos."

She steps back and lifts her slip and apron up to her chest. It's a bit shocking since I don't know her that well and, well, people don't usually go yanking their dresses above their heads in front of strangers, but she has on little black shorts and the word "scorched" spelled out across her stomach. She turns around and she has a huge tattoo of a violin in the middle of her back, its curves mimicking her curves.

I politely say, "Wow. Those are amazing." I try to give an admiring whistle, but since I really can't whistle, it comes out softer than a pussycat walking on the felt top of a pool table. There's some sort of electricity crackling between us and I am thinking I should hightail it out of here before trouble starts brewing. "Invitation to the Blues" changes into "Singapore" and with the opening chicken squawk his rough voice starts:

We sail tonight for Singapore
We're all as mad as hatters here…

With that I imagine myself sailing on a curvy Asian ship with a one-armed dwarf at the giant wooden wheel, sailing me through warm dark starlit skies…

She snaps me out of my daydream with a curt, "What can I do for you?"

I dig in my handbag for the key. I have put it inside a blue Tiffany's bag to keep it safe. "Well, I found this key and I've never seen a key like it and I'm wondering if you might know anything about it?"

She picks it up and examines it.

We sail tonight for Singapore
Don't fall asleep while you're ashore

She pulls a loupe out from behind the counter and affixes it to her eye, turning the key so she can see all sides. She is whispering to herself. She takes out a little cloth, pours some solution on it and rubs the grime off the key.

…While making feet for children's shoes
Through the alley back from hell
When you hear that steeple bell
You must say goodbye to me

The key starts to shine and catch the light, and I see there is a tiny red stone at the top. "Is that garnet?" I ask.

She shakes her head and says "ruby" as if finding a key

with a ruby embedded in it were common. I glance at Jimmy Tate who is distracted by a rusty curved scimitar that hangs on the wall over a sign written in black marker that reads, 'Strange women lying in ponds, distributing swords, is no basis for a system of government.'

Hunter asks, "Where did you find this?" She's looking at me with the loupe still attached to her eye like a Baron with a monocle

"Well, I had a bit of a scuffle last night in the Quarter and this got dropped and somehow ended up in my handbag..." I trail off, disconcerted by her intense gaze. "Can you tell me anything about it?"

She looks at Ed who is chewing on a cinnamon stick of some sort. I have no idea where he got it and I'm hoping he didn't just find it lying around here. He nods at her.

In the land of the blind the one-eyed man is King

Hunter hands me the loupe. "Look for yourself."

I'm not sure what she's getting at but I put the loupe in my eye as Jimmy Tate bursts out laughing and says, "You've gone from looking like Miss Scarlett to Colonel Mustard." I glare at him and take a very close look at the key. I can see the red jewel winking at me from the handle. I see tiny scratch marks on the side and when I look closer, I nearly shout, "Hey, there are letters on here." Jimmy Tate looks over my shoulder, but you really can't see them without a magnifier. "They spell out, "s-i-c-v-o-l-v-o-s-i-c-i-u-b-e-o." Hmmm, I have no idea what that might mean."

Jimmy Tate pulls out his phone. "On it! I'm googling. Say them again." I repeat the letters. "Yes! We got a few hits. According to this, the letters spell out latin words. The Latin dictionary says the phrase is "sic volvo sic iubeo."

Hunter says, "As I wish, thus I command."

Our heads swivel to look at her in unison and I laugh in surprise. "You speak latin?"

She shrugs. "Doesn't everybody?" She ignores us by pulling out a rag and wiping the counter.

"I have always wanted to learn Latin and Greek."

Then she really surprises me by saying, "There are things that can only be understood in ancient languages.

Ed gives a sharp whistle, better than mine, and snaps his fingers, "Bildung, Ladies and Gentlemen. Hunter teaches herself on her own for no damn reason other than to learn. It's a beautiful thing."

Hunter stops cleaning the counter and leans forward on her elbows, staring at me. I feel like a living butterfly pinned to a velvet board by her eyes.

Tom Waits sings, *You must say goodbye to me.*

I clear my throat and try to focus. "So, this little key of secrets has a ruby on it and a latin phrase: 'As I wish thus I command.'" I ask Hunter, "Have you ever seen a key like this?"

"No, I've seen similar keys, but not exactly like this. Of course there are local legends about powerful keys."

"What kinds of local legends?"

"Well, off the top of my head, The Quarto is one example."

Jimmy Tate is intrigued. "We know the Quarto. Any others?"

"There's also the key of Jean Lafitte."

"The pirate?"

"Yup. Supposedly he buried his treasure in the brick walls of his old blacksmith shop in the Quarter. Of course every person with a metal detector who comes to New Orleans has searched every inch of those walls, but legend says there's a key. And don't forget House of Rothschild. They, too, have key legends."

"What's House of Rothschild?" I ask.

Hunter is putting on a large pair of round goggles as she shrugs again. "Le Bon Temps Roule, Princess."

"Let the good times roll? How will that tell me about House of Rothschild?"

"The bar. Fausto can tell you everything about them. Tell

him I sent you. If there's a key, he knows the lock. I have to get back to work." She smiles at Ed. "Don't be a stranger, Woodcarver."

He nods. "Freret Street Gym tonight?"

She nods. "Every Friday. Come by. Actually, there's something I want to show you if you have a minute?" After *Singapore, Ruby's Arms* starts and I'm anxious to leave as this song always makes me cry.

She opens the gate at the end of the counter and Grandpa Boogie walks through. They disappear in the back, but then Hunter pops her head back in. "Oh, one more thing. 'Sic volvo sic iubeo' is also the motto for Comus." She laughs and pulls her goggles over her eyes before disappearing again.

Jimmy Tate and I look at each other. "Holy shit," we both say at the same time as we head outside. I pull out my phone and write down all our new clues. Comus, Quarto, Lafitte, Rothschild, so I can research them later and cross-reference them with Booth.

My screensaver is a photo of Grace Kelley in *Rear Window*, climbing a fire escape in her floral ball gown and kitten heels. It's my favorite nail-biting scene of all time in *Rear Window* when she decides to do her own detective work and climbs into the killer's apartment to look for clues.

If she can do it, so can I.

Happy and relieved to be back in familiar territory of sunshine, I take a deep breath and put on my pink cat-eye sunglasses. "Le Bon Temps Roule for an afternoon aperitif?"

"You read my mind," Jimmy Tate says, linking arms with me.

Chapter 10

Satan's Whiskers

(diabolical 1930's Hollywood cocktail)

Gin, Sweet and Dry Vermouth, Orange Curacao, Orange Bitters, OJ

We walk down the street to Le Bon Temps Roule. The bar is dark, seedy, and you have to yank your feet as you walk or they'll stick to the floor. It's not the type of place I would normally frequent, well, maybe in my Bukowski phase in my 20's when dark bars full of lost souls beckoned me like a live wire tricks a child into thinking it's a licorice stick. It took one deep scorch before I realized Bukowski was not the poet for me.

I walk up to the man wiping down the bar. "Fausto?" I ask. He is tall and muscular with his black hair combed back like an Italian bad boy from a 1950's movie. He is wearing a white t-shirt stretched tight across his chest and black jeans.

"Who wants to know?" he asks bluntly.

"Me. Us. Hunter sent us."

He motions to a dark booth in the corner. "That's Fausto." I can't see the face but I can see an arm sticking out of the booth.

"What's he drinking?"

"Whiskey, neat."

"We'll take three."

Jimmy Tate narrows his eyes at me. "Are we really going to do this? After drowning our sorrows at Commanders? We just sobered up five minutes ago."

"Shh." I say curtly. "There's a method to my madness."

The bartender pours and slides our drinks across the bar so they stop right in front of us without spilling a drop. Impressive.

We carry our shots over to the booth and I set the whiskey down in front of the mysterious man. He looks up at me through his little round glasses and he's not at all what I was expecting. He is small with a puff of gray hair, thick bushy eyebrows, and a beard to match. The table in front of him is loaded with books and notebooks and a small laptop with a beret perched on top of it. He is taking notes in a large notebook.

"Fausto?" I ask.

"Yes?" he answers in a raspy Italian accent. He sounds like an old-movie-mobster but looks more like he'd be riding an old bicycle through a little village with a baguette and a bouquet of flowers in the basket.

"Hunter told us where to find you."

"Ahhh, Hunter, how is that little lady?"

"Fine, I think." I plunge in. "It's kind of a long story, but we found a key and we are interested in learning more about organizations with key legends, like the House of Rothschild. Hunter told us if there is a key, you know the lock."

"Well, I do collect doorknobs. And books. Last count I had 50,000 doorknobs, and over 300,000 books." He lifts a book that was open facedown and there is a small silver doorknob, the kind you might find in a public restroom. He lifts his one wrinkly crooked finger to his lips and then points over his shoulder with his thumb. "Shhhh, don't tell the fuzz."

What have we gotten ourselves into?

He points at the whiskey. "Is that for me? Are you plying me with drinks? Do you think I'm that easy? Well, you're right, I am. Have a seat."

We sit down and Fausto says, "Down the hatch!" He and Jimmy Tate shoot down their drinks.

I lift the glass to my mouth and set it back down. It seems too much right now... this all seems too much. What am I doing here in a dark, seedy bar in the middle of the afternoon talking to a hobbit with a gnarled finger and a doorknob fetish?

Jimmy Tate yanks me out of my descent with a snap of his fingers in front of my face. "Ellington Martini! You drink that right now! I will not drink myself to oblivion alone."

"I just *can't* right now." I say. I lay my head on his shoulder. "I don't feel good."

Fausto looks at me with big teddy bear eyes under the thick brows. "House of Rothschild giving you the blues? They have a tendency to do that."

"I don't know anything about them. Are they a bank?"

"Oh, my dear, they are so much more than a bank," he says glancing over his shoulder. "They could buy and sell banks, governments, entire countries if they want. Of course their heyday was the 1800's and early 1900's," he lowers his voice, "but some people believe they are still in power, pulling strings behind the scenes." He holds his fingers like he's directing marionettes on a puppet stage.

"Do you think they are still around?" Jimmy Tate asks.

Fausto looks at us silently for long enough to make us squirm. Finally, he says, "Mayer Rothchild built his financial empire in Germany in the late 1700's and passed it down to his sons. The United States was a new unstable country then, so House of Rothschild sent emissaries over here. August Belmont was their bigwig in New York City and Judah Benjamin was sent to New Orleans, but both emissaries were completely tied up in New Orleans. Do you know John

Slidell?"

"Slidell as in Slidell—the town next to New Orleans?" I ask.

"Yup. Belmont married John Slidell's niece. John Slidell was a Louisiana senator." He is still pretending to work puppets, which is good because I'm getting more and more confused by all these names.

I hold up one finger for him to pause. "So, to clarify, Belmont was the House of Rothschild's financial wizard in the North and was married to power here in Louisiana?"

Jimmy Tate chimes in, "Belmont as in Belmont stakes?"

Fausto claps and points at him in excitement. "Yes! One and the same! Belmont eventually became a horse breeder but that's a different story." He waves his hands in front of his face like he's waving away a skeeter. "At the time, New Orleans was the wealthiest city in the country per capita with its cotton and sugar and its thriving port. House of Rothschild had its eyes on the prize. They wanted to control the entire economy of the new country, which is why they did the things they did."

"What did they do?" I ask, fascinated.

Fausto's eyes seem to be growing brighter as he counts on his puppet fingers to illustrate what he is saying. "Judah Benjamin's entire purpose was threefold: to come to the south, fund the confederacy and to foster a devastating Civil War. War is profitable and a split country is a weak country, easier to manipulate. After the South seceded, Judah Benjamin was a key figure in the Confederate government." Fausto counts on the fingers of his other hand. "He started out as attorney general, then became Secretary of State and then, head of Confederate intelligence under Jefferson Davis. Meanwhile, Belmont was up North with his Louisiana bride and a father-in-law senator in his pocket." He stops talking and abruptly says, "Show me the key."

He's making me nervous, but he's pretty small and pretty old, so if he tries any funny business I'm pretty sure I could take him. I dig the key back out of my bag and set it on the table in front of him. He promptly covers it with his hand, looking around again, and then turns to face the wall, pulling out a small pencil flashlight/magnifying glass contraption which he uses to look over every inch of the key.

"There are letters on here," he says, and he sounds exactly like my sister when she used to stick marshmallows in her cheeks and talk like Don Corleone.

Jimmy Tate and I nod. "We know."

"Sicvolvosiciubeo," he reads slowly as if it's one long word.

"As I wish, thus I command," I say.

"Sic Volvo Sic Iubeo, the motto of Comus," he says slowly, in four separate words. Then he says in an even slower, more rickety voice, "'Let me issue and control a nation's money and I care not who writes the laws.'"

"What's that?" I ask.

"Mayer Rothschild's most famous quote." He holds the key vertically and moves it back and forth in the light, like a hypnotist. "Legend says there is a locked box somewhere that contains all the skeletons of House of Rothschild, a box of evidence you might say."

"Evidence of what?" I ask.

"Their methods of holding power. Do you think the Hashashin worked alone?"

"Hashashin?" Now he's really losing me.

"The ancient secret society created by Hasan-I Sabbah in the mountains of Persia, the original 'Old Man of the Mountain'."

I shake my head and glance at Jimmy Tate who is also shaking his head. "We're not familiar…"

"You've never heard of Hashashin?" He shakes his head in disbelief and continues in his Don Corleone rasp, "When one has many enemies and no army, stealth killings of the powerful are an extremely effective means of warfare. Just read any historical book about royalty in any country from the

English to the Egyptians to Rome—they all used it. The Hashashin sect was special because it was organized. Hasan-I Sabbah created secret initiation rites involving mind-altering drugs." He leans towards us an whispers with wide eyes, "It is said his hold over his acolytes was so powerful they would gladly throw themselves off any parapet in the Islamic world."

"When was this?" Jimmy Tate asks.

"Eleventh, Twelfth and Thirteenth centuries."

"That was a long time ago. What would that have to do with anything today?" I ask.

Fausto sighs and roughly scrubs his beard, moving up to his eyebrows till all the hair on his face is sticking out like he's covered in zesty cat whiskers. He suddenly pounds the table with one stubby finger, "Hashashin is the first ruthless killing group we know about, and their legacy has informed every secret society since, especially House of Rothschild."

"Killing group?"

"The word 'hashashin' became assassin in English."

Jimmy Tate and I look at each other again. "Assassins?" Jimmy Tate and I ask simultaneously.

"Assassins as in the killing of presidents and kings?" I ask.

Fausto looks around and bounces his hand in the air, motioning us to be quiet. He drops his voice to a low whisper again, "House of Rothschild is responsible for nearly every assassination or attempted assassination in our country going back to the beginning. Harrison, Buchanan, Taylor, Lincoln. Of course they botched Buchanan, tried to poison him but he knew their tricks."

"Buchanan?"

"*President* Buchanan," Fausto says, gathering all his books and papers into one stack and sliding them into his satchel. "Jesus, what are they teaching in schools today? Buchanan's entire inaugural dinner was poisoned at the National Hotel in Washington D.C. in 1857. Everyone back then knew that Northern men drank tea and Southern men drank coffee.

Arsenic was sprinkled into the sugar for the tea and 38 people died."

"What?" I'm shocked. "I never learned that in history class."

Fausto laughs. "Of course you didn't. Buchanan knew he was probably poisoned and told his physician who was able to save him."

Jimmy Tate asks, "But why would House of Rothschild poison Buchanan?"

"He wanted a united country. He tried to clamp down on those who were fostering slavery and civil war and couldn't be bought. He declared no state could secede from the union. Harrison and Taylor were assassinated for the same reasons — interfering with interstate wars and trying to stop the spread of slavery into new states."

Fausto pulls his beret over one eye and slides to the end of the booth as if he's about to leave.

"Wait," I say, pulling out my phone and holding it up to him so he can see the antique photo. "Do you know any of the men in this photo?"

He narrows his eyes and sucks in his breath, letting out a low whistle as he stares at it, then stares at me. "Where did you get this?"

"It was passed to me last night along with the key."

"You are in a great deal of danger little lady. I don't know what you're mixed up in but I suggest you run. Fast."

"What do you mean?" I ask, feeling the fear rise up and choke me.

He stares at the photo on my phone, tapping the screen and splitting his fingers so the faces grow bigger. "That's Judah Benjamin, the House of Rothschild agent. The others are the Hashashin for Lincoln. There have always been rumors, but this is the first photo I've ever seen of all of them together. I'm sure you also know this group were the founders of Comus and the Freemasons here, both southern covers for the Illuminati."

"Comus is a cover for the Illuminati?" Jimmy Tate skeptically raises an eyebrow.

Fausto mumbles in answer, still scrolling over the details of the photo. "The Knights Templar disappeared into the Illuminati, and the Illuminati disappeared into... well ... other organizations. They went underground. They always had three centers, three being their sacred number, and at that time they were in Germany. Then they established Skull and Bones at Yale and they sent an agent down to New Orleans to establish their third section. They always had doctors as part of the Hashashin to make sure the assassinations were completed. Tulane Medical School was a big part..." he abruptly stops talking, looks at both of us, then shakes his head and says, "I have to go."

Even though I don't think he's playing with a full deck, I quickly ask him, "So if someone fell over on me last night and gave me the key and the photo and whispered, "Stop the killing of the king" before dying... what do you think that might mean?"

Fausto looks like he might faint. He stands up, his things in his hands, and turns back to us with a big huff, "The 'killing of the king' is the code used by the assassins to get into the highest tier of their front group, the Freemasons. To reach the thirty-third tier of the Freemasons, you had to complete the 'killing of the king' showing your devotion and ability to keep secrets. The thirty-third tier lived by the Assassins Creed, "Nothing is true, everything is permitted." Power, money, orgies, anything you can think of was at your fingertips." He backs away from our table. "I'm not going to ask anything else. Don't say another word to me. Just get as far from me as possible. You, and everyone around you, is in great, great danger."

Jimmy Tate and I look at each other and let out a long breath at the same time. I'm unnerved and as I feel the fear growing in my belly, I down my whiskey and feel the line of fire burn it away as my phone pings. It's a text from Ava.

"Bellamy needs help. I have to leave. Please hurry. At her mother's."

Chapter 11

Widow's Kiss

Apple Brandy, Yellow Chartreuse, Benedictine (A golden liqueur first produced by Benedictine monks in the 16th century), angostura bitters

Bellamy comes from an old New Orleans family mixed with Yankees. Her mother's house is Classic-Upper-Garden-District-Grandeur, with its fresh gray paint and black iron lace over every portico. Of course nothing in New Orleans stays fancy for long with the wet heat crumbling stones into decay in front of your eyes. The smell of honeysuckle drips in the air. Lush gardens and overgrown palms surround the house, with time-worn red brick pathways beckoning us to the over-sized front door. A massive stone fountain sits squarely on the brick path so we have to walk around it. The fountain is held aloft by the nine muses, an ode — I suppose — to the original street layout of the Garden District where every street was named for a different muse. In the spirit of Melpomene herself, the muse of tragedy, the Lower Garden District streets are now rundown and crime-ridden, but Bellamy's family is safely ensconced in Upper Garden District grandeur.

I knock on the enormous door and it's opened by the houseman, Hyacinth LcClote. His hair sprouts out of the top of his head in short dreadlocks like ladybug antennas even though he has tried to tie it back in a neat ponytail. He is small and wearing a white jacket and gloves. "Welcome," he says, bowing and ushering us into the green marble entryway. Bellamy is sitting in the gilded parlor to the right with her mother, who is wearing a black Chanel jacket with a knee-length black skirt and sensible Chanel pumps. She has her large diamonds and sapphire rings on her fingers and her nails are done in a perfect French manicure. Her silvery blonde hair is pulled up in a French twist and sprayed stiff. She and Bellamy are sitting in their green and ivory Louis X1V chairs at a round table near the front window holding teacups and saucers in their hands. A large silver tea tray sits between them.

Bellamy stands when she sees me and I rush to hug her. "Are you ok?"

Her eyes are red and swollen and she shakes her head. "I hadn't seen him in years, but to die such a violent death at such a young age... and to fall over on *you*... you probably have his blood on you somewhere."

I turn to her mother. "I'm so sorry Madame Banjeau."

"And I." Jimmy Tate says in what sounds like a clipped English accent, bowing his head toward Madame Banjeau with his hands clasped in front of him. He looks at me out of the corner of his eye and I can feel the inappropriate giggles bubbling up again. I suppress them.

Madame Banjeau dabs her temples with a monogrammed handkerchief. "Thank you for your condolences. This is a very difficult time for our family and such a loss to our community. Duncan had so much potential. Ellington, you must be even more traumatized than we are, with Duncan dying in your arms. Bellamy told me all about it, and I must say I was stunned. Last night sounds simply ghastly. Do tell me all the details, although I'm not sure I can bear to know them, yet I must."

I'm pretty sure neither she nor I want to go over the details of last night, but thank my lucky stars Bellamy jumps to my rescue. "Mama, leave Ellington alone. She has been through enough without living through it all again."

"Come now, Bellamy, it helps to talk about tragedies. As Shakespeare said, 'Give sorrow words. The grief that does not speak whispers the o'erfraught heart and bids it break.'"

"I don't know what to say, Madame Banjeau," I begin. I am interrupted by Bellamy, who says curtly, "Mama, I will not let you do this to my friend. She has been through enough. I already told you everything she told me. She does not need to relive it to satisfy your morbid curiosity."

Madame Baneau leans towards me and whispers, "I heard there was a key," as though Bellamy is not standing right next to us.

"Mama!" Bellamy interjects with such a forceful voice that her mother finally backs off.

"Alright, *my goodness*. Well, if Ellington wants to talk, I am here." She looks at me.

Bellamy rolls her eyes. "Goodness she's like a pitbull with a bone."

"Bellamy," says Madame Banjeau, "Don't you dare compare me to an animal. Especially such a trashy one."

"Mama, we are forgetting our manners." Bellamy says, firmly taking Madame Banjeau's arm. "Let's get our guests some tea."

Madame Banjeau walks over the window and pulls a long tasseled rope that must ring for Hyacinth. I can't help but think about the difference between this rope tassel and Hunter's homemade shotgun bell. It seems it's a day for people to 'ring' and I'm thinking I need a red velvet rope with a giant golden tassel over my bed so I can call Winston to bring me my golden slippers. I'm just imagining how these golden slippers would hug my feet in soft fur and turn up at the toe like a genie when Hyacinth silently appears.

"Madame?"

"Hyacinth, a tea tray for our guests."

He bows and disappears as Madame Banjeau excuses herself, and with her goes all the tension in the room.

Bellamy collapses on the couch in an unladylike slump, holding a tasseled pillow over her body like protection and I'm thinking what if bulletproof vests were covered in velvet with tassels? So much nicer. Of course it would be obvious when someone was wearing one, so there'd have to be a sleek version sans tassels for undercover work, but still velvet... my eye is caught by a framed photo of a man on a shelf I've never noticed before. He looks very familiar. I pull out my phone and look at the antique photo—same guy. "Bellamy, who is this?" I ask, holding up the framed photo.

"Great Granddaddy, Albert Pike. You've seen his picture before. They have that big oil painting of him down in city hall."

I hold up my phone so she and Jimmy Tate can see it. Jimmy Tate jumps up. "Oh my gawd!" he blurts. I know he's thinking the same thing as me: If Great Grandaddy Albert Pike is in this photo with Booth, then Fausto would say he was part of the assassination team.

"What's going on?" Bellamy asks as Hyacinth quietly returns with tea. "Why do you have a picture of my Great-Grandaddy on your phone?"

"This is the photo Duncan slipped me last night before he died. Winston took a picture of it before the police took it for evidence."

She stares at the photo, confused. "Duncan slipped you a picture of our Great Granddaddy? Why?"

"I don't know." He stuffed it in my hand. "But look who else is in it."

"Who?"

Jimmy Tate says, "You don't recognize John Wilkes Booth?"

She stares at us now. "What? John Wilkes Booth? Why

would I recognize such a heinous man? And why would he be in a photo with my Great Grandaddy?"

Jimmy Tate and I exchange a glance. I'm not sure I should fill her in on Crazy Fausto's theories just now, she's under enough pressure. "I don't know the answer to any of those questions. Was your grandfather into theater maybe? This photo was taken in 1864 when Booth performed in New Orleans. Maybe your grandfather went to see him? Booth wasn't a villain yet—he hadn't killed Lincoln. And he was a popular actor, so maybe your Great Grandaddy was a fan?"

She looks suspicious, but her brain is on overload so I see her decide to accept this as a possibility. "Could be. My grandfather was really into theatrics, rituals, drama, like you Ellington. He actually spent years recording and creating the rituals used by Freemasons throughout the world. He wrote this really long involved book explaining them called *Morals and Dogma of the Ancient and Accepted Scottish Rite of Freemasonry.*"

My heart starts pounding on my chest. "Freemason? Your grandfather was a Freemason?"

"Not just *any* freemason," she says, handing me back my phone and walking over to the tea tray. "He was the head honcho, supreme leader, grand poobah of southern Freemasons. In fact, he was sent down here from Boston to establish the first Freemasons here."

"You're kidding," Jimmy Tate says. "And he wrote a book explaining all the levels of Freemasonry? All thirty-three of them?"

"Thirty-two," Bellamy says, pouring tea into three cups. "The thirty-third level is top secret, only for the initiated." She puts air quotes around 'initiated'.

"Was your grandfather in the top level?" I ask.

"Of course. He wrote the book."

"Have you read it?" I ask.

"Heavens no! A million pages of boredom. I've tried, but could never make head or tails out of it." She holds a tiny pitcher and pours cream into her cup.

"Do you have a copy of it?" Jimmy Tate asks

"Sure, somewhere in this house. But the original handwritten manuscript is upstairs."

"Can we see it?" I ask. It might hold some clue to Fausto's theory.

Bellamy shakes her head. "No. It's so old it disintegrates in the air. It's written on some fragile paper made of rice or something. My mother keeps it in her temperature-controlled bedroom along with her shrunken head." She adds a sugar cube to her cup.

My mind is spiraling through the air like flying purple beads thrown off a balcony by beer-soaked hands. "Shrunken head?"

Jimmy Tate asks, "Why does your mother have a shrunken head?"

"You know she spent time with some remote tribes in the jungle when she was a student."

"No," Jimmy Tate shakes his head, his eyes huge in disbelief, "Somehow we missed that tidbit."

"It was a long time ago. She was like Jane Goodall, except she was studying the plants. She only stayed for a year."

"That's incredible," I say. "I can't even begin to picture your mother, the most non-earthy, non-adventurous, non-scientific person I have ever met, traipsing around the rainforest."

"I know, I can't either. She's always been a stick in the mud since I was born. She doesn't talk about it much. My grandmother said when she came back she wasn't the same. When she left she wanted to be a scientist; when she returned, she just wanted to stay inside a gated home."

"With a shrunken head in her bedroom?" Jimmy Tate says.

Bellamy shrugs. "It's actually really cool. Sparked my interest in medicine." While she's talking, Bellamy is dropping more cubes into her cup and stirring. Five cubes of sugar? In one little cup? You might as well fill a cup with sugar and sprinkle it with tea. I can't help but think of Fausto's story about the poisoned tea.

"You can't drink that," I say, taking it from her and before she can protest I've poured it into the nearest potted plant.

"What are you doing?" Bellamy asks, stupefied. Her hands are still frozen in a tea-stirring position.

I take the teapot and other cups and dump those too.

Bellamy says, "What in the world are you doing? Why are you acting so crazy?"

All I can hear in my head is Fausto's words, *Everyone around you is in great danger.* I glance at the entrance doors and see what looks like a pair of eyes watching me through the crack. Without thinking, I run to the door but no one is there.

Jimmy Tate comes over and takes my arm, whispering, "Pull yourself together Nancy Drew." He clears his throat and says to Bellamy, "I think I should get Mistress Minx home. She's obviously under a lot of stress."

"Absolutely, take her home and put her to bed," Bellamy says, hugging me tightly with a concerned look on her face. "Are you okay?" Then she pulls away and looks at both of us. "What are you two up to?"

"Ask us no questions, we'll tell you no lies," I say as I put on my sunglasses and move stealthily to the front door, my back against the wall, followed by Jimmy Tate. We nod at each other and fling open the door at the same time, bracing ourselves for gypsies, tramps, thieves, murderers, or whoever else might be lurking. There's no one there. I poke my head back into the living room. "Love you Bell. We're just a text away if you need us. And we shut the door behind us.

I link arms with Watson as we walk down the overgrown brick path."We make an excellent team, Watson."

"Watson? I'm not Watson. He's portly. I'd rather be one of the Hardy Boys. They were hot."

"Okay Joe, or Frank. You know I'm not going home, right? I have to meet Winston at The Columns for his faculty thing. Care to join me?"

"Why not? You've hijacked my entire afternoon. You might as well have the evening too."

How I adore a friend who will toss aside their own plans to come on an adventure with me. I turn and Bellamy is standing at the window with a worried look on her face. I wave at her and blow her a kiss with fake nonchalance, but I know she isn't fooled. Two cars are parking in front of her mother's house and elderly people are creaking their way out, straightening their clothing and juggling casserole dishes as they head up the pathway to the Banjeau house to pay their respects. Good. That should keep them busy for a while.

Chapter 12

Alleycat

Muddled Lime, Mint and Orange, Citrus Vodka, Orange Liqueur, Champagne Float

The Columns is a sprawling white mansion named for its enormous white pillars. It looks a lot like a plantation house with charm and character spilling out of its windows and looping through the dense trees that grow all around it. It's kind of a cross between *Gone With the Wind* and the *Haunted Mansion*. Jimmy Tate is escorting me and we climb the steep steps up to its genteel porch and see they are setting up for the Preservation Hall Jazz Band to play. I lean against a column and watch the musicians laughing as they tune their instruments. Jimmy Tate follows my lead and leans on the other side of the same column.

I sigh. "Oh how I love the smell of New Orleans air in the evening, heavy, wet, and stroking my skin like velvet." I let my riding coat slide down my arms, slow and sultry, and rub one hand up my arm with light fingers.

"I wish it made *my* skin feel like velvet. It makes me feel wet and sticky and my hair gets so frizzy I end up looking like a slutty drug addict." Jimmy Tate pats his hair.

The opening hallway of The Columns greets visitors with graceful statues of dancing women, glittering chandeliers, and ceilings so high it feels like you're in a palace. We walk right by the gleaming ballroom with its piano beckoning like a lover, past the streaming sunlight of the massive arched windows, and enter the cool dark bar. It looks haunted with its old paintings on the dark wood walls. There are photos of an old movie that was filmed here about a Storyville brothel and a knight in shining armor stands at attention in the corner.

"What's your poison?" Jimmy Tate asks me.

"Ha-Ha, very funny. I'm starving so I will of course have a Bloody Mary."

Jimmy Tate looks at me with one arched eyebrow. "Research?"

"Yup. Plus it's made with vegetables and spices, therefore qualifying as a healthy meal."

Jimmy Tate nods. "You're right. And it has vodka and spices to kill all germs. I'll have one, too."

While the bartender pours, I stare at the spiral staircase up to the hotel rooms. It's grand and if I blur my eyes so I don't see that chipped wood, I can picture Rhett carrying Scarlett up it, except it's my face on Scarlett's body.

Jimmy Tate notices. "Are you thinking about the time you stayed here when you had that gang of rats running around your house opening your cupboards and eating saltines on your Oscar De La Renta gowns?"

"I'm pretty sure there are more rats *here* than there were in my house. I think I nearly died of claustrophobia in that elevator." I lean close to his ear and whisper so as not to offend any eavesdropping staff, "Plus, that elevator is the kind with the metal grate instead of a door and it lurches and rattles and you can see all the insides of the dirty inner walls as you ride up and up. Honestly I was just waiting to see smears of blood or worse on those walls."

"I'm not sure what would be worse to see than smears of blood, but I hate those kinds of elevators. In fact, I'd always rather take the stairs."

I sigh. "Someday I want to be swept up in strong muscular arms and carried up a sweeping staircase."

"Don't look at me. I'm sore after working out all morning." He flexes one taut bicep. "Or maybe I could. My muscles are primed."

I poke him in the belly, and then poke him again. "Woah, Mr. Six-Pack. Your abs are hard as a washboard."

Jimmy Tate's smile is bigger than the sweeping staircase when he lifts his arms in triumph and swishes his hips side to side like a washing machine. "Anybody in this place need any washing done?" He points at his belly. "I got your washer right here."

I can't help laughing as people in the bar glance in our direction, but no one pays much attention. It takes a lot more than a shouting Pilates teacher with washboard abs to get attention in this town. Although you'd think the promise of handling one's laundry would make people at least inquire. I take a long sip of my extra spicy drink. "Do you know what would make this perfect?" Jimmy Tate shakes his head. "French fries."

"Yes!"

We order food to be sent out on the porch and head out to listen the band. Music just sounds better in this city, more soulful. I don't know why. The same band can play New Orleans music in another state, but it sounds different here. Something about the sumptuous air, maybe, caressing the instruments with its silken fingers, drawing unmatchable tones out of the instruments. With those first few notes, the outside world disappears, and the music infiltrates your body until you are pulled into its beautiful dream.

I sit at a small wrought iron table with curling elegant legs, (the table, not me), and rest my chin in my hand and let the music take me to a world where a hot New Orleans vampire that looks remarkably like Winston strides down the cobblestone street in a top hat and boots, and I'm thinking what an easy mark I would be, as my neck is such an erogenous zone that not only would I *not* run from a gorgeous vampire who approached me, I would probably tap him on the shoulder and *ask* him to sink his teeth into me. If you have to go, what a way to go. One explosively erotic moment... but then I feel actual lips on my neck and and I yank back to see who it is. *Please let it be Winston.*

"Winston!" I jump up and hug him. I feel like I've been sailing stormy seas all day and have finally reached safe harbor. He hugs me tight.

"How are you, my Love? I've been worried about you all day." He turns to Jimmy Tate and shakes his hand. "Hey Jimmy Tate, How are you?"

I recap my day for him starting with the police questioning, followed by the Mardi Gras Indians, Commander's Palace, the cemetery, Grandpa Boogie, the Locksmyth, Le Bon Temps Roule, and Madame Banjeau's house. Jimmy Tate adds extra details, mostly what people were wearing. I feel like we have had five days rolled into one.

The server comes out without our pommes frites and it's a perfect combination of salty and spicy and I feel the stress of the day melt off me. We're sitting so close to the band it's hard to talk while they're playing. And I cherish this time that allows me to be quiet with the music for a few minutes. Tired of fighting them, I close my eyes and let the images come. Handcuffs and opium pipes; pink feathers and fierce warrior painting and intricate beading; the glittering invitation and the look on Bellamy's face when she heard Duncan Pike's name; the tumbled tombstones and dancing woodcarver; the scimitar and the beautiful locksmith and when the leg trap comes into my mind I shiver and sit up straight.

"Did you just fall asleep?" Winston whispers in my ear.

"No, well, maybe a little bit. I think my brain is shutting down by itself." I take a long drink of cold water.

"Come dance with me." Winston takes my hand and puts his other hand firmly on my back, pulling me close to his chest. We rock back and forth and turn in a circle and since dancing isn't Winston's strong suit and there's a whole lot of stepping on toes, I break away and do my own dance while looking at him, letting the music enter every cell of my body and it feels wonderful and sultry and I hadn't realized how much I needed to dance. My axis mundi doing its thing, grounding me, filling me.

Winston swoops back in and wraps his arms around me and we do the three partner moves we know 'til the end of the song when we end in a deep dip that strains my neck. "Ow!" I yelp, grabbing my neck. Damn dip always throw something out. Winston helps me back to my chair. I'm not sure why I'm limping when it's my neck that hurts. When I plop down in my chair, I notice my handbag is gone. I forget all about my neck and start looking frantically around my chair, under the table, under everyone else's chairs. "Where's my handbag?" I say, trying not to panic. Winston and Jimmy Tate recognize the rising panic and immediately start looking around.

"Where was the last place you saw it?" Winston asks in a calm voice.

"Here! I put it under my chair. I was holding it between my feet when I got up to dance. I assumed it was safe because Jimmy Tate was at our table."

Winston looks under the table. "Are you sure you didn't leave it in the bar? Re-trace your steps."

"I know I had it here, I put my lipstick on after you arrived."

"I'll check the bar just in case."

Just then I see a red flash in the bushes. "There it is!" I yell and the thief erupts out of the bushes like a startled gecko and takes off running down the street. My heart is thumping louder as Winston and Jimmy Tate run after him with me following close behind. The thief is small and wiry and faster than a jackrabbit as he runs down St. Charles. He is wearing jeans and a collared shirt and I can see his preppy haircut from behind—unusual outfit for a criminal in New Orleans. I get a quick glimpse at his face when he turns and smiles at me. Creepy! Smiling *while* stealing? And I'm slowing down after the initial burst of adrenaline. My riding boots are not made for running but I clunk along behind Winston and Jimmy Tate who are gaining on the kid. Both of them may look like fops, but Winston was a high school track star and Jimmy Tate is an athlete.

The thief leads us off St. Charles into a neighborhood with bars over the front doors and sagging porches. A police car is parked at the corner and I can see the cops in uniform talking to kids on bikes in front of the liquor store. "Help!" I yell at the cops and the thief accidentally drops my handbag in the street. He stops to pick it up but Winston and Jimmy Tate are right on his heels and they grab at his jacket but he shrugs it off and changes direction into a side alley. He climbs a chain link fence into someone's yard and disappears. He's faster than a roach being chased by a shoe.

Winston tries to follow him over the fence, but he gets stuck on the metal spikes. I have turned around to grab my bag off the street before someone else takes off with it, you never know in this town. Jimmy Tate is bent over, his hands on his knees, huffing and puffing as Winston limps back to us. The cops are running toward us with their weapons drawn.

"What happened?"

"That thief stole my bag right off the porch at The Columns," I puff.

"Did you get a good look at him?"

"Not his face, but he was a white kid with short brown hair wearing jeans and a light shirt. He jumped that fence."

Jimmy Tate is holding the kid's denim jacket. He hands it to the police. "We pulled this off him."

The cops take it and run back to their car. They turn on their light and siren. I can hear them radio out a description and their location as they drive around the corner to see if they can spot the kid.

I kneel in the street with my bag, not caring that the pebbles are digging into my bare knees. I am a gris-gris bag that's lost its power to attract anything good; a deflated balloon after the parade is long gone; where's my mojo?

"What is going on with that purse?" Jimmy Tate asks. "It's a magnet for scoundrels and scalliwags. Did he take anything?"

I look: wallet, sunglasses, lipsticks, glitter gloss, invitation, and yes, the key is still there. "I don't think so."

By now a crowd of people from the neighborhood have been drawn out of their houses to watch the commotion. The group of kids on bicycles have parked in a half circle around us and are watching me carefully, shaking their heads. I can hear them saying things to each other, like "What a dumb ass goin' to all that trouble and then dropping your loot!" "Must have been those Brawlers from the Irish Channel."

Another kids says, "More like 'Bawlers', and they all laugh.

Winston helps me stand up and brush off my knees. He gives me a tight hug. "You all right?"

"Of course I am! But what's going on? Two crimes in two nights? It's like a voodoo hoodoo hex."

I look around at the faces of the kids and there are a lot more of them then us and they start to look like wolves who have suddenly realized they are hungry, and isn't this nice that a little orphaned lamb showed up on their doorstep. It feels like they are licking their chops, getting ready for the kill.

"Let's head back," I say briskly.

We walk back to the The Columns and I'm so jumpy it seems every tree is hiding a murderer. I'm relieved when I see the lights of The Columns, and the band is playing "Hattie Green" in the same old style as Dr. Hepcat. The music greets me like an old friend, wrapping my soul in joy.

Hattie, don't you hear your daddy callin' you? Now that gal, she can make it, or she can shake it...

Some of the other patrons and wait staff approach us as we climb the steps, shaking their heads, saying things like, "Unbelievable. That a thief would be so brazen and come all the way up onto this porch to steal a bag. Is no place sacred anymore? You can't even sit on a porch and feel safe?" One waiter shakes his head. "You got to keep an eye on your bag, Ma'am."

Unbelievable. I'm being blamed for the theft of my own bag. I would like to argue with them, but with the music playing, all I want to do is shake it. I shimmy my hips and shoulders, but can't really move my feet which feel like they're on fire after running through the streets wearing riding boots. Winston wraps his arms around me from behind and says in my ear, "Honey are you okay?" Winston asks. "Do you want to head home?"

"Hell no, Winston! If Rome's going to burn, I want a front row seat."

Jimmy Tate directs us, "You two sit down, this round is on me."

We march back to the bar—I feel safer here than on the porch. I whirl around to Winston and Jimmy Tate, holding my purse against my chest like a baby. "Hold on, I just thought of something. What if it's true that my handbag really is cursed?"

"Your handbag?" Winston asks. "The one you have been dreaming about ever since you saw it on Grace Kelly's arm? The one that cost nearly as much as a car? It's not your handbag, Love." He leads me to sit at a table in the corner as Jimmy Tate asks a server to bring me a tall ice water. "Wait!" I sit upright like I've been bitten by a snake. "Wait, wait, wait... keys, my handbag..." I gasp and jump up. "Winston! Jimmy Tate!"

"Are you hurt? Did you sit on a thumbtack?" Jimmy Tate asks.

"What if, *what if*," I'm pulling everything out of my handbag as I talk. "What if the key was already in my purse?

What if the victim, Duncan Pike, didn't drop it in my bag as a clue, but grabbed my bag because he was trying to find the key? What if the key was already in there?" I dig with both hands around the lining of my handbag and am rewarded when I find a hidden pocket. "Oh how the plot thickens! There's a fake bottom in this bag and an invisible pocket in it."

"How in the world did you find that?" Winston whispers, looking around the room to see if anyone is watching us.

"When I used to dance, I shared a dressing room with a magician who pulled little birds out of an invisible pocket in his top hat. Those damn birds used to fly around our dressing room scaring the daylights out of me. But you would never guess in a million years there was anything in his hat, even if you ran your hand around the inside. The only way you could find it is if he showed you." I demonstrate by showing Winston the empty purse. I take his hand so he can feel the hidden pocket. "This could have been why Duncan grabbed by purse. He was trying to get the key, not give me the key. But he died just as he was dragging it out of its hiding place so it dropped into my bag. And he had no choice but to whisper his secret to me. 'stop the killing of the king'. Whatever he was trying to accomplish, whatever he was trying to stop, he wanted me to do it for him."

Jimmy Tate sticks his hand in my bag to feel the pocket too.

"Winston, where did you get my handbag?" I ask.

"Bianca LeBlanc."

"Bianca's? How? She doesn't sell vintage."

"I went in there looking for a gift for you and she said she had the perfect thing. She went in the back and came out with the Kelly bag. She knew you had been longing for one for a long time. She had the certificate of authenticity and the original bag for it. I didn't ask her any other details."

"Do you remember anything else? Was she acting funny at all, like she wanted to get rid of it?"

"No, Ellington, she was Bianca, as lovely and elegant as

she always is. If the key *was* in there, she didn't know about it."

Jimmy Tate gasps. "What if she found out about it later and needed it back and told Duncan to get it from you? That would make her a suspect."

"Oh my god, Bianca?" I ask.

"I don't believe it." Winston says.

"Believe it or not, do you two understand the implications of this? This puts a new spin on the whole deal. I'm not sure what the spin is yet, but this is exciting isn't it?" My mind is turning like a slot machine jackpot at Harrah's.

Winston says, "Maybe you should get rid of that purse before it causes something worse to happen."

I nod as I pet my purse sadly. Of all the things to be trouble magnets... not my favorite handbag. "I suppose you're right. And Jimmy Tate, I think we need to go straight to Bianca LeBlanc's tomorrow."

"I agree, you need to start looking for a ballgown immediately..."

"Looking for a ballgown will be the perfect excuse to investigate Bianca and learn more about the Kelly."

Winston shakes his head. "You two playing Nancy Drew makes me very nervous."

I kiss him on the cheek. "Most things make you nervous. Don't you worry about me, Lover."

We are interrupted by a couple of professors from the university. One is portly with a band of gray hair around the sides and back of his head like Captain Stubing from the Love Boat, and the other is a wearing a white collar, a priest, with hair the color of a Dark and Stormy and crinkly eyes that look like he laughs a lot.

Winston stands up to introduce us. "Ellington and Jimmy Tate, this is Father Archer, the Provost of the university and Gerry Batracho, the new Dean of the Business School."

My favorite Dean was looted after the storm so badly he moved to Texas. The next Dean had a painkiller problem and after I found him stumbling around the playground, at Audubon Park, he got fired. Gerry Batracho is the new Dean, and he's meaner than a junkyard dog.

Father Archer looks at me with concern. "Winston told us about your night last night. That must have been horrible for you."

"Oh it was like a horror movie coming to life," I answer.

Gerry says, "I was at the Joan of Arc parade last night passing out wooden doubloons."

"I can't believe someone would have the audacity to commit such a crime in such a public space," Father Archer says. "This city can be so heartbreaking."

"Do they have any leads on the crime?" Gerry asks.

"They're working on it," I say, but I'm distracted as two police officers enter the bar. They look around and when they spot me, their postures change and one of them lifts his cell phone to his ear and starts talking.

Or is it just my imagination?

All heads at our table swivel to see what has caught my attention.

"Are they here to protect you?" Father Archer asks.

I laugh. "No, but that would be nice."

Gerry spits loudly, "It doesn't matter if they find the perpetrator or not, the Louisiana justice system is worse than a third world country. They should arm every person in this city so they can defend themselves, then we'll see how long those criminals last."

"I wouldn't live in a city full of people walking around with weapons," I say.

"You already do, Ms. Martini. But right now, only the bad guys have them." Gerry looks at my handbag in a way that makes me want to hide it. Either he's a cross-dressing Hermes-lover, or he knows about the key. Or my imagination is running away with me again. He excuses himself.

After he leaves, Father Archer laughs, dissolving the tension. "Gerry's quite passionate about his beliefs."

"Father Archer, Ellington was looking into some interesting characters from history today. If she keeps going she may turn traditional southern history on its head." He turns to me. "Tell Father Archer what you learned today. One of his Masters is in Southern history."

I'm trying to pay attention but the police are distracting me. "*One* of your Masters? How many do you have?"

Winston says, "He has four Masters degrees, and a PHD."

"What are you a Master at?" Jimmy Tate asks in a lascivious manner.

Oh no he is *not* flirting with a priest. Of course the priest at my wedding ended up passed out on a pool lounge with two crumpled bikinis under his chair, but that's another story.

"Linguistics with an emphasis on archaic languages, Economics, Southern History, and English," Father Archer answers.

"And your PHD?"

"Psychology."

"Ahhh, so your well-equipped to handle any issue that might arise at a university?"

He laughs. "I don't know about *any* issue, but you have my interest, what are you researching?"

I'm not sure we should be revealing pieces of our investigation to someone we don't know, and I'm trying to remember if Nancy Drew ran around telling people the clues she found before she solved the mystery? I seem to recall she didn't keep secrets but kept talking and learning until everything was sorted out. What about Sherlock? Or the Scooby Doo kids? I decide it's too complicated to think about. "We are researching an antique key and local key legends like the Quarto and House of Rothschild. Do you know anything about them?"

But now I see my detectives, Washington and Boudreau, walk in and stand with the officers at the bar. I don't know if this is good or bad. Will they be mad if they find out my bag was snatched and I didn't call them? Could that be construed as Obstruction of Justice if I didn't stick around to file a report? I try to ignore them while I figure out how to greet them.

"Oh well, do you have a few hours?" he asks with a laugh. "I have done quite a bit of research on both subjects. Of course there's infinitely more material on House of Rothschild than the Quarto. They were stunningly wealthy and their wealth only seemed to grow with each family member. They were everywhere, from the Rothschild Giraffe to the infamous wine, Mouton-Lafitte-Rothschild. They became nobility and had palaces all over Europe and even financed entire wars. They were able to stop governments, economies, and entire countries from crumbling with their loans."

"Do you know anything about their involvement in the Civil War here?" Jimmy Tate asks.

Father Archer looks at both of us and seems delighted by this question. "Oh sure. It would stand to reason if they were financing, managing, influencing, however you want to put it, England, France, Austria, and many other places in Europe, they would make a grab for this new country."

"What about John Wilkes Booth? Have you ever heard anything connecting House of Rothschild and Booth and Lincoln?"

"Sure, there are all sorts of conspiracy theories. It was obviously in the Rothschild's best interest to get rid of Lincoln so it's not a huge stretch to think they may have tried to get rid of him, although the last person I'd hire is an actor like Booth. Would have made more sense if the assassin had been done by a military man."

"Well Booth turned out to be very effective."

"Yes he did, sadly. The theory says that when the South seceded and took the U.S. Mint with them, Lincoln couldn't afford the war. Every bank turned him down or were charging massive interest rates. Lincoln even sent emissaries to other countries to request loans. In fact he sent a Louisiana senator, Slidell, to England. They all came back empty-handed."

My ears prick up at the mention of Slidell.

"Lincoln would not plunge his beloved country into debt so he talked to congress and they advised and approved the creation of new money to finance the war," Father Archer continues, "They were called "greenbacks" because the writing on the back of the bills was green. It was a brilliant move for our country, but incredibly threatening to other countries."

"How?"

"Well, a country that can make its own money is a massive threat to monarchies and dictatorships and especially to House of Rothschild who wanted to control our economy."

"And Booth was willing to die for House of Rothschild?"

"Hardly. There is all kinds of speculation that Booth didn't die. Rumors say the body was actually a confederate soldier named James William Boyd. There were a lot of unusual things done with the body after the shootout at Garrett's Barn. It was tied up in a horse blanket after he died on Garrett's porch and taken to Belle Plain where it was put on a steamer and transported up the Potomac to Alexandria and then transferred to a tugboat and then onto the Montauk at the Washington Navy Yard."

"What?" I ask. "That's a lot of moving for a dead body."

Father Archer laughs. "It doesn't end there. The Secretary of War ordered his body be buried in a cell at the Arsenal Prison, although some say the deputies were paid off to dump Boyd's body into an Arsenal Prison sinkhole used to dump dead horses. The body was supposedly exhumed and moved again and again, and positively identified as Booth, but who knows. They didn't have DNA testing back then. But, in connection to the greenbacks, here's an unusual coincidence: Captain Boyd worked in economics in New Orleans with the main banker at the time, Judah Benjamin."

"Judah Benjamin the main agent for House of Rothschild?"

"Yes." I take out my phone and show him the antique photo.

He looks at me with raised eyebrows. "Well that's an incriminating photo. Booth, Benjamin, Pike, and Baird all together. Wow, where'd you get …"

Before he can finish, Detective Washington and Detective Boudreau walk over to our table. Detective Washington looks at me with those arctic blue eyes and smiles warmly at Father Archer. "I hope we're not interrupting."

"Not at all. Please join us," I say.

"No, we wouldn't want to intrude," Detective Boudreau says. "We just have a few questions for Ms. Martini here."

"Well, I was about to excuse myself anyway," Father Archer says. "Ellington, Jimmy Tate, I hope we can talk again soon. Fascinating conversation." He shakes Winston's hand as he leaves and the detectives sit down.

"We wanted to talk to you about tonight's purse snatcher."

"How did you know about that?" Jimmy Tate asks.

"We received a report over the radio."

"Of a purse snatcher? But how did you know it was me? I didn't leave my name," I ask.

"The detective described the victim as a blonde with a tall dark-haired man with glasses and another man of medium build with brown hair, we thought it an awfully big coincidence if it wasn't you."

Jimmy Tate puts one hand on his hip. "Medium build? They described *me* as medium build? Not athletic? Ripped? Muscular? Could they have made me sound more boring?"

I lean over to pat his hard belly. "Don't worry Princess. They've never seen your abs up close." I turn back to the detectives. They are making me nervous. "How did you find us?"

"You mentioned to the officers you had been at The Columns when the crime occurred."

Detective Washington slips out a plain notebook, the kind

you actually write in with a pen, and Jimmy Tate bites his lower lip and whispers in my ear, "Oh-my-goddess, it's just like the movies."

I put my finger to my lips to say "Shhh" but it's a bad move because the detectives are watching.

"Is there something you need to tell us, Ms. Martini?" Detective Boudreau asks.

"No, nothing."

"You seem awfully cavalier for someone who witnessed a murder last night and got her purse snatched tonight."

I sigh, long and loud. "The *last* thing I am is cavalier. It's sink or swim for me right now and I am doing my darnedest to keep my head above water. One thing you will *never* find me doing is cowering in the corner."

"It's true. She is fearless," Winston says.

"I can vouch for her fearlessness too." Jimmy Tate lifts a hand. "The woman looks like a wilting flower but believe me, she has an iron will."

"*Wilting*? Really?"

"Wilting is not the right word. How do you say, a *petite fleur*? A *steel magnolia*?" He looks at me. "*Diamond cream puff?*"

I nod. "That's better."

"Can you tell us what happened tonight?"

"Of course."

We sit down across from them while they take notes and I recant the evening. Jimmy Tate watches in fascination and I feel like I should get him some popcorn so he can enjoy the show. Winston sits back down folding his arms.

Detective Boudreau asks, "Ms. Martini, any idea why so many people are after your purse?"

"No, and I would have stayed and filed a report but the thief dropped my bag so I figured, no harm no foul. Plus, we didn't feel safe standing on that dodgy street."

Detective Washington writes something in her notebook while saying quietly, "I live on that street."

Shit. That's right. Dryades. "Oh, well, it's not that it's a bad area. It was just dark and, well, you know…"

"Yes, *I know.*" She doesn't sound very happy.

Detective Boudreau says, "Do you mind if we take a look through your purse? We may be able to discern something you haven't."

Oh I don't like that idea at all. It's like they've asked if they can look through my underwear drawer.

"Well, that's the thing, Detective Boudreau. I have looked and looked through everything in my purse and it's just the same old stuff. I haven't a clue why it's so desirable." I've watched enough detective movies to know I could be in deep trouble for withholding evidence if they find that key right now. When I eventually turn it over to them I'm going to have to pretend I just barely discovered it. Also, they probably need a warrant to look through my personal belongings. My heart is pounding like I've been caught with my hand in a cookie jar. I kick Jimmy Tate under the table and he yelps like a puppy. When everyone looks at him, he pretends he's choking on his drink by repeating his yelp. "Excuse me," he says, patting his chest and yelping again, just to make it more believable.

I slap his back, making him yelp louder. He looks at me, distressed. I put a glass of water to his lips to help him drink which makes him choke even harder. I am trying to figure out how to telepathically communicate that I need to get the key out of my purse, but all I do is say the word 'key' without moving my lips and he has no idea what I'm talking about. I can't do anything further because the detectives are watching me. We both look like we're trying to cough up a hairball. Winston is also watching us, his face showing no emotion.

I walk to my chair, lean back, and drape my arm across the back of my chair, the picture of cool. I might say like Sharon Stone in *Basic Instinct* but don't worry, I will not be uncrossing my legs.

Detective Boudreau looks at me with his all-knowing eyes, eyes that say 'I know you've been up to something and

I'm going to find out'. "So you don't mind if we look through it?"

"Of course not," I say, but now I'm between a diamond and a platinum mine, (aka rock and a hard place). *How the heck do I get the key out without them knowing?* I decide my best chance is for me to show them my bag instead of letting them paw through it. I pull it onto the table and the detectives watch me closely as I slowly pull out every item in my purse. I quickly slide the key back into its invisible pocket with one hand while I pull out more lipstick with the other.

And everyone said all the time spent practicing magic tricks I learned in a library book were a waste of time. Ha! Learning sleight-of-hand is never a waste of time.

Finally Winston says, "Honey, how many lipsticks do you have?"

"I don't know, six, ten?" I answer, standing them all in a row so they form their own missile line. When everything is out, I turn my purse upside down and shake it, then hand it to the detectives who each look inside. They hand it back, but are still looking at me suspiciously.

"What did you think you might find in my bag? I mean, the guy last night didn't take anything, he *put* the photo *in* my bag. Maybe the theft tonight is unrelated."

"Awfully coincidental, don't you think? Two crimes in two nights, both revolving around your purse?"

"Do you mind if we look at each item. We may be able to notice something you're missing." Detective Boudreau asks.

I scoot over handfuls of lipstick. "Have at it. I would love to figure out what is going on. Believe me, I want to stop being accosted even more than you want me to stop being accosted." They start taking apart my lipsticks and I push over my wallet and hairbrush and everything else.

The officers roll every one of my lipsticks up and down and go carefully through each item. Finally, they scoot it all back to me so I can put it back in my bag and stand up.

"Well, Ms. Martini, we will file a report. If anything else

unusual happens, please don't leave the scene. Call us."

Winston puts an arm around my shoulders and squeezes. "We'll watch out for her, Detectives. Thank you for your help, and for working to keep New Orleans safe."

Jimmy Tate rolls his eyes. "New Orleans is anything *but* safe, when any hobo can walk in off the street and piss in your eucalyptus towels..."

I cut him off. "Jimmy Tate!" I shush. The detectives are now looking at him like someone has dropped an ice cube down their back. I link arms with Winston and Jimmy Tate, although I'd like to be covering his mouth, but instead I say, "Thank you for helping me, last night and tonight."

They finally leave. I turn to Winston. "Let's go. I feel like a zombie."

"Don't say that too loud around here," Jimmy Tate says. "People think they're real."

"They might be. I did a paper on zombies in college," I say.

"What? How would they allow that subject in a college paper?"

"It was a paper on the zombie symbology in *Wide Saragasso Sea*, Jean Rhys' book about the madwoman in the attic in Jane Eyre. I have a vivid image right now of a madwoman dancing in the flames."

"The Saragasso Sea is the sea that pulls people under, right?" Jimmy Tate asks.

"Exactly," I say with a shudder. "Let's go home

Chapter 13

Flambeau

Orange Juice, Amaretto, Cognac, Cinnamon Simple
Syrup, Bitters, Bookers, Lime

When I get home, I'm so tired I can't even make umbrellas. I fall into a deep slumber and awaken late the next morning to the smell of a cappuccino. I slide my pink silk eye mask up onto my forehead to let the light in. I lift my head slowly, feeling delicious in my pink silk, man pajamas. Winston is sitting on the edge of the bed in his suit and tie, handing me a foamy cappuccino. "Mmmm, what is this?" I take a sip and the warm liquid fills me. "Dear god every sip is like falling in love. Thank you. Thank you." I sit up in bed and prop myself against my pillows crossing my legs in front of me. "What are you doing home?"

"I have a break right now and decided to come check on you. You ok?"

Like a thumb over a garden hose that is suddenly lifted, all the events of the last two days come rushing back and I slide down my satin pillows like a heart-shaped balloon the week after valentine's. I let out a long long sigh. "Yeah. I'm ok."

"I have a surprise for you." He pulls a pen out of his pocket.

"A pen? For little ol' me? You shouldn't have."

"Not just any pen, my love. This, my dear, is a blacklight."

"Really? The invitation... I completely forgot." And now I'm back on golden ground. My invitation, the ball, shimmering gowns, oh yes, this is what I need to focus on, not crime. I set my cappuccino on my bedside table and pull my handbag and the invitation out from under my pillow. It made for lumpy sleeping but at least I knew it wasn't being stolen or accosted somewhere. "Where did you get it?"

"I asked my students if anyone knew where I could find one. One of the football players had one in his pocket if you can believe it. Apparently he works as a bouncer at frat parties and was in his same clothes from last night."

"That's kind of gross but thank you. I can't believe you remembered." I turn over the invitation so the back is showing. It seems the paper is swirling like a vortex straight out of the twilight zone, but I blink my eyes to steady.

"Ready?" Winston asks, walking over to close the drapes to make it as dark as possible.

I nod. "Ready as I'll ever be. I just hope it doesn't say something super creepy, like a dead monk will fall over on you, a purse snatcher will accost you, and then... what could possibly happen next?"

He flips on the blacklight and shines it over the invitation. A symbol appears in the middle of the invitation. It's looks like the outer edges of a fleur de lis, the symbol for New Orleans, but there are other lines and designs intersecting it at different angles. "Hmmmm, it's a... what is it?"

"Who knows? The new logo for Rex?"

"New logo? Rex has been around for 150 years and they're going to create a new logo?"

"Well, it means nothing to either of us."

I point at the feathered arcs surrounding the symbol. "Do these look like the wings of Isis to you? I did an Isis dance in my showgirl days so I know Isis wings when I see them. This is always how they are represented, arcing upward surrounding something. In Egyptian symbology, the wings of Isis breathe life into the dead. She fanned her wings over her beloved Osiris to bring him back to life so she could get pregnant with her son, Horus."

"So she's like a zombie-maker?"

I laugh and pick up my coffee—I need fuel. "No, the Egyptians didn't need zombies when they had mummies. Isis fans the flames of creativity *symbolically* with her golden wings. She awakens dormant creativity and inspires it to take action, at least that's how I always viewed my dance." I take a drink, the warmth spreading through my body like true love. I can't help but moan a little in pleasure.

"Like your cappuccino?" Winston says. "Fanning you back to life as we speak."

"Exactly." I wrap both hands around the cup to savor its warmth as I gaze at the symbol waiting for it to reveal its meaning."But maybe it's just a random design." My shoulders slump over.

Winston laughs. "What did you think was going to be on there? A message from the queen?"

"I was hoping there would be some secret message just for mè, maybe that they had picked me to be the queen of Rex this year, or at least made me part of the tableau."

"What is this tableau you keep fantasizing about?" he asks.

The cappuccino is taking effect and I speak quickly. "They do a living tableau where they have people wear costumes and re-enact some famous scene from mythology. We used to open my burlesque show with a Greek tableau with all the dancers. It was a little taste of what's to come. We wore Jean Harlow wigs and white togas over our shoulder with golden ropes around our waist. Of course we had our Harlow wigs washed and set for opening night and when we got them back that afternoon, they looked more like Barbara Bush than Jean

Harlow. And it was too late to fix them and we had to perform that night anyway." I shake my head. "I loved that opening number though. I was draped across a pink velvet chaise lounge while another dancer, the fire eater, fed me grapes."

"Fire eater?"

"She was the super wild nasty one. I won't even tell you where she had fiery flames tattooed on her body. Suffice to say it had to have really hurt. She also had two Chihuahuas that wore mink stoles. They came to all the shows and waited for her in the dressing room," I get up to brush my teeth and Winston follows me, leaning against the door frame.

"You seem to have zoos going on in your dressing rooms."

"And I haven't even told you about the baby kangaroo. Those things have a powerful kick," I say through foaming teeth. I rinse and dry my mouth and walk over to my dressing table to brush my hair, talking loudly to Winston can hear me. "Anyway, the theme of Rex is fire this year, so it will probably have something to do with fire gods and goddesses, Brigid, Pele, or who's the guy who stole fire from the gods?"

"Prometheus?"

"Exactly. Maybe it's good I'm not performing. I can relax and enjoy the ball as a guest."

"What are you doing today? I don't think you should leave the house without protection."

"Seriously? Winston, we've talked about this. If you get scared of criminals, they win."

"I know, but that was when crime happened to other people. Now it's erupted in our lives and I need to know you're safe."

"Winston, honey, you know I can take care of myself. I have danced with remote tribes in the bush in Africa. I have traveled alone in the most dangerous places in the world, Mexico City, Egypt, Panama. I think I can handle New Orleans."

"I know, I just worry about you."

"Well, don't. I'm perfectly capable of taking care of myself."

"I know." He kisses my neck and I wrap my arms around him.

Then my legs.

He laughs. "Calm down Tiger. There is nothing I would love more than some morning delight, but I have to get back to work. I can come back for lunch," he says, kissing me so deeply I can feel it in my toes and various other body parts spring to life. I pick up the remote on my side table and turn on the Stones. Nothing makes Winston surrender to my charms faster than *Sticky Fingers*.

"Oh forget it, work can wait." He tackles me onto our luxurious sheets and by the time "Wild Horses" comes on I'm getting a thigh workout stronger than any P90X video and by the time "Moonlight Mile" comes on we are both lying on our backs, our limbs spread out in sweaty sexy glory. "Now I really have to go," Winston says, slipping back into his suit and kissing me on the cheek. "Just please text me often all day long so I know you're safe."

I salute him. "Roger, Cowboy. Will do."

He leaves and I'm thinking Winston would make an excellent cowboy with a hat and a low-slung belt. He'd bust through the swinging doors just in time to catch my fall from the second floor and then we'd fall in love and jump on his horse and gallop off to a little cottage surrounded by fields of wildflowers where butterflies would land in my hair and... I snap my own fingers in front of my eyes to bring myself back to reality and I pull my hair up on top of my head in a messy bun and pin two big pink flowers on either side of my head. Thank goodness I don't have to make an impression on any police today and can wear whatever floats my boat. I put on a short pink Hellbunny sundress with a fluffy slip underneath to make it puff out, a cozy white 1950's sweater with pearl buttons and ballet flats. I look in the mirror, and yes, I look like a large pink peony, but I don't care. Pink delights me.

It's time to ditch the Kelly bag, it's attracting too much negativity. I move all the contents to my pink marabou backpack, which never leaves my body and would be impossible to steal out from under me. I pull the key out and look at it for a few minutes. I really should turn it into the police, but I'm making excellent progress on solving this mystery. Plus, it will look suspicious to turn it in so quickly after last night. Plus, I'm *dying* to find the lock that fits this key. What if it's an ancient treasure so great I'd be rolling in real gold doubloons? I could buy ten mansions on St. Charles and put schools in them.

But then I remember that I need to bring my Kelly to Bianca's so I can investigate her involvement in the mystery bag. I decide to wrap it in a green fringe shawl, and put it in a Fleur De Paris hatbox for safekeeping. No one will guess what's in there, it just looks like I've been shopping. I text Ava that I'm ready and head outside to sit on my porch swing and wait for her.

She arrives in her retro Cadillac and it smells like pencils and licorice. She pushes stacks of crumpled wrappers off the passenger seat so I can sit down. I think I might be sitting in melted taffy as my dress is sticking to the seat. Hopefully, it matches my dress. She is listening to WWOZ and I fill her in on the events of last night. She just shakes her head after every few sentences. "I can't believe it, Ellington Martini. How in the world did your beautiful world get filled with so much darkness?"

"I don't know, but if anything bad happens to me, you are a witness to my final wishes—bury me under a pile of tutus, sparkling eyeshadow, crowns, feathers, and pink cupcakes."

"I thought you wanted your ashes spread over a sunflower field?"

"I changed my mind. I think. The only thing that is definite, non-negotiable—is that I want a New Orleans funeral. Before I can finish, the song "Dixieland Funeral" by

Chuck E. Weiss comes on the radio. We both look at each other with our mouths wide open. "What the ...? That's eerie."

She laughs. "That, I believe, is called synchronicity." She cranks up the volume and when the marching band drums kick in, we drum on her dashboard as she turns down Washington Street.

"I thought we were going to the Quarter?"

"We are, but I told Bellamy we'd pick her up. She needs to get away from her mother and she also needs costume stuff for the Pussyfooters."

"Well I'm glad to see she's got her priorities. The world might be falling apart but we're going to look good while it does. My mama always said the best defense against a cruel world is a beautiful pair of shoes." The Pussyfooters is an all-girl marching band for women over thirty. They wear adorable matching costumes, usually corsets and tutus and tall white marching boots, and they all look amazing no matter their age or body type. I've always wanted majorette boots and a hat, like Shirley McLaine in *Sweet Charity*. I've been on the waitlist to get into the Pussyfooters or Cherry Bombs for two years, but alas, I'm still waiting. The Bearded Oysters and Lady Cameltoe Steppers both had a spot for me, but I'm holding out so I can join with Ava or Bellamy. I hate waitlists. There's nothing magical about waitlists.

We stop the Cadillac in front of Bellamy's and she storms into the car. She must have been sitting on the porch waiting for us. "Bell! How are you? How are things at Melpomene Manor?"

"Melpomene Manor is an Edvard Munch nightmare. My Mama is in Full-Out-Code-Red-Drama-Creating mode and the house, well the house is full of fainting spells, swooning maidens, and pissing contests."

"Pissing contests?"

"Yes."

"Give us an example."

"Ok, last night my second cousin, Honey, came over with her new husband." She drops her voice to a whisper even though it's only us in the car. "Her first husband died in a car crash. Very tragic." She resumes regular volume. "We are all thrilled for her to have found love again, but boy is he challenging—some sort of snobby bombastic lawyer who drinks too much. Never stopped talking about the wine my mother was serving. Gushing about the 'necklace' and 'this wine has legs' and 'Mmmmm, smell the bouquet'. Dear Lord Sir, are you going to drink it or fuck it?"

Ava gasps out loud. "Did you really say that?"

"Of course not! I just thought it."

"Goodness," is all I can say.

"Then my Uncle Beau puffs out his barrel chest and says 'wait till you taste mine.' He disappears for twenty minutes, and returns with five bottles of some rare wine, Chateau Lafitte-Rothschild. Or Mouton-Rothschild. Uncle Beau said he planned to drink every last bottle he owned before Duncan's funeral, and I think he has several hundred so that should be fun to watch. Drunk Uncle Beau is not a pretty sight."

My ears prick up at the mention of Rothschild. Didn't Fausto or Father Archer say the Rothschild family were involved with vineyards at some point? I think so. Coincidence? I think not. "Is Uncle Beau Duncan's father? Your mother's brother?"

"That's the one, Beauregard Pike, Duncan's father. He's a hot mess with all this going on. One minute he's sobbing and the next he's swearing revenge on the murderer and the next he's plotting his next financial coup at the bank."

"Does he know who the murderer is?" I ask.

"No, but he seems determined to find them and make them pay in some scary way." She closes her eyes and makes the lion face we learned in yoga where you open your eyes and mouth really wide, stick out your tongue as far as you can and make a "blaaaaah" sound. It stretches your face into freaky contortions, but does wonders for releasing tension.

"Can we talk about something else? I can't bear anymore gloom and doom. I need a bit of frivolity."

Ava squeezes her hand. "Absolutely. Frivolity is our specialty."

Chapter 14

LetMeEntertainYou

Peach Schnapps, Blood Orange Puree, Champagne

The Quarter is a different place by the light of the day. The street washers move slowly down the streets like enormous bush pigs looking for truffles. We park on Governor Nicholls and walk down Royal. As soon as I see the colorful windows of Fifi Mahoney's with their massive wigs in the window, I feel at peace inside. One window has a waist-length pink wig that has been teased and ratted and festooned with cupcakes in various sizes. It sits on a mannequin head wearing big red heart-shaped sunglasses. The other is a blue wig that is teased so high it could hold a schooner, and it is. Bellamy lowers her sunglasses, "Lord have mercy is that a pirate ship in the wig?"

"Looks like it," I say, feeling my heart speed up with delight. "And look at the tiny treasure chest and golden sparkles falling out of it. Ooooooh! The sparkles cascade like the treasure is spilling out of the chest and down the hair. Fantastic!"

"I *must* have that," she says. "We have a pirate theme for our pre-Pussyfooters ball party. I have thigh-high boots and I'll wear that wig."

I have a theory that every woman has a special place in their souls that loves sparkles and costumes and dressing up, but maybe I'm just pinning my own inner landscape to others. Ava has scurried inside to see what treasures she can spot first, and I follow her, reveling in the sparkling beauty of the shop.

Like Tiffany's was to Holly Golightly, Fifi Mahoney's is to me. Holly was looking for the illusion of safety that comes with financial security. I am always looking for glamour, magic, and adventure and Fifi Mahoney's is all three rolled into one, splitting at the seams. Costume and wig shops are usually in the skankiest part of town right next tattoo parlors and porn shops. But in New Orleans they put their showgirl shop right in the heart of the French Quarter on Royal Street, right where it should be—on a street with 'Royal' in the name. The staff people are devoted costume lovers who seem to delight in their customers, with swivel beautician chairs and a big mirror so you can sit down while they try different wigs on you. And they treat everyone equally, from drag queens to cancer patients, strippers, moms, lawyers. We even brought Ava's 95-year-old grandmother in in here to get a wig and a group of men wearing glitter eyeshadow and wigs resembling Cher, Barbra Streisand, and Hilary Clinton all cheered for each new look as the staff tried different wigs on her.

I inhale the smell of powder and glitter eyeshadow as I study the wigs displayed on a high shelf circling the ceiling. One is bright pink with high pigtails and pink firecracker tinsel adorning it and the other is orange with monarch butterflies on wires starting in the hair and swirling up and out so it looks like butterflies are flying around the head. I wonder if Hunter would like that. But I glance down and am taken by the glass cases of tiaras and feather headpieces. Oh goodness, I can feel my wallet starting to shiver in anticipation. Peacock feathers shimmer in emerald green and sapphire blue under the lighting, hypnotizing me with their beauty.

I am looking at the crowns in the window when I see a flash of a denim jacket walk by. It makes my heart pound and I lean forward to see if it's the purse snatcher, but the jacket has disappeared. I hurry over to stand close to my friends — protection in numbers.

Bellamy wastes no time and is already sitting in a chair with a wig cap waiting for the pirate ship wig to be brought to her. Ava who is rattling on about the Great Gatsby theme of the Cherry Bomb ball and how she needs a flapper wig.

I think the denim jacket has scared me so badly, my hearing has gone wonky. It sounds like Ava is speaking through a tunnel. "We have a Great Gatsby theme this year and I found this stunning beaded, champagne flapper dress. I have stockings, shoes, long necklaces and now I need a big boa and headpiece."

"Ladies!" We hear Bellamy calling us from the other room. "Come give me your opinions."

I shake off my trepidation and we walk into the wig room where Bellamy is smiling like a lottery winner sitting in her swivel chair. "Wow Bellamy!" Ava says, "That is a showstopper. Oh my Goddess, look at those sparkles. You will be the only one with a pirate ship in their hair."

Bellamy looks at the pink-haired shopboy. "You haven't sold another wig like this, have you?"

"No, no, every wig is a one-of-a-kind. I put this one together myself." He is adjusting the hair around Bellamy's face with flair.

Ava gasps as she spots a short black flapper wig cut in a blunt bob. "That might be perfect? Can I try?"

A girl with baby blue hair and matching nails appears. She uses a long rod to pull it down from the high shelf. She puts the wig on Ava and adds a sparkling rose-colored flapper headband with matching ostrich feather.

"Those are incredible on your olive skin," Bellamy says.

And it's true, the rose color makes her glow.

Bellamy turns her long swan neck side to side admiring

herself when Jimmy Tate enters wearing one of the peacock headpieces. He puts his hands on his hips and says in a perfect Bette Davis imitation, "What a dump!"

"Jimmy Tate! How did you know we were here?" I ask, rushing over and hugging him a little too tight.

"Psychic powers," he says in a deep gruff voice.

"I texted him on the way here," Bellamy says.

"Did you see anyone out front?" I ask him.

"Why?"

I hear the bell on the front door tinkle and I'm relieved when two women enter the shop.

"Did you see anyone in a denim jacket?" I ask.

Jimmy Tate looks at me with concern. "Oh my darling, are you thinking about last night?" He guides me to the red velvet couch shaped like lips and tries to take my Fleur De Paris hatbox from me. I hold it to my chest, shaking my head. I'm not letting this out of my sight. I hear him tell Bellamy to find me some cold water.

Ava is staring at me, wearing her flapper wig. She sits next to me and squeezes my hand. "Everything is going to be all right, Ellington. It's hot in here. You just need some nice cold water to cool off."

I nod. I don't really feel like talking.

Bellamy returns with a cold bottle of water. I lift it to my lips and see written in small letters on the label, 'Sic volvo sic iubeo.' When I look up, the thief in the denim jacket is looking at me from the doorway with a sick smile. I scream and throw the water bottle at him. He disappears as it slaps against the wall and sloshes water across the floor.

I have no time to think as I run after him. My ballet flats are impeding my speed so I kick them off as I run, barefoot, after him. My marabou backpack is bouncing up and down on my back as I run, and it's not that easy to run carrying a heavy hatbox. The thief is speeding down Royal and makes a right down Ursuline. He is fast and spry and in better shape than me. I make it about three blocks before my chest is heaving so hard it feels like it might explode and I have to stop. I can hear my friends shouting behind me and Jimmy Tate sprints past me, chasing the vermin. I stop, my hands on my hips. The flowers have bounced out of my hair and Ava has them both in her hand along with my shoes. "Are you okay?" she asks, panting.

Bellamy is right behind her. They are both still wearing their wigs and the blue-haired girl has followed them. "Oh shoot, we have to pay for our wigs." They are both panting. "We're coming."

The shopgirl folds her arms and says, "I'll walk back with you."

Bellamy says in her firm authoritarian voice, "We left our handbags with all our money back in the shop. You can head back there and ring us up and by the time you're finished, we'll be there paying."

The girl looks at all of us suspiciously.

"Really?" asks Bellamy. "Do you think we are a gang of wig thieves and this is our diabolical plan? To try on wigs then run out of the store and leave our purses behind for two wigs? Believe me, Honey, we are all 40ish and none of us want to run full speed anywhere."

The girl is still staring with narrowed eyes. "Oh for heaven's sake," Bellamy says, taking off her wig and handing it to the girl shaking out her own hair. Ava hands over her wig too and the blue-haired girl marches away, saying, "These will be at the shop and you can take them *after* you pay for them."

Bellamy sees my foot and says, "Oh my god you have cut your foot. Sit down." The doctor in her has taken over and she makes me sit on the curb while she looks at the cut.

Just then a bell rings and the street fills with young girls wearing school uniforms, carrying books. Bellamy helps me scoot back to lean against the moss-covered brick wall of the Ursuline Convent, famous for educating girls when many girls were shut out of schools. Built in 1727, it is known to be the oldest building in the Mississippi River Valley, but it is probably *most* famous for the vampires. When the first nuns arrived in New Orleans, they saw a need for girls and requested them to be sent form the convents of Europe. The "Casket Girls" arrived with trunks called "casquettes" that were shaped like coffins. It is said the trunks weren't full of clothing, but were instead filled with vampires, and that their caskets are still stored on the third floor. The third floor windows have always been completely nailed shut. For the past three hundred years, it has been said that bodies drained of blood were often found on the front steps of the convent.

Now the blood of my cut foot is staining the dirty sidewalk. Ava hands me a tissue and Bellamy applies direct pressure to stop the bleeding. Ava sits down next to me. "Sugar, who was that boy you were chasing?"

"That's the thief from last night, the one who tried to steal my purse," I say, breathless. "And Bellamy, where did you get that water bottle? He had written on it."

She looks guilty. "The shop didn't have any water and I went to cross the street to buy some from the coffee shop and a guy offered it to me."

"What? You took water from a stranger?"

"Well the bottle was sealed," she says, her accent thicker when she feels guilty. "He said he had overheard that I needed water for a friend and he had an extra bottle if I wanted it. I *thought* he was being nice. I grabbed it and ran back to you. What writing was on it?"

Jimmy Tate is back and interrupts. "That little freak crossed Esplanade and I lost him." He looks at me. "That was the dude from last night, right? How did he find us here?"

"He must have followed us. Jimmy Tate, this whole thing has to be tied to Comus." I tell him how Bellamy got the bottle of water and the words written on the label.

Jimmy Tate nods. "And Fausto said that's Comus' motto."

Bellamy looks at both of us. "Who the heck is Fausto? And what do you mean your purse got stolen last night? You didn't tell me any of this." We fill Ava and Bellamy in on everything we've learned and they are flabbergasted.

Ava cannot contain herself. "*Fausto? House of Rothschild?* What do they have to do with any of this?"

"Ava, calm down. Fausto is a harmless doorknob collector and House of Rothschild isn't dangerous, they lost their power a hundred years ago," I say.

She hisses, "That's what *you* think. Do you know how deep their tentacles go? They can destroy or create countries with a swish of their pen. And Fausto, a doorknob collector? Fausto is the nation's leading scholar on secret societies. Some say he may even be deeply involved in them, a kind of covert agent like John Brown. "

"John Brown?" Jimmy Tate is confused.

"Of Harper's Ferry. John Brown was always deeply involved in the most secret sects of the Freemasons. When the Freemasons connected with House of Rothschild, they needed secret agents to instigate war. It was in their best interest to keep the north and south separate—it was easier to control the economies of smaller countries that way. They had John Brown renounce secret societies and pretend to be a regular citizen so he could raid Harper's ferry and help foster war.

"How do you know these things?" Jimmy Tate asks. "And how do you remember them? I can't even remember what I had for breakfast yesterday."

"Is Fausto in House of Rothschild? Or Comus?" I ask.

She shakes her head. "Comus is defunct, remember? He's in Rex. They are the power krewe now. And of course the Freemasons are always operating right under everybody's noses. Fausto could be a thirty-third degree Mason."

Jimmy Tate puts his hands on his hips, "Nobody ever asks *me* to be part of a secret society."

"That's because you can't keep a secret," I say.

Bellamy jumps in with a loud whisper. "What about Skull and Bones, the secret society at Yale? Is there a section of it here? My cousin that was murdered, Duncan, was a member when he went to Yale. In fact, so was his father, my Uncle Beau, and our grandfather, back four generations at least. But they always said Skull and Bones was just a boys club for business networking."

Ava rolls her eyes. "That's always the excuse."

I feel an icy hand across my neck and I turn around but no one is there. I feel like crying, but I won't. I'm going to keep plowing forward. "Here's a possible twist," I say. "Last night, I remembered this magician I used to work with who kept a secret pocket in his top hat, which led me to the one thing that linked me to the murder *and* the purse snatching."

They are all quiet. Ava finally says, "What?"

"My vintage handbag." A collective gasp. I tell them about them about the secret pocket and my suspicions that Duncan may have targeted me.

They gasp again in perfect unison.

"Oh my god!" Bellamy says.

I nod. "I know. Creepy."

"But he didn't take it from you," Ava says.

"Exactly," I answer. "Maybe he tried to take it but he got stabbed before he could."

"You are freaking me out, Ellington Martini," Bellamy says.

"I'm freaking *myself* out. That's why I am not carrying my handbag out in the open today. It's here in this hatbox."

"I was wondering why you were holding that like some sort of bag lady," Jimmy Tate says. "Once I went to a Bourbon Street Strip Club, the one with Chris Owens, and the stripper on stage stumbled through her whole dance clutching her purse to her chest." Chris Owens was a famous New Orleans stripper back in the old days. Now she runs the Easter parade through the French Quarter, which is one of the reasons I fell in love with this place. Any city who's Easter parade is run by a showgirl wearing a fabulous hat is the city for me.

"*Anyway*," I continue, "It seems people are out to get that bag, although I'd punch them in the face if they took it."

"Where did Winston get it?"

"Bianca LeBlanc's." I glance at my Tank watch. "Shall we head over there now and look for clues and ballgowns?"

Bellamy shakes her head. "You can think of ballgowns at a time like this?"

"Bellamy," I say, "It is times like these, times when chaos and mayhem try to get the best of us that it is most important to cling to beauty." I stand up and brush the rocks off my derriere. "When Frida Kahlo had that car accident and she was in so much pain the rest of her life, her friends said that the more pain she felt, the more elaborate her outfits. Velvet, silk, beautiful colors... these are the things that get us through rainy days, and it doesn't get much rainier than this."

Just then pink bubbles start to surround us, and the sound of a turntable playing Nellie Lutcher. We all look up at the wrought iron balcony across the street from us. It is filled with potted palms and there's no one on it, but the bubbles keep coming.

Chapter 15

Pink Lady

Gin, Grenadine, Egg White, Cream, Ice

On the way to Bianca's, I say, "Now listen everyone, don't bring up the handbag right away. I have to feel out the situation and figure out the best way to ask Bianca without making it seem like I don't like my gift.

Ava pulls into a parking space. "We understand. You don't want her to be insulted."

Jimmy Tate adjusts his mirrored Gucci sunglasses. "*And you want to make sure she still feels inspired to suggest gifts for you to Winston. We understand.*" He gets out of the car, and in his best Mae West impressions says, "Keep those gifts coming!"

As we walk down the sidewalk, I jump when a purple dragonfly zooms by. I keep walking. I can feel a soft warm breeze coming off the Mississippi with its rank flowery, mud smell. When I met Bianca at a party, she invited me to her shop, and it was like stepping into someone's dream. I didn't even know shops like this still existed outside old Technicolor musicals. Bianca bought the shop as a young debutante in the 1950's, and expanded it into her version of "civilized" shopping. She put in three runways for each fitting room: the Bridal room, Ballgown room and Mother-of-the-Bride Room. The runways are a place where women can walk, twirl, and stoop, observing their gowns from all angles. They are surrounded with comfy chairs where friends can sit and drink champagne. It's just like the shopping scene in *How to Marry a Millionaire* with Marilyn Monroe, Betty Grable and Lauren Bacall modeling clothes in a shopping fashion show. I always want a glass of champagne and a fashion show when I shop— they're like tiny parades.

Entering the shop, we are all assailed by the smell of jasmine. I like jasmine, but the shop smells so pungent I feel like a hot baguette dipped in a steaming pot of gumbo. Bianca says she chose jasmine because she used to wear it in her hair as a child. I wonder if she knows that jasmine was code for sex in the Storyville brothels. Ladies of the night used to wear jasmine corsages so men could identify them. They would ask potential clients, 'Would you like some jas?' Winston told me this is where the word 'jazz' comes from. Bianca is so ladylike, though, she probably would have chosen a different flower if she'd known the story. Although flowers are basically sex on a stem and so is jazz for that matter.

When we enter, there is a dapper man wearing a cheap suit and diamond cufflinks standing at a booth covered in purple. It's the perfume counter and he holds a tasseled atomizer, waiting to spray any willing woman. Ava heads over and holds out her wrists with big smile. I quickly turn the opposite direction—if I get sprayed I will never get that smell off my skin. It's the kind of smell that moves in for good, putting its feet up on the couch and being generally offensive, kind of like Winston's mother.

Bellamy and Jimmy Tate have entered the tunnel of boas and ballgowns straight ahead like Lewis and Clark on an expedition. They start calling my name.

"Ellington... Oh Ellington... you must come immediately."

I enter the tunnel of shimmery hoop skirts ala Scarlett O'Hara hanging from the ceiling, surrounded by flapper dresses and Rita-Hayworth-Style slinky silk gowns. Oh dear Goddess, I want to lie down and roll in the clouds of silk. And with Sinatra playing over the speakers, all jagged edges full of thieves and murderers disappear and are replaced with soft romantic dreams.

Jimmy Tate and Bellamy take my arm. "Honey, have you floated away? Come back to earth, we have something to show you." They move aside two fluffy black boas and I see a tower of pink satin sleeping eye masks, some with eyes painted on the outside. There's also oversized men's button down white shirts for sleeping, elbow length gloves, enormous hats, and a retro telephone in a suitcase with a high heel shoe. I clap my hand over my mouth so I don't scream, but a little squeak escapes. "*Breakfast at Tiffany's*? Oh Bianca! She has truly outdone herself now."

Bellamy and Jimmy Tate laugh in delight, as I run from display to display. "I knew she'd love this room the best," Bellamy says, "She's obsessed with Holly Golightly."

I turn to them with two large purple boas around my neck and an eye mask over my eyes. "I can hear you, you know. You're acting like I'm not here."

Bellamy puts on a large hat and big sunglasses from a display. "Actually, you're kind of not here. It seems you've disappeared in a cloud of feathers."

Jimmy Tate throws a boa across his neck and we all laugh as he spits out a mouthful of pink feathers. "Dear god has Bianca totally lost her mind? This place is fabulously insane."

I have pulled on evening gloves and am strutting around the room practicing my Audrey Hepburn poses when Bellamy grabs my arms. "Sugar, we are getting distracted." I look at her in the big hat and sunglasses and then to Jimmy Tate who is smoking a candy cigarette while pretending to talk on the retro phone.

She might be right.

She takes my face in her hands. "We need to focus. Ballgown. Clues. Ballgown. Clues. Say it with me."

"Ballgown. Clues. Ok, you're right." I reluctantly put the sleeping eye mask back on the rack and start to pull off the gloves, tugging on each finger. But then Dr. Micheal White's "Minnie the Moocher" comes over the speakers, the absolute best song for pulling off evening gloves and various other clothing. I start to move my hips, and bend my entire body over one leg in a dramatic drop, slowly rising like a phoenix from the flames. I pull off the gloves to the beat, finger by finger, with my teeth. Jimmy Tate isn't paying attention, he's too busy writhing on the nearest tower rack like a pole dancer. I have to say that pilates pays off, his leg extension is epic. When I get to the part where I throw the gloves over my shoulder onto the floor, I realize I'm going to have to buy them.

Ava appears through the boa tunnel. "There y'all are. Pull yourselves together and follow me."

She's so commanding we all follow her no questions asked. We walk behind her through a narrow hallway of glittering evening handbags, through the section of seersucker sundresses and giant sunhats for long brunches, and into the bride room.

The bride room.

The crowning glory of the shop.

It looks like a wedding cake mated with a swan and they had a giant baby full of feathers and tiers of tulle. Massive hoop dresses hanging from the ceiling and line the walls. In the center are antique carousel horses with antique dolls riding on them, their glass eyes staring out. These design choices push the beautiful shop out of beauty and into creepy. I can imagine this being the perfect scene for a murder, and last night crashes back like a tsunami.

I have to sit down.

I half stumble to the closest pink pillow chair and collapse. Bellamy sits beside me. "You ok, Sugar?"

"I just need to sit for a minute." I'm trying to block all the blood and the whispers and the sick smile from my mind. I feel like I might suffocate and when Bellamy hears me trying to catch my breath, she immediately rubs my back and makes me take deep breaths with her. With every breath, I get calmer. Jimmy Tate throws a white marabou stole over my shoulders and whispers, "Stay with us, Darling. Do *not* go down that dark rabbit hole. Bury your face in this fluff and all your troubles will disappear. Pouf," He blows the feathers so they flutter lightly.

If there's one thing I'm really good at it's pretending, so I pretend I'm fine. The music switches again to Louis Armstrong; charming, jubilant Satchmo. He always brings me back to my joyful self.

Just then Bianca rushes into the room with two women and a child. They are talking bridesmaids' dresses and Bianca has a stack of chiffon and silk dresses draped over her arm as she talks while waving around the other arm. One of the women is wearing a navy cotton safari-type dress with a fedora and navy wedges and a large totebag that matches. She has a little girl with ringlet pigtails and big pink ribbons tied in her hair. The child is running across the displayed wedding dresses in her shiny mary janes and hand-smocked dress, crawling behind the mannequins, causing them to wobble dangerously. Her mother says sternly, "Elizabeth! Come here right now. You will ruin those gorgeous dresses with your shoes."

To my great delight, Bianca says in her thick molasses drawl, "Oh let her plaaaayyyy! What *woooon*derful memories she's creating. Just imagine how nice it would be if these were our own childhood memories. Let her play. She's just fine."

This is one of the reasons I love Bianca—her generous spirit. Plus after having eight kids of her own, nothing seems to rattle her.

She smiles happily when she finally notices me draped over her couch. "Ellington, how wonderful to see you my darling." She floats over to kiss me on the cheek, and I notice how thick her lashes are around her big brown eyes. She either has the Elizabeth Taylor birth defect of double lashes or has an amazing mascara. Mental note: ask Bianca what mascara she uses. Her hair is gathered on top of her head in a victorian bun showing off her luminescent long pale neck. I think Bianca's dark luscious hair might be the best-kept secret in New Orleans. She never wears it down, but if you catch her at the right moment when she pulls out the pins, her hair falls to her waist like the theater drapes at the end of Gypsy Rose Lee's finale dance. She envelops me in a cloud of even stronger jasmine, then notices Bellamy and Jimmy Tate. "Well you've brought your royal court. Hello Mr. Tate. Welcome." She warmly kisses him on both sides of his cheeks. She takes Bellamy's face in her hands. "Miss Bellamy, I am so sorry to hear about your cousin. Such a tragedy. My heart goes out to you and your family."

Bellamy drops her head like a weeping tomb statue. "Thank you."

Bianca introduces us to her customers, Adelaide and Alice Desjardins and I can see they are dying to know what the tragedy is, but their southern manners outweigh their curiosity and they don't ask. Upon closer inspection, I see Alice Desjardin is the blonde dandelion puff server from Crepe Nanou, the night of the murder. I didn't recognize her looking so glamorous, wearing a long sleeved silk blouse in a champagne color with matching pants, her hair neatly tied up in a French twist. My head feels hot with the memory of those last joyful moments before the darkness descended, and all those dangerous thoughts that start with two words: "if only."

Before I descend further, Alice says, "Your name is Ellington? Were you named after the Duke?"

Happy to be re-directed, I say. "My parents were huge jazz lovers. They played *Such Sweet Thunder* in the delivery room."

Bianca says, "How could I have known you all these years

and have never heard that story?"

"Oh each of us were born to a different iconic jazz album: *Round Midnight, Love Supreme...* My parents were completely obsessed with music, and they wanted the first thing we heard when we entered the world to be jazz."

Bellamy says, "I think if I was naming my future children after a meaningful theme in my life, it might be Margarita, Manhattan, and Cosmopolitan.

Bianca laughs, "Calling 'Manhattan! Supper's ready' is quite a mouthful."

Jimmy Tate says, "You could call her Hattie for short. I love Hattie. Mine would be Dior, Louboutin, and Hermes. I could call them Di, Lou, and Mes for short."

"Mes like Mezz Mezzrow, the jazz clarinetist. I like that." I start singing a little of Fats Waller's Viper Song, the part with Mezz's name in it. *I dreamed about a reefer, five feet long, the Mighty Mezz, but not too strong. You'll be high, but not for long, when you're a viper.*

Jimmy Tate says to the group, "That's her signature song when she's had too much wine and ends up lying on the piano at Marcello's singing for the Never-Lefts."

Adelaide tilts her head. "The Never-Lefts?"

"That group of people who come to visit New Orleans for a weekend and end up staying forever?"

Alice looks confused. "And Mezz Mezzrow is a jazz player?"

I nod. "He was a famous jazz clarinet player back in the day. He wrote *Really the Blues.* "

Jimmy Tate holds pinched fingers up to his lips like he's smoking a fatty. "He also was famous for selling the best weed. So famous they named it after him — the *Mighty Mezz.*"

"I would name my children Cream Puff, Cupcake, and Éclair." I say, giving my muffin top an affectionate squeeze and whispering "Love you." Everyone looks at me. "What? I recently read that if you tell your cellulite and muffin top that you love them, you'll improve your body esteem and the fat will melt."

Jimmy Tate says, "Girl, you worry me sometimes."

"I'd name my kids Desdemona, Ophelia, and Juliet," Alice says with a big wistful smile.

"Ah Shakespeare. *Such Sweet Thunder* is actually based on a the works of Shakespeare. 'If music be the food of love, play on!'" I say exuberantly. "Also, I was Peasblossom in *Midsummer Night's Dream*." I say.

"The fairies are my favorite," she says.

"Me too! Except I had to wear a green, handpainted unitard which is not my most flattering outfit and at the end I had to slide out of the ceiling upside down on a rope. Of course I got terrible rope burns on my ankle."

Jimmy Tate is staring at me, holding his fingers to his temples. "Hold on, hold on, this is an image I want to keep forever, you in a green unitard sliding out of the ceiling on a rope. I *really* wish I had seen that in person. Green unitard."

Adelaide puts her arm around Alice. "That's our Alice. If there's a tragic heroine around, she wants to join the drama."

"At least I'm not marrying a man I don't love," Alice says with a sweet smile.

Adelaide's face turns red but she has a big smile on her face. "I do love him."

"You love his wallet."

Bianca stops them. "Oh ladies, we do have so much more to discuss before the big day." She ushers them from the room, and I sink back into the couch and close my eyes and breathe deeply, trying to bring in peace and let go of fear when I hear a whisper in my ear, "Green unitard." I throw a pillow at Jimmy Tate just as Bianca returns.

Her eyebrows are raised when she sees the flying pillow and I once again feel that queasy 'principal's office' feeling. I've been trying to decide how best to approach Bianca about the bag, but I finally decide to just shop and let the subject into the conversation naturally. "Bianca, I haven't even told you yet but I have exciting news." I pause for dramatic effect.

She opens her hands. "Well?"

"We're invited to the Rex Ball!" I can't stop myself from shouting it like I'm on a game show and have just won a trip to Hawaii.

"You're joking."

I shake my head happily. "No, I'm not. And I need a dress."

She claps. "Well of course you do, Sugar. Oh now, *this* is going to fun. Sit right here," she motions for me to sit on a round pink chair. She calls over one of her many daughters who work at the shop." Flora, I need a notebook and a pen." Flora nods and disappears. "Now," Bianca continues, "Let me tell you how this all works. One of the best parts of the ball is deciding what to wear. Usually, I have my clients brainstorm a list of ideas for what they envision, for what suits their personality, mood, and how they want the night to go. A kind of vision board." Bianca can see my eyes glazing over. "Don't you worry about a vision board, Sugar, you only have two weeks, so let's get down to the first essentials."

Bianca is in her happy place with her notebook and pink clipboard. "Now, do you want a showstopper dress with no regard for comfort? Or are you more concerned with being able to eat a few extra cream puffs? Of course that's why the good lord invented corsets."

"Corsets? What kind of corset? Do you mean a full boned one like Scarlett O'Hara wore? Or one of those elastic ones?"

"Oh, Ellington, honey, don't you wear corsets? You're in the south now, Sugar! Things expand in this heat, and a lady always must do what she can to keep certain muffins from rising."

I take a deep breath. "Well I tried wearing a corset for the first time two weeks ago on a date with Winston. My waist was tiny and adorable, but I only got two blocks in the car before I had to lift up my dress, unhook the darn thing and throw it in the back seat. I can tell you Winston was very confused—he was driving."

Jimmy Tate and Bellamy are laughing while Bianca looks simply horrified.

"Then, I walked into the restaurant for our romantic dinner and realized my dress was tucked up my back, so I had to scoot sideways along the wall to the powder room to handle things. It is there I couldn't take my too-tight, thigh-high stockings for one more minute, so I tore those off and tossed them in the trash."

Now Bianca has one perfectly manicured hand over her mouth, her eyes wide.

"Apparently, the stockings and corset had cut off the blood flow to my brain, or I drank a little too much wine, but I read the dessert menu, my favorite part, and they were serving "Ladyfingers", which struck me as the funniest word I had ever heard, so I couldn't stop laughing. I can tell you a stockingless woman laughing until her face is beet red with tears running her makeup is not a pretty sight. Then we went to a nightclub, where I eventually reached my final breaking point: I threw my underwire bra in the trash in the Ladies room, and eventually, my too-tight dress as well. Luckily I had my long faux fur coat with me so I wore it home. But I have to wonder, who invents these torturous things?"

Bianca speaks in a hushed voice. "Oh Ellington, please don't tell me you rode home from a nightclub in your underwear?"

"I was covered! I had on my coat."

"Oh I am simply mortified."

I pat her back. "Sorry, Bianca. I hope I haven't completely offended your sense of decorum. Winston was a little taken aback himself, but I think he was more worried I was going to get arrested."

Jimmy Tate and Bellamy laugh my favorite laugh, the deep hearty laugh of drunken pirates, until Jimmy Tate snaps again and says, "Ladies? It's ballgown time." Probably the only thing that can keep us from a world-class laughing fit is ballgown shopping.

Like a monarch in a field of lavendar, Bianca flutters through her domain. She sits next to me and Bellamy and Jimmy Tate have collapsed on the nearest velvet settee while another daughter, Violet, enters carrying champagne for all of us. Bianca gets down to business, "These balls are your chance to go all out with dress, to live out any dress fantasy you have ever dreamed about. Sometimes the queens come in and order their fantasy dress which we design and make from scratch by hand. We don't have time for that, so tell me if you prefer a large hoop ballgown or something more silky and streamlined? Or something in between?"

"I have no idea. I have always wanted to wear a real ballgown complete with hoop skirt, but I don't want to be fussing with it all night. I want to be able to sit down comfortably. I know the balls can last eight hours and I do not want to be miserable."

"Yes, it *can* be a very long night so comfort is key for someone as sensitive as you." Bianca is sketching while she talks to me. "Did you wear a hoop gown to your wedding?"

"No, I wore a red bikini."

She stops sketching and stares at me. "Pardon me? What did you say?"

"I said, I wore a red bikini."

She clears her throat and pats her chest like she's having a hard time swallowing. "I'm sorry, did you say you wore a red bikini?"

I nod.

"Why on god's green earth would you have done that?"

"Well, at the time it was the cutest thing I owned. And I didn't feel like dress shopping by myself since my family and friends lives across the country. I had just moved here and hadn't made any close friends yet."

Bianca is staring at me like a dog that had been waiting for a favorite treat but instead of giving it to her I ate it myself. She looks so forlorn I put my arms around her. "Bianca, I didn't know my choice of wedding clothing would shock you so. If it makes you feel better, I didn't get married in a church."

"Well thank our lucky stars for that."

"Winston and I eloped to an island. We got married barefoot under the stars with orchids hanging from the palm trees and the warm waters lapping our ankles."

She swallows. "And Winston? Did he wear a bathing suit as well?"

I laugh. "No, no, Winston wanted to live out his James Bond fantasy. He wore black pants with a white tux coat. Very debonair."

Bianca pats her chest again. "Well thank god for that, at least."

"But he was in flip flops."

She rubs her temple with one perfectly manicured finger. "You could have spared me that little tidbit." She lets out a long sigh. "I suppose if the waves were lapping at you, shoes wouldn't have worked. I do feel *strongly*, however, that men should just keep their feet covered. It is *not* their best feature."

Ava has been missing for some time and she comes around the corner wearing a soft blue seersucker halter sundress and large straw hat with cat eye sunglasses. She is carrying a little straw handbag shaped like a picnic basket with cherries on the handle. "What do you think? Isn't this perfect for brunch at Galatoires? Can't you just see me drinking Mint Juleps on the balcony?" She pretends to stand on a balcony, laughing and talking to invisible friends and waving at us.

Bellamy cheers. "Yes! You look amazing! That outfit is perfect from head to toe. Where did you find it? I need a brunch outfit." She rises. "Take me to the 'Brunch on a Balcony' section."

Jimmy Tate stands up to follow her as well. "Me, too. Do they have mens seersucker as well? I need a vest and a bowtie for my new look."

Bianca nods. "You do. That would be perfect for you,

along with a bowler hat and a cane."

Ava puts her hands on his chest in excitement. "Just like a Tennessee Williams character."

The image of Jimmy Tate with a cane brings back the Joan of Arc parade as I think about the monk and his desperate frightened eyes. I involuntarily jump back in my chair. Bianca doesn't know the cane details about the night before and I don't want to tell her. Bellamy, Jimmy Tate, and Ava all look at me with concern. I jump up from my seat so Bianca can't see the tears in my eyes. "Let me see that adorable handbag Ava." I walk over to her and examine it with its red lining and charming perkiness. It cheers me up, and I have to wonder if there's something wrong with my morality that a man can practically die in my arms yet the memory evaporates at the sight of an amazing handbag?

I start to chatter so they can't ask me if I'm all right. "I love this. The sunglasses, dress, bag, the whole kit and caboodle. It's fabulous on you. Why don't you all go into the brunch room while I talk to Bianca?"

Bianca seems to sense that something isn't right and in her elegant way, makes a suggestion. "Sometimes the easiest way to decide on a direction is to pull a few pieces that call to you and try them on. That way you can see what makes you feel the most beautiful while still staying comfortable and we can work from there. Yes?"

"Perfect." I'm relieved. It's not her style to be nosy and pry into people's affairs. I can see she knows something is up, but with her excellent manners she won't ask.

She pats my back. "It's settled then. I'll take Ellington around, pull some pieces, and you all meet us back here in a half hour or so for more pink champagne and a fashion show."

I'm so grateful to have missed a meltdown. "Bianca, you are singing my tune. I would like to climb into a little flute of champagne right now and swim around in pink bubbles for the rest of the day."

Ava squeezes my hand while Jimmy Tate smiles and wiggles his eyebrows at me. Bellamy is already sauntering to the brunch room. "Toodles Ell! See you in a few. Just hoot like an owl if you need us." Our laughter reassures me and Bianca and I look at each other.

"Let's do it."

With a steady hand, Bianca starts pulling dresses, and she's not pulling the demure ones. She holds up a long ivory silk Harlow gown with a plunging back and sheer ribbons holding the back together. My heart jumps back to its delighted rhythm as I surrender to sartorial splendor with a long deep sigh. Bianca doesn't even have to ask me if I like it, the look on my face tells her and she drapes it over her arms with a big smile on her face. She swaggers into the non-bridal ballgown room and calls, "Come along Dear."

I enter the next room with every color of gown winking at me, taunting me with beauty. Bianca has hung the ivory Harlow in a large dressing room on the side, and when I say dressing room I mean hot pink tufted velvet walls, hooks everywhere, and a bench to sit in between trying on. Fiona comes in from a different door with another tray of champagne glasses. She hands one to me with a big smile of perfectly straight teeth. "Here you are, Miss Ellington. Why don't you sit right here and relax while we explore your options?"

I sit down in the ivory sequined chair she is pointing to with my flute of champagne. It's such a beautiful word, *champagne*. No wonder people love it so much. It's pink, has bubbles, and has a beautiful name. But would people still drink it if it was called, say, Grimaulder? Or Saugus? Or Herpedorkson? I doubt it. Amazing the power of names, and speaking of names, Bianca is holding up a stunning cherry red Christian Dior. It is strapless with a laced up bodice and full hoop skirt—very Scarlett O'Hara. It looks lush and it's the shining fabric that makes it such a stunner. "Wow!" Have I died and gone to heaven, drinking pink champagne and looking at luxurious dresses?

Bianca is delighted herself. "Isn't it stunning? It's vintage Dior. They don't make them like this anymore." She cradles it in her arms as she walks it over to my dressing room. This is my chance to ask about my vintage bag. I hate to break the spell, but, "Bianca, I didn't know you carried vintage?"

"We sure do. There's a high demand for vintage everything. They don't make things with the quality they used to, or if they do, they charge $50,000 for a dress, which no one in their right mind would pay. Vintage allows people to get one-of-a-kind highest quality items at affordable prices, with the added benefit of eco-chic."

"Like my Hermes Kelly bag?" I ask, holding the bag up for her to see.

"Exactly." She smiles. "That bag is spectacular, and they only made one or two in that color. It's extremely rare. Winston came to me looking for the perfect item for you, and I knew you and that bag were a match. Nothing thrills me more than making a match."

"Where did you get it? I mean, if I wanted to see what else the seller might have, who would I call?"

She smiles elegantly. "Oh my Ellington, if I gave away my secrets, I wouldn't have a business, would I? If there's something you want, you ask me and I will try to find it for you." I'm starting to see why she's been in business for 50 years, and it's not just because of her beautiful shop. The woman has the business acumen of a hedgefund ninja.

She guides me back to my dressing room. "Now remember, we can work wonders with undergarments so don't worry about tiny imperfections. And I'll make sure your undergarments are comfortable. Fiona and I are right here if you need any help. And what size shoe do you wear?"

"Seven, although the way my feet swell at night I usually buy an eight or nine."

"These are a nine." She hands me a pair of slip-on heels from the row next to the dressing room. "They are just for trying on so we can gauge the hem. I'll go get your friends so they're ready for your grand entrance. Your champagne can wait right here." She takes my glass out of my hand and sets it on a small roundtable covered in feathered headpieces.

I decide to start with the burgundy velvet gown. It has a side zipper and it's a little snug, so after a lot of wiggling and jumping to help the zipper finish zipping, I'm finally in. It is very fitted and pools at the bottom like a mermaid tail, very glamorous. I can hear Bianca herding my group into chairs around the runway as I slip into the kitten heels and exit my room. Jimmy Tate cheers when he sees me and Ava and Bellamy both gush "Oh Ellington. You look stunning."

I walk up the stairs and saunter down the runway as my posse 'ooohs' and 'aaahs.' With their encouragement, I swing my hips, and boy are they showcased in this dress. I turn and look in the 3-part mirror, trying to see my back side.

Bianca is following me with a pin cushion on her wrist. "It looks stunning from every angle and fits you like a glove," she coos in her southern drawl. She calls to Fiona who has been watching from the doorway. "Fiona, can you bring us some of the black crystal necklaces and the dangling ruby necklaces?" Fiona nods and disappears.

I am peering at my very round behind in the mirror and I squeeze my glutes to check out my wiggle room. I notice you can see every action of my muscles from the back.

Bianca shakes her head. "That's why the good lord invented Spanx."

"But look how revealing." I bounce on my heels and my whole backside jiggles up and down. "You don't think it's a little snug?"

Bellamy laughs, "I don't think you'll be bouncing up and down at the ball will you?"

"Well, I don't know, what if I dance? Or what if they ask a question and I'm raising my hand and I have to jump up and down so they see me in the crowd?"

Bellamy looks thoughtful. "I can't imagine why that

would ever happen at a ball. It's not a classroom. And there's no reason why you can't dance without bouncing."

I squeeze my glutes again and Jimmy Tate and Ava double over laughing.

I raise my eyebrows. "Spit it out. What are you trying to say?"

Ava tried to pull herself together. "You look beautiful, you really do, but when you squeeze your tush like that, well, it looks like two prairie dogs wrestling under a blanket."

"I knew it! This dress is too ass-ish."

Jimmy Tate composes himself to sound like a professor, "Yes indeed, the dress is 'ass-ish' but showing of off one's derriere is all the rage these days. As the nobel Sir Mix-A-Lot once said…" He stands up and pretends to be a gangsta, *I like big butts and I can not lie…*

I look around for something to throw at him but all I have on me are my shoes and I don't want to injure him. Bianca and Fiona climb up on the runway to adjust things. They place a black sparkling choker around my neck with dangling black crystals and slide elbow length black gloves on my arms. They clip dangling rubies on my ears and Bianca is fooling with a piece of black silk around my hips. "Now see here, Darling? Any flaw can be turned into an asset with the right tools." With their magical accessories, the dress has gone from stunning to show-stopping. And the silk has been placed so my assets are more hidden and not so… displayed.

Jimmy Tate has recovered, but can't resist shouting, "Your *ass*ets be looking mighty fine, Miss Ellington."

I realize I should have brought a stack of pillows to throw at his head.

I saunter up and down the aisle a few more times and decide this is a definite possibility. More champagne is poured as I head back to the dressing room to try on Gown #2: the Bronze Goddess. It takes a few minutes to take off my jewelry and I can hear the voices and laughter growing louder outside with every sip. I slip on the dress. This one is much easier to zip with its super-plunging neckline. There are lots of oohs and aahs as I swizzle up the stairs to the runway. Bianca pulls the back of the gown and clips it so I can see what it will look like when it's tailored, but the bottom is still so long it pools around my feet and drags behind me, but not in a glamorous train sort of way—more like I'm a little girl wearing her mother's nightgown.

Ava's brown eyes are huge as she looks up at me over her glass. "You look like a goddess. An Amazon warrior from Paradise Island."

Bellamy nods. "Yup. You could definitely be a Warrior Princess in that. I think that would be amazing with that slicked-back high ponytail you have and a spray tan to show off your gorgeous shoulders."

Jimmy Tate knocks back his drink. "Careful, spray tan with a bronze dress and you'll end up looking like an Oscar."

"Oh my goodness I *do* look like an Oscar. Except not as slim and statuesque." I mutter as I shuffle back to my dressing room so I don't step on the dress. "And what could be worse than a chubby Oscar."

Bianca and Fiona are standing at the edge of the runway with their hands full of bronze and gold cuffs and collars as I head back. "That's it? You don't like that one?"

"I love it but it's not suited to me right now. I felt much more connected to the crimson velvet. I'm trying on the next one." I shut my dressing room door before they can talk me into another catwalk as the chunky Oscar. The next dress is the vintage Dior ballgown, and when I say ballgown, I mean a GOWN in capital letters. It's glamorous, classic, and edgy all at the same time. The fabric is stunning by itself—thick gorgeous silk. It looks pretty small but I manage to squeeze myself into it. The structure of it is another of its magical properties—it has a built-in corset so it's designed to support and "hold in" without layering. I have to flip the hooks to the front to hook it properly, then suck in my stomach to alien proportions to scoot the hooks to the back, and I still can't reach the top hooks. Darn! Dresses that need a second person to finish putting on are a pain in the ass.

"Bianca?" I call in a singsong voice.

She appears in a flash.

"That was fast."

She nods. "Need some help?"

"Yes! These last hooks…"

"Yes, they can be challenging, but are usually worth the effort." She is obviously an expert and she pushes my extra muffins down with her fingers while hooking hooks.

Goodness.

She takes a break to poke her head outside and call Fiona. She whispers something to her and finishes hooking just as Fiona arrives with her arms full of sparkles: this time it's a vintage necklace of dripping diamonds with a sapphire drop; antique bracelets with at least three inches of sparkle for each wrist; and even a diamond upper arm band; no less sparkly than the real thing. Bianca and Fiona pull elbow length black evening gloves onto me, then expertly hook all the jewelry.

They clip up my hair and Bianca hands me my handbag saying only two words, "Lipstick, Dear." She's right. You can't get a decent idea of an outfit, especially a ballgown, when you have pale lips that disappear into your face. Bianca and Fiona wrap their arms around each other happily while they look at me, happy with their creation. If they weren't such ladies I think they would be high-fiving each other.

Fiona opens my dressing room door. "Stay here, let me present you properly."

I can hear my very loud friends stop talking and laughing when Fiona climbs the runway. In a perfect impression of Joel Grey in Cabaret, she says, "Madames and Monsieurs, Ladies and Gentlemen, I now present to you, that international sensation, Ellington Martini, in vintage Dior." She runs back down the steps so she can help me fluff the back of my dress as I walk out. The effect is exactly what a ballgown should evoke. There is a collective gasp followed by a hushed reverence like we are at church, and then, a burst of applause as they jump to their feet for a standing ovation. Oh how I love a standing O. I soak in the adulation. Call me shallow, call me a clap whore, but give me applause and I'm like a starving kitten given a bowl of cream. I don't even talk, I just slowly float to the runway and parade back and forth making various actions that I might make at a ball; bowing to people, throwing my head back to laugh at someone witty, sipping a drink.

And so, after only one visit to Bianca Le Blanc, I have found *The One*. It's done. While Bianca is tying up my treasures in beautiful boxes with ribbons, I sigh. Since I'm drunk on the power of my own shopping prowess and it's always easier to approach a shop owner about a delicate situation when you've just spent a truckload of money at their shop, I decide to take a risk and ask Bianca straight out about where she got the bag.

She lightly touches her elegant fingers to her throat. "I operate with absolute and total discretion, otherwise I"d be out of business."

"Yes I completely respect that, but Miss Bianca, a man is dead. He died *on me*." I take a tissue from the box on the counter to pat the tears that obstinately insist on returning. "I would never ask you to do anything that would put your livelihood in jeapardy, but this is *murder* we are talking about."

She hesitates and takes a deep breath. "You're right, and I'd rather tell you than the police." She scoots closer to me and like a shaken champagne bottle that is suddenly uncorked, she gushes in a whisper, "It was Madame Banjeau, Bellamy's mother." She sees my look of horror and nods her head up and down. "I know, I know, shocking. She consigned the Kelly, four Birkin bags, and eleven Chanel clutches."

Now I'm truly flabbergasted. How in the world does she have such a collection? She's not exactly the picture of fashion, although now that I think about it, she always does look well-put-together, but in such a drab way I never even noticed.

Bianca says, "The best thing she consigned was the Anne Maris of Paris Champagne Bucket handbag."

Now I'm speechless, or at least I *feel* speechless but I can't help blurting out, "Shut the front door! The Anne Marie Champagne Bucket Handbag? That has been on my "I-will-but-it-if-I-ever-see-it-no-matter-the-price-list for years! It's *impossible* to find. Jimmy Tate has one in his collection in a glass case and I visit it on a regular basis. It's beyond amazing and makes no sense that Bellamy's mother would own one. I have to think about that more, but right now, the most important thing I need to know is, do you still have that bag? I'll buy that baby right now!"

Bianca laughs. "Oh that is an incredible collector's piece. I actually kept it for myself. She points behind me to a glass display case I hadn't noticed and flips a switch. It's like a choir of angels start singing when her collection shows up. She has several of the Anne Marie handbags including the Sugar Bowl and the Poker Dice. Anne Marie had a shop in the Hotel Meurice in Paris back in the 30's where she sold her incredibly detailed whimsical bags. The champagne bucket is my favorite and I screamed when I saw it the first time — an actual glamorous black suede ice bucket with gold plated hardware and 'Champagne, Reims, France' written on the front in gold. The best part is the top, which is covered in Lucite ice with the top of a champagne bottle sticking out. My heart is wild with joy at such beauty. "Bianca, I need this bag for the ball. It would be perfect with my gown."

She laughs, that low elegant laugh. "Ah, Ellington, if I ever decide to give this one up, it's yours."

It's so close I can taste it, but I try not to look to disappointed. "And you'll keep your eyes open in case another crosses your path?"

"Of course."

When I exit the office, Jimmy Tate, Bellamy, and Ava are back in the *Breakfast at Tiffany's* section trying on hats and sunglasses. When they see me they all crowd around me. "Is everything okay?" Ava asks.

"I'll tell you all about it in the car. Let's roll." When we head outside I rest my back against the nearest oak tree. "I just need a minute." I take a few deep breaths and feel better with the solid old trunk supporting me. My tribe is checking their phones and waiting for me to center myself. Finally I say, "Okay, I'm ready. " We walk to the car and the fresh air clears my head swimming with beautiful handbags, gowns... It's time to head to Madame Banjeau's and find out what's going on with this handbag.

Chapter 16

Blood Orange Sidecar

Brandy, Blood Orange Juice, Triple Sec

When we arrive at Bellamy's, Hyacinth opens the door and Madame Banjeau is right behind him. "Bellamy, where have you been? You didn't tell anyone you were leaving. You haven't been answering any of my phone calls or texts. You had me worried sick. You can't disappear like this when our family is going through such a tragedy."

"I'm sorry, Mama. I just needed to get out for a little bit. But here I am now."

Madame Banjeau sighs heavily and places her hand over her heart, her rings sparkling over the pale pink Chanel blouse she is wearing. "I've got to sit down. The stress..." Bellamy rolls her eyes at us behind her mother's back as she leads her to the living room.

"Should I get her some water?" I ask.

"Hyacinth will bring it," Bellamy answers and like a genie popping out of a bottle, Hyacinth arrives with a cold glass of water.

Ava says, "I'll get her a cold towel for her forehead." She goes into the guest bathroom and returns holding a wet linen towel.

Bellamy places it on her mother's forehead, and when her mother feels the cold, she lifts it off her forehead and protests. "Not a guest towel, Bellamy. These are my good towels." She is talking to Bellamy but she knows damn well its Ava who brought her that towel.

"We don't want to intrude," I say, "We just wanted to drop Bellamy off safely," but I'm looking at the living room with new eyes after hearing about Freemasons and shrunken heads and gorgeous handbags. There's more to this woman than I could have ever guessed. Everything in here takes on new meaning. The white couch, the pristine décor, it all screams cold, rational, and completely controlled. But there are hints at what lies underneath. The silver compass lying on a large leather atlas in front of a large free-standing brown globe; the large oil painting of Madame Banjeau as a young woman in an evening gown. For the first time I notice in the painting her hand is resting on a book called *Morals and Dogma*.

Madame Beanjeau opens her eyes and sees me looking at the painting. "That was commissioned by my parents at my debut."

Jimmy Tate softly says, "Bellamy, do you mind if I use the little boys room?"

She's distracted. "Of course not. Help yourself."

I sit down. "Can you tell us about your debutante ball? Was it magical? I'm so excited to go to my first ball I could just pop."

Bellamy excuses herself and leaves the room as her mother starts talking. "It *was* magical. Of course at the time I didn't appreciate it the way I do now, but it was a night to remember. My escort was a military man, James Long, a direct descendant of Huey P. Long. It was very romantic." She gazes up at the photo. "It took more than a year to make that dress. It was couture of course, handmade by a designer in the Quarter. She dyed it herself to get the right color of gold to match my hair. It had more than a thousand handsewn beads on the skirt alone." She smiles to herself. "I must have had twenty-five fittings for that dress."

Ava says, "Do you still have the dress?"

Madame Banjeau's eyes light up. "I sure do. Would you like to see it? I could use a little uplifting break from all this tragedy."

We hear a loud clatter upstairs and Madame Banjeau's head snaps backward at the sound. She rushes up the stairs followed by me and Ava.

In the hallway Bellamy and Jimmy Tate are on their hands and knees on the floor, breathless, their faces red. They spot us and freeze in an unusual position, almost a starting wrestling position. I'm dying to know what is going on but I know they won't say until we are alone. Bellamy immediately drops to her belly and says, "Jimmy Tate was just teaching me a new pilates move." She moves her arms like she's swimming underwater, her feet glued together like a mermaid.

Madame Banjeau isn't buying it. Her face looks pinched when she says, "On the floor in the hallway?"

Bellamy pushes on the thick oriental hallway rug. "This was the perfect spot, cushy but not too soft."

They get up and brush themselves off while I jump in and try to change the subject. "Your mama is showing us her Rex gown from fifty years ago."

She looks at them sharply. "*Forty* years ago." She says, massaging her forehead at the thought. We walk into her large dressing room, which is its own room surrounded by mirrors. "Please have a seat," she says, showing us a soft floral bench on the side while she goes to the back of the room and pulls out a hanging bag. She hangs it on a hook, unzips the bag, and gently removes it. The gown is a shimmering gold.

"It's stunning," I say in a quiet tone.

She nods and her face has softened as she gazes lovingly on the dress. "Yes it is, isn't it?"

"It's a work of art," Ava says.

Jimmy Tate says, "Is that made by Mademoiselle Rose in the Quarter? The couturier?"

She nods. "Yes, hand dyed, hand sewn and beaded. It took her a year to make it."

"Madame Banjeau, you must have made the most beautiful queen ever. I bet it even still fits you."

She smiles at him and I can see a glimpse of the lovely girl she must have been once before bitterness and anger took over. I use my speed reading scan skills to scan her dressing room. I see clothes are organized by color. There are shelves of handbags and shoes, most in boxes to keep the dust away, but nothing unusual. Hmmm. If I saw this closet, I would never guess this woman owns several Hermes bags and definitely not an Anne Marie. Either it's a collection she had from her younger days, or she got the bags somewhere else.

I'm dying to see the shrunken head, but I don't know how to maneuver my way into the bedroom without outright asking, so with extreme tact, I blurt it out. "Bellamy said you have a shrunken head. Can we see it?"

Madame Banjeau slowly turns her regal head to Bellamy, who shrugs her shoulders and winces saying, "Sorry. It came up."

Madame Banjeau sighs and appears to be thinking. "I don't like to talk about that part of my life, and I would appreciate your discretion," she's looking straight at me and Jimmy Tate. We are both famous for our inability to keep secrets. "Follow me, please." We follow her into the recesses of her bedroom which looks like a movie set straight out of the House of Tudor. One thing I love about New Orleans décor is they are not minimalists. There is nothing austere, spare, or simple about this room. It is rich, over-the-top, royal furniture—a canopied bed, ornate golden chairs with red and gold cushions, and fur blankets lying stacked on a large antique Louis Vuitton steamer trunk. Against one wall is a large glass case on a pedestal, and inside, the shrunken head. I don't really want to see it, but I can't take my eyes off it. I've never seen a real one. The head is the size of my fist with dark leathery skin and long black straight hair. It's freakish and horrifying to see its eyes and mouth sewn shut, and I shudder and back away. "Okay, I've seen it."

But Jimmy Tate and Ava are fascinated, looking at it from all angles.

"It looks like a wrinkly baseball with a scary face drawn on it," Ava says.

"It looks like my Aunt Edna after a night out drinking," Jimmy Tate says.

I see an orange tabby cat curled up sleeping on a cushion by the window. Ahhh, normalcy. I coo and walk over to pet the kitty to try to forget what I've just seen, but when I reach over to touch it, it is stiff and obviously not alive. I scream and leap back, which makes Jimmy Tate and Ava scream. Madame Banjeau claps her hands, completely delighted, almost laughing, which I've never seen her do. "I have always dreamed of someone having that reaction to Fifi, but you're the first."

"These things don't scare you in your bedroom? I would have nightmares if I had a shrunken head and a stuffed dead cat in my room."

"Quite the contrary, dear, they remind me of the brutal truth. Every day we are one step closer to our death. And no one, *no one*, escapes. Nothing can be truly elegant if it is decaying before our eyes."

I wonder if that will be me someday, a bitter old woman reliving my memories through my ballgown. I decide that won't be me and I have got to focus for god's sake. I scan the bedroom for anything else that might stand out as a clue. I see the glass display with the Albert Pike book in it. I look at it but can't read the tiny print through the glass. That has to hold some clues, but when I ask Madame Banjeau if I can hold it, she says no, it will disintegrate under human fingers. Damn it.

When we get to the car, I ask Jimmy Tate, "What the hell was going on up there?"

He laughs. "Let's just say Bellamy caught me with my hand in a cookie jar."

"What cookie jar?"

Jimmy Tate pounds his hips. "This cookie jar." He reaches into the back of his pants and pulls out the *Morals and Dogma*.

"Holy Shit Jimmy Tate, you stole it?"

"She wasn't going to loan it to us. And they won't even notice it's missing."

"I thought Bellamy said it was on display in her mother's bedroom."

"It was in that glass case with a few other antique books. They all looked alike. I replaced it with an antique book with a similar binding that I found on the hallway bookshelves."

"You are so lucky she didn't catch you. Madame Banjeau would have never let us in her house again." I take the book from him. "Poor Albert Pike, if he had known his *Morals and Dogma* book was going to end up down the pants of a scandalous pilates teacher... Tell us what happened upstairs."

"It took me a few minutes to get the book, but I had just replaced it with one that was a close match but not the real thing. I heard Bellamy coming up the stairs and I ran into the Madame's bathroom and guess what I found? That woman is a one-woman pharmaceutical company: Xanax, Oxycontin, you name it. When Bellamy heard me in there she had an absolute fit and started knocking. I came out and asked her if her mother would mind if I took a few bottles home with me, one should always have a steady supply of valium on hand at any given moment. Then she attacked me."

"Bellamy attacked you? That's ridiculous."

"I know, but it happened. She was trying to wrestle the bottles from me. She could have asked, I would have given them to her."

"I'm sure she asked, just as I'm sure you held it above your head to tease her. No wonder she wrestled you to the ground."

He laughs as he says, "You know me too well. She got the

one in my hand, but she didn't get the one down my pants." He pulls a bottle of Percocet out of his underwear.

"*Oh my god* Jimmy Tate! You did *not* just steal from Bellamy's house."

"Not Bellamy, Darlin. Madame Banjeau. And just one tiny bottle. I'm not kidding when I say she had dozens of bottles up there."

Ava shakes her head. "Have we become common thieves?"

Jimmy Tate leans forward in his best Jimmy Durante impression says, "Listen, Shweetheart, this ain't no time for morals and dogma. Something is rotten in Denmark and it's up to us to figure it out. Bellamy will thank us when this is all over. But in the meantime, I'll be pain-free."

He pops a Percocet and I drop my head in my hands. I say, "You are incorrigible."

"I hope so."

Chapter 17

Blood and Sand

(Created in 1922 and named after Valentino's movie)

Scotch, Cherry Brandy, Sweet Vermouth, Orange Juice

Later that night, I've filled Winston in on everything, well, everything except the stealing of the book. Then I talked him into a light workout before we head to dinner at Cure. I'm at a loss for my next step, so I'm secretly hoping to run into Hunter at the gym so I can probe her for information and find Fausto again. I went by Le Bon Temps Roule but they said they hadn't seen him.

Winston is suspicious. He knows the only exercise I like is the ab crunch I get reaching for chocolate truffles while I lie in my hot bath at night. He's even more suspicious when I direct him to the gym Hunter mentioned on Freret Street, a street that is making a comeback, but at the moment is of dubious reputation. We park across the street from the gym by a dirty broken white picket fence. On the fence is a mural of a Second Line Brass Band in silhouette, beautiful dark figures playing their horns while dancing.

"Winston, look at that," I say as we park. "I love it when

artists just take over a piece of ugliness and make it beautiful."
I pull the rear view mirror toward me to refresh my lipstick.
"What is that quote by Anais Nin about art not being an
escape?

Winston is looking up the quote on his phone before I'm
even done talking. He is the James Bond of tech gadgetry.
Why use one's mind if one can use one's search engine?

But I remember it first: "'We do not escape into
philosophy, psychology, and art—we go there to restore our
shattered selves into whole ones'."

He finds the quote on his phone and shows it to me.
"You're right. That's it. How do you remember something like
that?"

I answer in a thick southern accent, "Oh Winston, you
know what my Daddy always said about me—my best quality
is my memory. My older sister has 'legs like Cyd Charisse',
my little sister has 'eyes like Ava Gardner'." Me? I have an
excellent memory."

Winston laughs and nibbles my ear, sending instant chills
across my body. "It's true, it wasn't your gorgeous face I was
attracted to when I saw you for the first time, it was your
memory." He pulls back. "What is that smell?"

I laugh. "Bubblegum lip gloss."

He makes a face as he hates the smell of anything sweet:
fruity, vanilla-y, cupcake-y, bubblegum-y...

"Oh Winston, I know you don't like bubble gum but they
were all out of the smell of the interior of an Aston Martin." I
blow him a kiss with my shiny pink lips.

The street is quiet and desolate as we cross it. Up and
down both sides of the street are broken shotgun cottages,
shuttered shops now piled in rusting car parts, and weeds
growing out of crumpled concrete. Even the chain link fences
are lying broken on the ground. The only thing alive on this
block is the glowing front lights of the gym.

We enter the gym and I am totally unprepared for the
assault on my senses.

And totally unprepared for this type of gym.

There are punching bags hanging from hooks all over the room, like the carcasses of gazelles hanging from the trees in leopard territory. The walls are dirty and in the middle of the room on a massive platform is a giant boxing ring. I had expected treadmills and rowing machines and Lulu Lemon, not this.

There are two sweating bleeding men in the ring punching each other in the face. The smell of sweat and blood repels me and I think I might vomit. I am transported immediately back to Jackson Square and the night of the murder. Torches and chanting monks; deep drums and medieval women on horseback; screaming people; dancing skeletons; light and dark; chaos and order; Dionysus and Apollo. And I always loved Dionysus more, the wine, the pleasure, the sensuality. Apollo was for bankers. But lately I've been thinking I prefer the Apollonian world-rational order, logic, clean-cut people. The Dionysian side has become too unpredictable and scary. But there's no Apollo here.

Here is the dark side of Dionysus.

I feel something deep in my bones shift, a primal awakening I haven't felt in a long time.

Winston takes my hand. "You ok?"

His touch immediately anchors me and I nod as I watch the two men in the ring dance around each other between punches. They are as light on their feet as Fred Estaire, but these guys aren't Fred. Their muscles are bulging making ridges in their skin, accentuated by their glistening sweat.

Plus, Fred never ignited my deepest most secret innermost self like this.

Oh my goddess, I need to get hold of myself, take a deep breath and become grace and power. I lift my chin, move my feet apart, and put my hands on my hips.

"What are you doing?" Winston whispers to me.

"Raising my power," I whisper back.

Winston squeezes my shoulders. "What are we doing

here? Let's go." Winston is a pacifist and this is probably worse for him than me. I would love to be a pacifist but there are just too many people who could really use a punch in the nose.

Just then Father Archer walks up to us in a black tank and shorts. "Winston, how are you?"

I say, "I didn't recognize you out of your collar." I have to avert my eyes. He looks naked without his collar.

He laughs and says to Winston, "I didn't know you were a fighter."

"I'm not."

I interject. "You are a fascinating paradox, Father Archer—a fighting priest. I know the Jesuits are a kind of renegade intellectual priests, but this takes 'renegade priest' to a whole new level."

"The body is a temple, Miss Martini. Nothing better than a great workout."

"True, but if your body is a temple, what about the other guy? His temple needs to be squashed?"

He laughs again and says, "Sometimes." Winston asks him if he's fighting tonight.

"Not tonight. Just working out. I fight one Friday a month, usually Roughhouse Boxing, but I work out every day."

I raise my eyebrows. "Roughouse Boxing?"

"Boxing without gloves," he says, wiping the sweat from his forehead with a black towel.

I am struggling hard to synthesize the contradiction of Father Archer, but I'm going to have to file this one in my 'I'll never understand' file. I have enough contradiction going on in my own world to keep me occupied.

He leans forward to speak quietly to Winston. "Hey, remember how you were asking about the antique ceremonial dagger in my office yesterday?"

"Sure. The one used for scalping?" Winston turns to me. "Father Archer has a collection of ceremonial tribal tools in his office."

I nod as if to say, *Ahhh, how nice for you,* but in my mind I'm thinking, *What the hell?* I am as surprised by his collection as I am that Winston would ever admire a dagger. He hates weapons almost as much as I hate cockroaches. In fact, we have had many cockroach wars in our relationship as the roaches in New Orleans are the size of small ponies and I have a primal fear of them, almost like I'm a caveman and roaches are flesh-eating dinosaurs. I can't bear to hear them skittering around my house, and Winston refuses to harm them and will only 'handle' them after a great deal of dramatic screaming by me. And by 'handle', I mean he will spend about an hour or so cursing and talking to the little beast as he tries to catch it in a big pan to throw outside, so it can return momentarily after summoning its friends to seek revenge on me.

"I have something to show you," Father Archer says, and walks us over to the bar on the side of the gym.

A bar in a gym.

There is a velvet portrait of Don Quixote on the wall, and a man with a Don Quixote beard stands behind the bar. He smiles at me and I smile back.

Father Archer grabs his gym bag from behind the bar and pulls out a notebook and pen, which he pushes towards Winston. "Write me a note."

Winston writes "Hello" on it.

Father Archer says, "Now click the top like you're retracting the ink."

Winston pushes the top down and a small sharp dagger shoots out the end. It startles both of us and Father Archer is delighted. "I found that at an antique weapon shop. Isn't that clever?"

We both nod. It's definitely clever but also disturbing. And while I'm very anti-weapon, I could probably use a hidden weapon on me at all times with the way my life is going, and a hidden dagger inside a pen would be perfect. "Which shop?"

Winston shoots me a look like he knows exactly what I'm thinking.

Father Archer reaches his hand into his bag again and pulls out large coin that looks like a silver dollar. "See this coin?" He pulls the coin apart, revealing a sharp circular blade, which he uses to slice a piece of notebook paper apart. Winston is impressed, pacifism be damned in the face of a cool gadget.

"Woah," he says, looking at it closely.

"Do you actually carry these with you for protection or do you just collect?" I ask.

Father Archer flips the coin in his fingers like a blackjack dealer. "We do live in one of the most dangerous cities in the country, so you can never be too careful. But I'm a collector as well as a protector. Even the saints carried weapons. In some cases, God gave them weapons."

"Like Joan of Arc?"

"Exactly like Joan of Arc. God told her where to find her sword and led her to victory. I am also a warrior, but since I can't exactly carry a sword around my body, I have to conceal my weapons." He is carefully putting his weapons away like a jeweler puts away his most expensive necklaces.

This guy is jamming my mind with his diametrically opposed existence. But it suddenly occurs to me he might be helpful. "Have you ever heard of a colichemarde?"

He answers slowly. "Have *I* ever heard of a colichemarde?"

I hear a loud grunt and a see a spray of blood shoot right toward me from the ring. The man in the ring goes down and I jump back. The bloodied man in the ring standing over his victim looks familiar, and through the swollen face I see it's Gerry Batracho. What the hell is going on here? A boxing gym full of priests and professors?

"Come with me," Father Archer says. We follow him through the gym, past the light-footed musclemen, to the back of the gym. He pushes open a heavy red door and instead of being outside in an alley, we are in another gym, a bit smaller. Inside there are two people wearing white with big black screened masks like beekeepers. Standing on the sides watching are three men wearing brown vests and bowler hats holding canes. The two in the middle of the room raise swords to each other and start sparring.

"They teach fencing here?" I am surprised.

"Fencing, yes, but not just regular fencing. This is a Bartitsu Club."

"Bartitsu?" I ask, unable to take my eyes off the grace and elegance of the fencers.

"The 'gentlemanly art of self-defense'. It's a style of fighting from Victorian London. Men and women, practice fighting using different antique weapons, and everyday items such as canes, umbrellas, parasols, even snuff boxes." He points to a wall that could be a Louis Vuitton display wall, but instead of handbags it is full of antique weapons.

"Is that a colichemarde?" I ask, pointing to the antique cane/sword in the center, even though I'm sickened by the sight.

Father Archer is delighted. "Ahhhh, you know something about antique weaponry."

"I actually know nothing, but have learned quickly. The colichemarde was the weapon used in that murder the other night."

"Oh no, I'm so sorry."

"No, no, it's ok. I'd actually like to know more about it. Where would someone get something like this?"

"They aren't that common, although you could probably find them at a flea market or antique show. These came from a family's estate, passed down through the generations."

"Do they ever come off the walls?"

"All the time. It's what we use for fighting practice."

I have the same sinking feeling in my belly as when I saw the leg trap at the Locksmith. On the wall are swords, canes, umbrellas, even axes. Standing in front of it is a case of smaller weapons like daggers and hatchets. One item in the case is a key that looks very similar to my key.

"Father Archer, what's this? Do you use keys to fight?"

"Keys actually make pretty effective weapons when held in the hands, like brass knuckles, but that particular key is an 1850's Jailers key and 32-caliber black powder gun."

"A key *and* a gun?"

"Yes Ma'am. Prison guards would use the key to unlock jail cells, and if a situation called for a weapon, the guard was prepared without even touching his holster."

I look at it carefully. "Is there a trigger? It looks just like a regular key."

"No trigger. The guard could touch his cigar to the black powder hole on top of the key and it would discharge perfectly. It fires in a surprisingly straight line."

"Incredible." I whisper, wondering if my key has a hole with black powder in it.

One of the fencers loses the sparring match and when I glance up, the winner is looking right at me. I can see the eyes behind the mask, but I can't tell where he is looking. The winner pulls off the mask and shakes her hair out.

It's Hunter.

She smiles and I feel my insides melt like the inner core of a hot molten chocolate lava cake.

Oh Goddess.

"Well if it isn't the infamous Ms. Martini," she says, walking over to me. "It seems everywhere I go I hear your name."

"All scandalous I hope."

"Of course," she says.

She's looking at me like I'm dessert and I'm hoping Winston doesn't notice.

I introduce her to Winston and Father Archer.

She nods at both of them and then glances at me and the key in the case. "You seem to have a thing for keys."

I laugh a little too melodically for this environment. "They seem to be following me around these days. Have you seen this one? It's really cool. It's a key *and* a gun."

"Oh I've seen it all right. I'm the one who brought it in." She says while picking up a bottle of water from the floor and taking a big swig, wiping her mouth with the back of her hand.

"Oh that makes perfect sense. You must get a lot of interesting keys crossing your path."

"You, too." There's an awkward pause as I notice how different she looks covered in head-to-toe white, like an angel, or an astronaut. I can't see her body tattoos, even the neck one is hidden by her fencing suit. "So," she says, "what are you doing here?"

"I came here to work out of course." I say, jogging in place to show her my skills. I can feel Winston's eyes on me and I know exactly what he's thinking. He's putting two and two together, figuring out that I came here to find Hunter.

But as Dashiell Hammett said so eloquently, sometimes two and two is four, and sometimes it's twenty-two.

"Do you spar?" she asks, tossing her head to the fencing equipment lying in wait against the wall.

"Yes I do."

"Great, let's get you into some gear and we'll have a match." She swaggers over to the equipment and starts finding me stuff.

"Ellington," Winston says, folding his arms, "What are you doing? You have never fenced in your life."

"Actually, Winston, I have. I learned to fence in my Shakespearean class in high school. As you know, I was Peasblossom in *Midsummer Night's Dream*."

"I know, I know, and you came out of the ceiling upside down on a rope. But the fairies never fenced, and I'm pretty sure you never played Hamlet."

"There are many things you don't know about me Winston Martini. Plan to be surprised the rest of your days." I saunter to Hunter, who is bringing me an epee to try. I hold it in my hand and practice a couple of blocks. "This is light."

Hunter picks up a chest guard and a beekeeper mask from the corner of the room and brings them to me. I hold my arms out for her to fasten on the chest guard while she holds it out to me to put on myself. Embarrassing! "Oh sorry, I can put it on."

"No, I got it," she says and loops the straps onto my shoulders. She leans in close to me to wrap the straps around my back.

Oh dear.

"Is it too tight?" she says softly.

"No, feels good," I whisper, although I'm not sure why I'm whispering.

She walks around to my back to secure it. I glance at Winston and he is watching me, but seems not to notice the crackling energy between us, although he is pretty good at masking his emotions so who knows what he's noticing. I put the helmet/mask thing over my head with relief. Hiding my face seems like a really good idea right now. Hunter and I assume the basic fencing position, knees bent, rapiers raised tip-to-tip. And before I know it she has me backed against a wall at sword point.

What just happened? My skills are rusty, and hers are fresh, so maybe this wasn't a good idea. I lift my mask. "Can we maybe go slowly over hits and blocks one time before we start, just to refresh my memory?"

She nods and we start again, going slowly over the moves. Muscle memory is coming back to me, and as we go over the movements over and over until my arm feels like it might fall off. Titania's monologue starts running through my mind and as our swords pick up speed. I say the words quietly to myself. *Out of this wood do not desire to go. Thou wilt remain here whether thou wilt or no.*

Hunter is moving me backward again toward the wall when I hear her say, "I am a spirit of no common rate." She pins me, and I whip off my helmet. Did she really say that? Or am I hearing things? My blood is pumping me with vitality and I toss my hair in a dramatic head flip just like Kelly in Charlie's Angels. I like this feeling, this flirtatious dance, although it feels dangerous, but dangerous in a good way. Maybe that's what I am, in fact that's what I definitely am at the moment... a Girl Marked Danger.

"Drink?" I say in a cavalier way, shaking out my sore arm.

Hunter pulls off her own helmet, panting. "I have one, thanks." And she picks up her water bottle sitting on the floor. We both chug water and I'm pretty impressed with my athletic skills. Except now that my adrenaline is waning, I slide down to sit on the floor against the wall, my chest panting with the unusual sensation of exercise.

Winston walks over to me. "You ok?" I look into his face he's like a warm chocolate cookie for my soul — something about Hunter gives me vertigo — everything about Winston centers me.

"I feel great. I haven't fenced in a long time. I'm rusty. If I'm going to hone my detective skills I should brush up on my fighting."

I thought we were far enough away from Hunter that she couldn't hear me, but she did. "Detective?" she says, her face showing no emotion.

"Well, not officially. I'm pretty good at noticing things other people don't."

"Sherlock?"

"Exactly."

She looks at Winston. "And are you her Watson?" Her eyes travel from his face down to his crotch and back up, slowly, seductively. Now what's she up to? Seducing both of us? What a minx. As usual Winston is oblivious. I swear Elizabeth Taylor could bat her eyelashes at him and he wouldn't notice, although maybe he's just pretending with that nonchalant face he likes to play.

Winston laughs, relaxing me out of my twisting thoughts. "Most definitely. I am her Watson. And Watson is ready for a cocktail. Sherlock?"

"Almost, although we haven't worked out yet," I say, bending over to touch my toes. There's no way in tarnation I'm leaving until I've worked Hunter over for clues.

"That fencing counted," Winston says.

"You didn't fence."

"I know, but watching you was exhausting. Plus, I'm too thirsty to work out."

Father Archer has picked up an epee. He is going through a series of thrusts and blocks with it as he makes his way over to our group. He's pretty handy with a sword.

Two men in vests, white shirts and bowler hats saunter out to the middle of the mats. One is tall, handsome, and lean with sweeping sideburns and big dark eyes, the other is softer and rounder. They are pretending to walk by each other when one grabs the other and they start fighting with an umbrella and a cane. I am captivated. "That's impressive they can fight like that without knocking off their hats. I'd love to learn how to fight without messing up my hat."

Father Archer laughs and asks, "You should join us. We meet nearly every Friday night."

All of our attention is drawn to the center mats when the handsome sideburn-bowler-hat-man knocks the other to the ground and holds an umbrella to his throat. It must be the end signal because the fight finishes and the round gentleman fighter walks to the water fountain while a third short muscular man, also wearing a white shirt and vest walks briskly towards the winner. They start a series of moves, and the new gentleman pulls out an antique snuffbox as his weapon. They are throwing punches and dodging them in what looks like a staged barroom brawl.

I'm dying to jump in the middle. "I'd like to learn some of those moves with my purse after what I've been through."

"Hunter can teach you a few moves," Father Archer motions to Hunter who nods at me.

My heart does a little twirl. "Okay."

The handsome umbrella fighter has conquered the snuff man and as they move off the mats to make room for Hunter and me, he flashes a smile at me and I see his incisors are bigger and sharper than normal, like a vampire's. Shit. Did I really just see that? I watch him walk over to get a drink, his sideburns chugging as he drinks. He looks perfectly normal when he doesn't smile. I look at Hunter who laughs at the expression on my face. "Is he a vampire?" I ask.

"Don't worry about Terrence. He had vampire teeth implanted by his dentist."

"Why would he do that?"

She shrugs. "He likes vampires. A lot. That's why he moved to New Orleans in the first place. Vampire aspirants love it here."

Hunter shows me the moves and blocks of Bartitsu. It's a blend of martial arts, kickboxing and wrestling and it's completely awesome. I feel so powerful. Next time a monk falls on me or someone tries to snatch my purse, he's going to get a conk on the head. She moves to stand very close behind me, adjusting my arms, sliding her hand up my back to make it more erect. I can feel her body heat from feet to the top of my head. She says softly but I can hear her clearly since her lips are so close to my ear, "Bend your knees."

I bend my knees and she puts her hands on my hips, pushing them down and tilting them with a masterful hand until they're just right. "You've got nice hips."

I wiggle my lower half and say, "Why, thank you," like a fool. And I swear if she was a vampire I would let her bite me right now, she's that hot.

When I look over her shoulder, I see Winston watching me, and as much fun as I'm having, all I really want to do is sink into Winston's arms. I'm not that good at probing information out of people, at least not tonight. I move over to Winston, mastering my fight moves on the way. He laughs when I push my backside into him like I'm going to flip him over my shoulder. "Ready?" he asks, kissing the top of my

head.
"Ready."

Chapter 18

Tickle Your Brain

Cachaca Rum, Strawberry Puree, Lime Juice,
Champagne Float

Originally a fire station built in 1910, Cure has character in its
very bones. It's spacious with high ceilings and opens onto a
courtyard where they originally kept the fire horses. It's dark
and glamorous with shelves of gorgeous liquor, a fabulous
menu of tiny food and lots of candlelight. Winston orders a
dry martini and I order the Huckleberry with lavender and
thyme. I'm feeling earthy after facing all that violence.

Father Archer walks into the bar wearing his collar. He
immediately spots us and walks over. There goes our private
table, but I smile politely.

"We seem to be running into each other all over the
place," he says. "I swear I'm not following you. I'm actually
meeting some colleagues here. So do you think you're going
to take up Bartitsu?"

"Maybe. Then I can clobber the next kook who tries to
mess with me. I'm actually glad you're here. I have a question
for you. The other night at The Columns you were telling us
about the conspiracy theories?"

"Yes. I'm not saying I believe any of them, I'm just saying the stories are out there."

"Did you ever hear of any stories related to the Mardi Gras krewes or the Freemasons in connection to the House of Rothschild?"

"Oh sure. For example, after Lincoln was killed, Andrew Johnson, a notable Freemason, succeeded him and promptly reinstated confederate-friendly governments all over the South, effectively cutting off Reconstruction at the knees. Lincoln had wanted only Union sympathizers in local governments in the South to guide reconstruction, but the South was able to continue their racism. They created the Black Codes to make sure slaves had no rights and no way to move through society freely, and of course, the creation of the KKK."

I lean forward and whisper, "Is the KKK connected to Rex? Their outfits look so similar — just Rex puts sequins on theirs. Whenever I go to the Rex parade, their costumes freak me out. I was driving down Claiborne one Mardi Gras morning and there they were with their pointed hoods and capes, galloping down the street on huge horses."

He shakes his head. "They're spooky aren't they? I don't know the history of their costumes but I know a lot of Rex men and they are definitely not KKK. In fact, they are just the opposite — working to make the community better for every-one." Just then three professors enter the bar, including Gerry Batracho. Oh god, I can't talk to him. I excuse myself and head to the powder room to escape any interaction.

When I'm on my way back, Hunter walks in.

She seems out of place, like a jaguar walking around the lobby of the Ritz Carlton, way too wild and sultry for a place like this. In fact, she looks like she could tear the place apart with her teeth if she so desired.

I am so excited to see her. "Hunter, what are you doing here?"

"Having a drink."

"Come sit with us."

She doesn't want to intrude, but I convince her to sit down for one drink. She orders a double whiskey on the rocks.

"Hunter, I know you study the classics. Have either of you ever heard of *The Morals and Dogma of the Ancient Order of the Scottish Rite*?"

"Morals and dogma, two things I despise more than anything else," she says.

"So you haven't heard of it?"

She shakes her head. "No. But I've heard of the Scottish Rite Freemasons."

"Oh well, this is their main book, like their Bible. Only it's difficult to read and some parts were written to be interpreted only by the highest Freemasons."

"Ancient Rome did the same along with many other cultures." Hunter says. "Vestal virgins and carefully chosen priests were the only ones allowed the sacred knowledge that was deemed too powerful for regular people."

I reach into my bag and pull out a piece of velvet tied with a burgundy tassel rope. I delight in the theatricality of slowly opening it without explaining anything. It's like unveiling a pirate's treasure. My audience is riveted. When I pull out the antique book, I whisper, "First edition with the author's notes in the margins."

Both of them lean over me to get a better look. "You can only look at it in dim light," I say, "so it doesn't fall apart or fade."

Winston uses gentle hands to open it up. Inside the opening cover, he reads the words written in light pencil, "Fictions are necessary for the people, and the Truth becomes deadly to those who are not strong enough to contemplate it in all its brilliance. In fact, what can there be in common between the vile multitude and sublime wisdom? The Truth must be kept secret, and the masses need a teaching proportioned to their imperfect reason."

"Weird. It's saying exactly what Hunter just said." I ask Hunter, "What *is* the Scottish Rite of Freemasonry? I mean I know there are many high-profile Freemasons, including many of our own Presidents, but I don't know about this group."

Hunter says, "I'm sure you know masons were medieval stone cutters and builders, and there were different levels of skills, just like the Masonic lodges. They were in such high demand that they had unusual freedom to travel from place-to-place. They had all sorts of secret knowledge regarding building so that extended into keeping other secrets and combining with other secret groups like the Knights Templar and the Illuminati. As far as I know, the Scottish Rite is a branch that practiced rituals based in Scottish culture. What those might be, I'm not sure."

Winston offers, "Eating haggis while doing a highland jig in a kilt and listening to bagpipes?"

I gasp. "Winston, there were bagpipes in the Joan of Arc parade. Maybe the Scottish Rite were there. Maybe they killed Duncan."

Hunter says quietly, "Oh the puzzle…"

"Whitman?" I ask, incredulous.

She leans back and spreads her arms across the back of the booth. "'To court destruction with taunts—with invitations…' An overarching theme of my life."

Winston stands up. "And on that note, 'I rise thither with my inebriated soul.'" He heads to the men's room and I look at Hunter who is smiling.

"Clever."

"*One Hour to Madness and Joy* is one of my all-time favorite poems."

Hunter lifts her glass. "To 'savage and tender achings.'"

"To drinking the 'mystic deliria deeper than any other'."

She looks at me as she swallows her drink in one swig and slams her glass down on the table like we're playing a drinking game. "I've never met another person who had that poem committed to memory. Very interesting, Ellington Martini."

Winston has returned, and I'm not sure what he has heard but I can feel my face grow hot as he enters this electric space at our table, at least *I'm* vibrating. He stands for a minute before sitting back down, and looks at me and Hunter, then looks at our empty glasses. "Poetry?

I giggle. "I make Winston read me passages from *Leaves of Grass* or *Ulysses* as foreplay."

"Or dessert menus," he says.

I giggle again. "Nothing lights my fire like dessert.

"And on that note, I must be going," Hunter says suddenly standing up and leaving.

I lean over to Winston, my lips touching his ear. "I mind how once we laid on such a transparent summer morning, how you settled your head athwart my hips, and plunged your tongue to my bare-stript heart…"

And we can't pay the check fast enough.

Chapter 19

Fuzzy Navel

Peach Schnapps, Orange Juice

The next morning I show up at Jimmy Tate's Pilates Studio ready for a workout. I need to get strong! I absolutely despise workout wear like yoga pants, which reveal far more about people's nether regions than I ever want to know. So, what do I wear so my instructor can see my body alignment but the world can't see my hoo-ha? I opt for a tennis skirt over leggings and a fitted halter tank top. If I had long legs it might be cute but I can't get over the feeling I look like one of those dancing hippos in the tutus in *Fantasia*.

When I walk into the pilates studio, Jimmy Tate is in a precarious position. He is standing about four feet off the ground on the Cadillac, the big Pilates equipment that looks a lot like monkey bars on top of a massage table. With closer observation, I see he is actually standing on a woman wearing a navy blue leotard with matching tights ala Bob Fosse from 1979. She is on her back with her legs curled up, her knees near her ears, and he is standing on the back of her thighs. When they hear me walk in the door, she is unable to turn her head, and probably can't hear anyway with her knees covering her ears like that, but Jimmy Tate sees me and waves cheerily, hooting with glee. "Now you know our secret!" He and the person under him laugh loudly as he gently steps off her. "Norma, we got caught."

Norma looks at me, giggling like a child even though she's not a day under seventy. "Oh boy, you caught us... It's not what you think." She laughs uproariously at her own joke as she slowly sits up. She nudges Jimmy Tate with her elbow. "Imagine if we'd been flagrante delicto," she says, gleefully pronouncing the words with sharp consonants.

He snorts with laughter. "Now that would have been a sight." They have their arms around each other and he fans his face with his free hand. "Norma Chance, meet Ellington Martini. Ellington is a fabulous romance novelist."

Norma reaches out one soft pale hand. "Is that right? I love a good romance novel." She leans in close to me. "Lots of sex?"

"There are a few sex scenes, sure." It's a bit jarring coming from someone of her age who actually looks quite elegant in her leotard. Is that even possible? Leotard elegance?

"Good girl! Sex scenes are my favorite part of any book." She pinches my butt and I jump, which she and Jimmy Tate find hilarious. She says, "I have to pinch your ass for good luck," and then to make matters worse, she kisses her fingers and shakes them at me, shouting "For luck!"

"Do mine too," Jimmy Tate says, turning around so she can pinch his behind as well. What is happening here? She pinches Jimmy Tate and kisses her fingers again shouting "For luck!" Jimmy Tate is doubled over laughing. He turns up his work-out music, which is some sort of 1920's Charleston music. He and Norma put their arms around each other again and do little kicks. He turns to me. "Norma was a Rockette!" he shouts over the music. "Aren't her legs fabulous?"

Ahhh, that explains the leotard. "Yes!" I shout back. "I wish I had legs like yours."

They put their arms around me so I have to join their

kickline. Norma breaks off, dancing around Jimmy Tate's gym by herself, her kicks getting higher and higher till I'm afraid she's going to fall over. Jimmy Tate must be thinking the same thing because he runs over and turns the music off. She laughs again. "You're a doll, both of you. And I have to go meet my sons for lunch at Antoine's. I had to do extra leg lifts today so I can have the shrimp remoulade."

I'm out of breath, leaning forward with my hands on my hips. I can't believe this elderly woman is in better shape than me. "How many sons do you have?"

"Two." She puts her hand by her mouth like she's telling me a secret. "They're total squares. Bankers if you can believe it. Who grows up and wants to be a banker? They don't even smoke weed." She is pulling on a short floral skirt, which is actually quite flattering with her leotard, a black leather motorcycle jacket and a black fishing hat covered in purple roses. "You never know with children. They're tricky. I raised them to follow the beat of their own drummers and honestly, what drummer leads someone to banking?"

"The drummer that likes money?"

"Ha! What kind of goal is making money? It's all luck. Pinches of luck. Take it where you can get it is my motto." She pinches her own behind, kisses her fingers, and shouts, "For luck!" as she walks out the door. She pops her head back in. "Nice to meet you," And disappears again.

I turn to Jimmy Tate. "Seems like she might be a good match for Grandpa Boogie."

"If nothing else they could dance the night away." Jimmy Tate hands me a cool towel scented with peppermint oil. "Bury your face in this. I always feel so much better afterwards."

I rub my face and inhale, followed by a sigh. "Mmmm, that smells good."

"Peppermint oil is the ticket."

Just as I'm inhaling the door opens again and Bellamy walks in. "Well, color me happy with red stripes — it smells like a candy cane forest in here."

Jimmy Tate and I laugh, but I'm instantly wary. Her tone of voice is off and she doesn't sound happy. Plus, I thought Jimmy Tate and I had a private. I look at him and he shrugs his shoulders in the universal symbol for 'don't ask me.'

I walk over to give Bellamy a hug, but she quickly sits down on a mat to stretch before I can touch her. She is in exercise clothes but is still wearing her big baby blue Chanel sunglasses. I ask her, "Are you taking class with me today?"

"Has something happened?" Jimmy Tate is treading lightly.

"*Has something happened?* You mean besides my cousin dropping over dead on my best friend? Besides my family's house exploding into the darkest swampland? Everywhere I turn is a snapping alligator with my uncles and aunts and cousins. I try to go to my *own* home for some peace and quiet but my mother is making me feel so guilty I cannot stay away from *her* house."

I have never heard Bellamy so curt. She is sitting in the straddles, touching her toes, still wearing her sunglasses. Her face looks swollen from drinking or crying, or maybe both. She obviously doesn't want a hug, so I sit on the Reformer next to her and start doing mermaid stretches while I talk to her.

"Is there anything I can do to help?" I ask gently.

"No you've done quite enough, thank you."

"What do you mean?"

"You *know* what I mean. Why were you in the Quarter that night anyway? Why were you running around that stupid parade in the first place? Did you see Duncan before he was killed in cold blood and died on your fucking toes? Did you talk to him? Out of all the people in New Orleans he just happened to stumble onto *you*? I find that incredibly suspicious."

"*Suspicious?* In what way? Bellamy, what are you talking about?"

"I can't take it!" she shouts. "I'm leaving this city. I'm moving far far away where no one knows me or my fucked-up family." Tears start falling so fast she can't hide them with her sunglasses or wipe them fast enough.

"Bellamy, what happened?" I say, making a move to put my arms around her.

"Don't you *dare* hug me I will collapse completely," she says in a deep raspy voice straight out of The Exorcist. I'm afraid her head might start spinning around any second, but she rolls backward in a ball and shoots her legs up into a shoulder stand. I keep stretching like a mermaid since I don't know what else to do. I glance at the unusually silent Jimmy Tate in the mirror and see him hiding by the peppermint towels, listening to us. Finally, she sniffs and says, "Last night, Uncle Beau came over late to talk to my mother. I was upstairs taking a bath. They stepped outside to speak on the sleeping porch, and they were trying to speak quietly, but they don't know there is a copper drainpipe out there that amplifies voices straight into the bathroom. I could hear every unthinkable word. Enough to make me sick."

She stops talking, and I'm frozen in a sideways stretch, not wanting to interrupt her flow, but if I don't sit up soon I'll be stuck this way. Finally, she starts again. "Ellington, the things they said. I don't even know if I believe them. Terrible things about my family. You know my family. They might be stiff but they are good people, honorable people, and we have been in New Orleans for generations."

"Of course."

"They said Duncan excelled at Yale and worked his way up to the top of Skull and Bones. They said he was nearly there with the New Orleans group."

"I didn't know New Orleans had a Skull and Bones?"

"Me neither because it has a different name here, Knights of the Sun or the Golden Circles, or something like that. They said Duncan's medical school was part of the secret club and he was about to be inducted into the highest level of the secret club called the Thirty-Third Degree."

"The thirty-third degree as in the freemasons?" I ask. "What does Med School have to do with the Freemasons?" Oh shit, that rings a bell. Didn't Fausto say the secret societies always had medical doctors on call to complete the assassinations?

"I don't know anything about freemasons. I just heard them say thirty-third degree and that excelling at Tulane Medical School was necessary. They never told *me* anything about any clubs. They never even mentioned Yale to me. I went to Tulane for fucking med school but nobody said a word about inducting me into any Golden Circles or Skull and Bones or Craniums and Hoo-Has… whatever you want to call it. And I am sure it's because I'm a woman. Fucking misogynists." Now that she's mad she's stopped crying. "And then they started in on great-great granddaddy."

"Albert?"

"The one and the same. All these years, all these stories about my illustrious family. 'Oh Bellamy, your great grandfather was such a brave and honorable lawyer, a poet, a philosopher, a war hero. He negotiated peace treaties with the Native Americans. He was a lauded poet and scholar. He wrote books. They have his portrait at City Hall for Christ's sake and a giant statue of him at the foot of Capitol Fucking Hill in Washington D.C. I'm sure if there was ever a knight prancing around a golden circle, it would be him."

She stops talking again and moves into cat-cow stretches on her hands and knees accompanied by deep breathing so loud I'm pretty sure it can be heard outside. I try to make eye contact with Jimmy Tate to silently ask him what to do. He gets my message and shrugs, but he finally walks over and hands us both peppermint towels to wipe our faces. Bellamy rolls over on her back. "Jimmy Tate, do you think smelling like a damn candy cane forest solves anything?"

"No, but it certainly doesn't make things worse. Plus, peppermint oil is refreshing. It clears the mind and makes you tingle."

I hold it to my nose. It really *is* refreshing. Apparently it has refreshed Bellamy too because she moves to her knees like a ten-year-old at a slumber party and starts talking fast. "So, ever since I was a little girl, I was told how my family is one of the most prominent philanthropic old families in the South. She lowers her voice to a whisper. "But last night, Uncle Beau and my mother said my great-great grandfather was indicted for *treason* back in the 1800's."

"What?" Jimmy Tate and I both sit down on her mat close to her.

"I know. *Treason!* Can you believe it? The great Pike family with a dark stain like that. It's like the Kennedy's with their murderous frat boy. And Ol' Granddaddy Albert wasn't indicted by some president nobody ever heard of either. He was indicted under orders from Abraham Lincoln himself."

"What?" We both say again. Apparently it's the only word we can gasp right now.

"I know. I can't believe it either. I love Lincoln. The greatest President our country has ever seen. And he indicted my very own grandfather for treason. Could a story get any worse? That's like being kicked out of the catholic church by Mother Teresa herself."

Jimmy Tate scoots in closer. "But, what treason did he commit? Was he a spy?"

"I don't exactly know, but they don't indict people for no reason. I have always been told Albert Pike was an exemplary figure. I mean, why would they put a giant statue up in our country's capitol of a traitor?"

She's so upset I want to pat her back to make her feel better, but she doesn't seem like she'd be receptive to any comfort at the moment so I say, "This all sounds terrible, but why were they talking about your family's dirty laundry last night? I mean, every family has skeletons in their closet. What does this have to do with your cousin Duncan?"

"That's the worst part of all of it. They said they thought

Duncan had committed a heinous crime." She grabs at her stomach like she's going to vomit. "Oh my god my family is unraveling. We could never survive something like this. We will be the most hated and reviled family in the South if he did this."

"Did what?" Jimmy Tate and I both say at the same time.

"They said, they said..." she looks at me with her big blue eyes and I've never seen her so miserable. She breathes out slowly and collects herself. "They said he murdered his girlfriend in cold blood, poisoned her, and then committed suicide. They just found her body last night."

I gasp. "His girlfriend was murdered the same night he died? His girlfriend, as in the mayor's daughter?"

She is shaking. "That's the one." She breaks out in fresh sobs. "That poor, poor girl."

My arms have broken out in goose bumps at the thought of Duncan being a murderer. What if he had been on a murder spree before he caught up with me? He could have easily stabbed me in that crowd. But none of this makes sense. "Bellamy, this is not even possible. There's no way Duncan could have killed himself with a long antique sword. His arms aren't long enough."

"I know it's crazy, but they said he went berserk. He apparently had enough poison in his bloodstream to kill an elephant. They found his girlfriend poisoned to death back in his apartment. They said he was under enormous stress and he must have snapped. But what in the world kind of stress causes that?"

"Bellamy, none of this is making sense. Duncan was fatally stabbed. The *police told* me he was stabbed. I saw the blood myself. Why would he poison himself then stab himself? And if he killed himself, why would he fall on me in such a state of panic and whisper a message in my ear?"

"I don't know, but that's where things get even worse."

"Worse? How?"

She looks at me tearfully. "They think you're making this

stuff up, Ellington. They said you made up the message he whispered."

Now I feel frozen. "Why would I do that?"

"They said either you made it up, or you really think you heard it, even though it's not true."

I feel my blood starting to boil. "This is absurd! I saw the blood on his body myself. He was absolutely killed by stabbing. I would *never* make something like this up. Have they talked to the police? They'll tell them." I breathe out to calm myself. I look into her miserable face. "Bellamy, you don't believe them do you?"

"Of course not, but I don't know what to believe right now. I know you would never make something like this up. But it is true that the brain can rewire under stress. The neural pathways connect in unusual ways, making us see, hear, or experience things in different ways. Do you think it's possible you heard something that wasn't said? In the heat and drama of the moment?"

"Bellamy, I know exactly what I heard from that poor man. It was clear as a bell. And I know what I saw. How do you explain the photo? And the key in my handbag? You were with me when I found it."

"Ellington, it's a vintage handbag with a secret pocket. That key could have come from any previous owner."

"OK, you're right, that key could have come from a previous owner, but it's awfully coincidental that my bag keeps being targeted for some random reason. I went and talked to the police the morning after Duncan's death. They showed me the type of weapon used in the murder. It was long. There's no way someone could stab themselves with it. Why would they? When there are a million other ways to do it that don't involve having gorilla arms?"

"I don't know! My Uncle said they found books in Duncan's apartment on harey-scary or whatever that ancient Japanese ritual of suicide is called. They said he just snapped."

"But Bellamy, this is all completely absurd. It makes no

sense."

"Ellington, why would they make it up? It puts my family in a terrible light. What could possibly be worse than having a murderer in the family? It will ruin our family tree forever. If they were going to make something up, wouldn't they create a story that put us in a good light?"

She sees the clock. "Oh shit," she sniffs. "I used up all my exercise time talking. I have to go get ready for the funeral."

I swallow my anger and confusion and try to be supportive. "Bellamy, we will figure this out. Just please don't let them turn you against me. My brain is just fine. No rewiring. Ava, Jimmy Tate, Winston and I will all be at the funeral tonight. We'll see you there."

Bellamy presses her lips together. "Can you all keep a low profile... a very low profile. I snuck out before breakfast this morning so I could avoid my mother, but I know she was going to ask me to tell you all to stay away from the funeral. But I really need you there. You're my true family."

I'm furious that Bellamy's family is blaming me and trying to drive a wedge between us at a time when we both really need each other. I swallow my anger. "We'll be there for you, Bell. And we'll definitely keep a low profile."

Jimmy Tate hugs her. "They won't even know we're there. We'll blend in with the crowd. But we'll be there for you, my darling."

Bellamy throws her arms around me. "I love you Ellington Martini. No matter what, that never changes. Pinky swear." She links pinkies with mine before she heads out the door. We love our pinky swears. They make us feel like kids again before things got so... convoluted.

I turn to Jimmy Tate. "What the fuck?"

Chapter 20

Bees knees

Gin, Honey, Lemon Juice

Later that afternoon, my doorbell rings and I shout, "Come in." Jimmy Tate walks in my front door followed closely by Ava. "Look what the cat dragged in!" Jimmy Tate yells. "Good Lawdy Lady, this house smells like Willy Wonka's wet dream. What is going on in here?"

They walk into my kitchen carrying garment bags. We are all going to get ready together for the funeral. I am wearing my glitter apron with my hair piled on top of my head, making chocolate croissants and listening to Ella Fitzgerald, my antidote to extreme stress. They hang their bags on the back of my barstools as I attempt to wipe some of the melted chocolate off the front of my apron. I only succeed in spreading it around, and when I say around, I mean all over the front of my apron, onto my chin and forehead and even a little in my hair when I try to sweep my bangs to the side.

Ava looks at my pot of melted chocolate. "Have I died and gone to heaven? This place smells so good my toes aren't even touching the floor. I floated in here." She takes a large wooden spoon and dips it in the chocolate, then puts it in her mouth, sighing and closing her eyes. "Mmmmmm," she moans, slow and deep. Jimmy Tate looks at me and I can see he is trying to smother his laughter. Ava has an erotic connection to chocolate that is almost obscene to watch.

I get two tiny bowls from my cupboard. "You two sit down and I'll make you little tasting bowls, and a little splash of Burgundy to enhance the flavor of the chocolate. Then, tell me everything you learned about the mystery today."

I pour them two small glasses of wine to go with their chocolate and get back to stirring. Jimmy Tate looks at me suspiciously. "You're awfully chipper for someone who was just accused of having a rewired brain."

"I am thinking quite clearly, as I always do when I'm baking and eating chocolate." I wipe my hands on my apron. "Can you believe Bellamy today? She was all over the place."

"I hope she's okay." Ava looks worried. "She's buckling under all this stress. I wish there was something we could do to help."

With all the chocolate my brain is speeding up. My mouth is barely able to keep up. "Did you find anything else out about Duncan or her great-great-grandfather? Do you really think Duncan murdered his girlfriend? Creepy! Is it true Lincoln indicted for Albert Pike for treason?" I gasp and clap my hand over my mouth, saying between my fingers, "What if the Pikes are some sort of assassination team and when Duncan said 'stop the killing of the king' he meant POTUS?"

"What the heck is POTUS?" Ava asks.

"President of the United States."

Jimmy Tate looks at me in disbelief. "You think there's a secret society in New Orleans right now plotting to assassinate our president? That doesn't seem a bit farfetched to you?"

Ava looks at Jimmy Tate. "I'll think you find that's not a farfetched theory at all once you hear what I've learned."

Jimmy Tate says, "Spill, girl."

Ava looks at her notes, "Okay, this is going to sound crazy, but here is my theory. The Illuminati hid themselves in the Skull and Bones and the Freemasons. They planned to create a kind of New World Order funded by House of Rothschild."

Jimmy Tate rolls his eyes. "Girl, the men in white coats are going to come take you away. We'll bring you cookies and slip them under the door."

Ava says, "I know it sounds insane, but just hear me out. Ellington, Duncan didn't know you well, but he could have recognized you as Bellamy's friend or knew what you looked like from your book jackets. Let's just suppose that House of Rothschild or the Freemasons are trying to resurrect their power in some way, or maintain it if you believe the conspiracy theorists. What if Duncan had gotten involved, maybe when he was at Yale, and once he knew the crimes committed by the top tier, he wanted out? These people are not going to let someone with that knowledge walk free, they could destroy countless powerful people. If they were after him and he knew he wasn't going to survive, maybe he wanted the truth to come out."

Jimmy Tate slaps the counter enthusiastically. "That makes sense. Ellington, he chose to give you the pieces of the truth because he knows how nosy writers are and that you can't resist a good story, and even better, you have the power to tell millions of others through your books."

"I was chosen?" This is a disturbing thought, but also a boost, like being picked first for the dodgeball team. "I guess that does make sense, at least it makes more sense than anything else right now. So let's go with this, but what about the key?"

"Ellington, these flavors, the combination is just insane," Jimmy Tate says after a chocolate-wine taste.

I laugh. "I told you. Ava, take a lick and a sip before your chocolate cools off. The flavor is amplified when it's warm."

She does, and now she and Jimmy Tate are both moaning with their eyes closed when Winston comes in wearing a suit. He nods, his lips pressed together. "It seems I'm interrupting something?" He sets his briefcase down.

"Divine decadence," I say, kissing him.

He licks his lips. "You taste like my idea of heaven."

Jimmy Tate says, "I feel like we've been caught in bed with your wife."

Ava nods enthusiastically. "We are having intimate relations with this chocolate."

"So, what were you saying about Freemasons in between all the moaning?"

I hug his waist. "Winston has always been interested in the economic aspect of the Freemasons."

"Like their symbology on the dollar bill?" Ava asks.

"I've heard this before but can't remember," Jimmy Tate says. "What are the freemason symbols?"

Winston rattles off the facts: "The pyramid with the all-seeing eye at the top is one of their symbols. Their sacred number is thirteen, and it is encoded in the bundle of thirteen arrows held by the eagle, the thirteen stripes on the shield, the thirteen stars and the thirteen steps up the pyramid on the reverse side."

Ava hops up and down in her seat. "Oh, I forgot to tell you. Ever wondered why there are thirteen stars on the confederate flag when only eleven states seceded?"

My eyes grow huge. "You're kidding? A Freemason secret sign?"

"Yup, they wanted everyone 'in the know' to know who created the war. The Freemasons were so powerful, they had secret agents all over fomenting war."

"Like who?" Jimmy Tate asks.

"Well, besides John Brown and Harper's Ferry, August Belmont, our House of Rothschild agent in New York designed the Kansas-Nebraska line. Nebraska was split and half was allowed to have slavery. That allowed for closer geographical proximity to create the war."

"Ava, you are blowing my mind," I interrupt. "I can't keep track of all these people and names and places..."

Ava cuts me off and says in an excited voice, "Oh, I forgot to tell you about Pike and his treason." She looks at a piece of paper in front of her. "Ok, he negotiated many treaties for local Native Americans and they joined his troops when the War started. They actually won a famous battle called The Battle of Pea Ridge, but then, Pike was charged with training his troops inappropriately."

"What does that mean? He didn't have them do hundreds of pushups?" Jimmy Tate asks. "Judging from his photos, Pike preferred chocolate to pushups."

"That *means* his Native American troops were scalping people in battle, a practice apparently frowned upon by the military," Ava says.

"Oooh," Jimmy Raye and I both moan in horror at the same time.

"Hold on, how is that considered treason? Winston asks.

"Witnesses said some of the soldiers were still alive when they scalped them, and some were mutilated even worse."

I shudder. "I can't imagine what could be worse than being scalped alive."

"Anyway, Pike was arrested for treason, but there was insufficient evidence and they allowed him to resign from the military.

Jimmy Tate says, "Um-hm Girl, insufficient evidence *my ass*. He knew somebody."

"He may have gotten in trouble for that, but that's still not treason." Winston asks.

Ava shrugs. "I don't know but that wasn't the only charge. They said he also mishandled military money."

"There has to be more to that story," I say, thinking. "Was this before or after he wrote the book on Freemason rituals?"

"He wrote the book later. I hope he's innocent of all wrongdoing, for Bellamy's sake," I say.

Winston asks, "Who erected his statue in Washington D.C.?"

"I can tell you," Ava says, shuffling paper. "The Supreme

Council of the Scottish Rite. And it's visited and cared for by the Daughters of the Confederacy. And he is holding a copy of his *Morals and Dogma* book in his hand."

"He's holding his secret ritual book? I want a job like that, developing rituals of some crazy club," I say. "What a cool job. We would start every meeting with Burgundy and Chocolate."

"Followed by some barefoot dancing under the moonlight?" Winston laughs.

"Exactly."

Jimmy Tate adds, "With umbrellas that sparkle under the moonlight?"

"Yes!"

Ava says, "I'm in. When you start the 'Order of the Dancing Barefoot Under the Moonlight with Sparkling Umbrellas' I'll be your first member."

"Me too, but I want to be Grand Sovereign Taster of the Alchemical Combination of Burgundy and Chocolate."

"Yes! Let's start it." I run to my kitchen bookshelf. "Wait, I was just reading this fabulous book on Old-Time Hollywood scandal called *Of All the Gin Joints...*"

Jimmy Tate gasps, "I love *Casablanca*."

"Me too. Anyway, it was talking about how many of the actors were barred from the upscale clubs for being Jewish or poor or... just for being actors. So John Wayne and a few others started their own club called..." I find the page..."The Young Men's Purity Total Abstinence and Snooker Pool Association."

Ava says, "Wait, no way John Wayne was a teetotaler."

"No, it was a joke. They wrote in the club's notes that the official goal of the club was 'To promulgate the cause of alcoholism.'"

Winston pours himself some wine. "Now there's a mission statement I can get behind."

"But wait, it gets even better. They later changed their name to 'The Young Men's Purity Total Abstinence and

Yachting Association' and wore seafaring blazers covered in insignias. It says at their first annual St. Patrick's Day dinner they met at the Coconut Grove but were thrown out when a food fight erupted."

Jimmy Tate laughs. "They should have come to New Orleans. We celebrate St. Patrick's Day with city-wide parade-level food fights."

"Oh my god," Ava says, "Last year at the parade I was hit in the head by a *cabbage* thrown off a float. Nearly threw my neck out. I had to sit down!"

"I was with you, poor thing. Those cabbages are practically lethal weapons. I'm surprised there aren't more deaths at those parades with flying cabbages."

"What about the potatoes? Those hurt too."

"Oh my god the potatoes. They *do* hurt. I have gotten hit by those more than once."

Winston says, "Like getting hit in the head by the golden coconuts at Zulu. I have sworn off parades forever."

Ava is staring at him. "Wait, you got a golden coconut? I have never caught one."

"That's me and Muses." I say. "I attend every year, front and center, and I have yet to actually catch a shoe. It's my dream to catch a shoe."

Jimmy Tate says, "Hey, I have given you at least five glitter shoes that I personally caught at Muses."

"Yes, and I love them, but it's not the same as catching one yourself. The magic lies in the catching." I pour myself another tiny splash of wine.

"Look at this magic trick," Ava says. "I can pick up my croissant crumbs with one finger." She presses her finger to her plate and lifts it covered with croissant flakes. She slowly lifts her finger to her mouth and raises one eyebrow, staring at Jimmy Tate.

Jimmy Tate frowns and says slowly. "Don't. you. dare."

Winston is puzzled. "Dare to what?"

I laugh. "Jimmy Tate has a thing about people licking

their fingers. Ava loves to do it in front of him."

Ava gleefully sticks out her tongue, still staring at him. "Oh help me, somebody stop me," she says in a thick southern accent.

Jimmy Tate covers his eyes with his hands. "Go ahead you little trollop. I'm not watching."

Ava whispers, "Oh Jimmy, oh Jimmy, open your eyes…"

"Oh for god's sake you two," I say. I look at the kitchen clock, which I found at an old abandoned train station in Paris when I was backpacking. I lugged the thing around for weeks, but it made me happy whenever I looked at it, and it still does. "Guys, we've lost track of time. We have less than an hour to get to the funeral."

We race each other upstairs to get ready except Winston, who pours himself another glass of wine.

Chapter 21

Sazerac

(Invented in New Orleans)

Whiskey, Bitters, Sugar Cube

For the funeral, Ava has loaned me a gorgeous fitted black satin dress, and on me... it's extra fitted so I look like a satin cinnamon bear. I wanted to wear my Naughty Monkey glitter wedges, but Ava said no, too scandalous, and made me wear my black Chanel T-straps with sheer black stockings. When I emerge from my dressing room wearing a royal blue fascinator with a veil, Ava tries to put the kibosh on that too, saying it is too dramatic for someone who isn't a member of the family, and all hats must be black as a sign of respect. But Jimmy Tate points out that might be true in Kansas, but is not true in New Orleans where funerals are unique and often outlandish. Of course he is wearing a black fedora with a leopard-print band with his black 70's suit—very pimp-chic. Ava wears a simple black suit with a gray silk blouse and damn if she doesn't look amazing. I swear, if I wore that outfit, I'd look so boring they would send me straight to a nursing home for boring dressers, but she manages to look sexy and spicy in anything. Winston is wearing the same dark suit he wore to teach and it fits him like Cary Grant in *North by Northwest*. I don't know how he manages to look so fabulous with such little effort.

Because Bellamy asked us to come incognito, we all have on large sunglasses and scarves around our necks to lift over our faces if need be. Except for Winston who refuses to wear a silk scarf, or arrive incognito.

When we arrive at the cathedral, Jimmy Tate grabs our arms. "Oh Em Gee Willikers… would you look at that?"

Instead of a hearse, the Pikes are using a black horse-drawn carriage as a hearse for Duncan pulled by four fantastic black Arabian horses. The horses paw the ground with their elegant hooves and their black silky manes glimmer blue in the sunlight. Ava whispers to us that she read in Duncan's obituary he was a major equestrian, which is why they used horses to pull his last trip through the city. We slip in the back of the cathedral and find a pew to sit in, and as always I am both awed by the gothic arches and mortified by the violence in the religious paintings. Bloody stabbings, bleeding crowns of thorns, weeping and suffering everywhere. The whole place smells like incense and I see little boys in robes on both sides swinging golden orbs as they walk in circles singing with voices as clear as frozen vodka, and quite frankly, I could use a frozen vodka right now.

I close my eyes and listen to the choir sing "Come Home" when I am startled awake by Jimmy Tate's elbow. Disoriented after my short nap, I elbow Winston next to me who is discreetly playing Solitaire on his phone, hiding it under his hymn book.

It's boring as hell, but I'm just glad they aren't subjecting us to the latest New Orleans funeral fad like Granny Juncadelia, a subject of one of my articles. Granny Juncadelia was propped up wearing her favorite Saints jersey, with Mardi Gras beads around her neck and a glass of bourbon in her hand. They did her hair, put sunglasses on her and everyone milled around her dead body like it was any Sunday. It was funny in a macabre way, and I'm not sure it's any worse than looking at the dead body lying sleeping in a coffin, but I prefer my funerals with a closed casket. Then I can pretend the person just went on a long trip.

It's finally over and when the family walks by our pew, Madame Banjeau is staring right at me with narrowed eyes. She glances sharply at Bellamy who ignores her and smiles at us, squeezing Ava's shoulder as she passes. Uncle Beau also passes with a disapproving sideways glance at me—I'm guessing it's Uncle Beau as I haven't seen him in a while and this gentleman looks like the extra-large version of the old Uncle Beau.

When we get outside, there is a band on the steps playing "Amazing Grace" and every person leaving the church is handed a little white box shaped like a pyramid and told not to open it yet. Once everyone is outside spilling into the square, Uncle Beau quiets everyone with a wave of his hand. "In honor of our beautiful boy, Duncan, and all the hope and promise that was taken from our family and our city when he took his last breath, please open your white boxes and set his soul free."

Everyone opens up their boxes and out flutter small orange butterflies. The sun shines through their sheer gossamer wings as they take flight. I open my box and the butterfly doesn't flutter out but lies there stuck to its chrysalis, with one wing open but the other still sticky and closed. "Oh Winston," I say, "My butterfly is stuck."

"Don't touch it," he says. "The wings will dry out and it will fly."

"This is a bad omen," I say, peering into the box.

"It's not an omen. It's just not ready."

I can feel my panic rising in me like pan of raw bread dough on a warm windowsill. "You don't think it's a sign for me personally? That maybe I'm in over my head? That my wings are broken?"

"Honey, your wings aren't broken. *Your* wings are strong. The butterfly's wings aren't broken either, they are just still emerging from the chrysalis and you can't rush it. You have to let the wings unfold in their own time."

I burst into tears and all the tension and fear of the past few days comes flooding out. Winston puts his arms around me while Jimmy Tate and Ava rub my back. "Honey, the butterfly is fine, she's just taking her time emerging. Set the open box in the sunshine and when the wings are ready, the butterfly will fly out."

I nod and with tears running down my face, I find a safe place to set the box on top of a bush so the sun will warm it. Winston hands me his pocket square and winces when I blow my nose in it, but that's what pocket hankies are for, even silky Hermes ones.

The coffin makes its final circle around the Square before it makes its way towards the cemetery. As it disappears from view, the band finally breaks into a jazzy New Orleans song and umbrellas and boas are passed out and every last person on the steps starts dancing. They can't help themselves. The Second Line parade is my favorite part of every New Orleans funeral.

I am handed an umbrella and we all dance around the square, by the Cabildo and Pontalba buildings, down Decatur and back through the park by the statue of Andrew Jackson. People come out on their balconies, drinks in hand, to smile at us and dance with us... their way, I suppose, of showing their support. One woman is wearing a slip just like the Stella shouting contest. Every Spring the French Quarter hosts the Tennessee Williams Literary Festival. A woman in a slip stands on the balcony of the Pontalba building and people on the sidewalk practice shouting "Stella" to her and tearing their shirts. It's one of my favorite events in the Quarter, and I'm thinking I'd like to tear my too-tight dress off about now and dance around in *my* slip.

The brass band takes off their marching band hats and

wipes their dripping brows. We are all sweating too from dancing a little too wildly in our fancy clothes.

"I'm thirsty," I shout over the tuba.

"Follow me!" Jimmy Tate says and he leads the way to Muriel's Bar on the corner. Famous for its resident ghost, Muriel's Bar overlooks Jackson Square. The top floor is a séance room complete with statues and red tassels and an Egyptian sarcophagus. In its dark carriageway, there is always a table laid out for its ghost. The restaurant staff say if they don't leave the table set at all times, wine glasses mysteriously fly across the room and smash against the brick walls. Jimmy Tate and I have been here many times, hoping to catch sight of a flying glass, but so far, no luck. Today we sit in the cool lush courtyard to order our drinks, surrounded by palm trees and soft sunlight.

The courtyard air immediately cools my sweating skin when all of a sudden the smell of roses erupts around me. I sniff my forearm. "Oh my god. My sweat smells like roses. I can't believe it. My magic has finally taken over my entire body so that even my sweat smells like roses." I hold my wrists out to Jimmy Tate, Ava, and Winston to smell. "I will be famous for my scent, like Cleopatra when she dipped the purple sails of her barge in rose oil so people could smell roses long before she arrived."

Ava rolls her eyes and pushes my arm away. "Oh my god, girl, that's *me*. I just put rose oil on." She holds up a little tiny jar of rose oil, smaller than my pinky.

"Oh." How deflating.

I lift my glass. "To Duncan. Wherever he is, I hope he is at peace."

My phone pings with a text from Hunter. *Can you meet me at Jean Lafitte's Tavern right now?*

I text back, *yes.*

"Wait, what about Bellamy?" Ava asks. "We told her we'd come to the funeral."

"We did go to the funeral. There's no way I'm going to

Uncle Beau's house. Did you see the daggers he was throwing at me with his eyes? He hates me right now. Text Bellamy and see if she can slip away."

"I already did," a voice says behind me. Bellamy pulls up a chair and sits down at our table. "I can't take any more funeral crap. My mother will be furious but I don't care. What are we drinking?" I order Bellamy a margarita. They're powerful at Muriel's and will make her feel better. The last time we had margaritas here we ended up hiring a horse and buggy to drive us around the Quarter for two hours and told each other ghost stories. Then we ended up on Bourbon Street where Ava danced with a pole onstage during someone else's show and Bellamy borrowed the "Big Ass Beers" sign from the front of a store and danced down Bourbon Street with it. And I have the pictures to prove it.

I receive another text. *Bring the key.*

I text, *Got it.*

Chapter 22

Obituary Cocktail

(Created at Jean Laffite's Blacksmith Shop in the early 1900's)
Gin, Vermouth, Absinthe

We arrive at Jean Lafitte's Blacksmith shop, with its exposed brick, catawumpus roof, dormer windows, and shutters instead of doors. The building oozes charm and smells like whiskey, wood, smoke and peat moss. Known as the longest continuously running bar in the country, the buccaneer Jean Lafitte would have been proud of its tenacity. Not even Katrina could shut it down — the bartenders just kept shotguns behind the bar and poured drinks for those who stuck around. A crooked stone fireplace stands in the middle of the room, silent witness to hundreds of years of drinking, brawling, storytelling, and while it once held fires, it now holds only ghost stories.

We sit at the bar, our knees against the brick underbelly of the wooden bar while we wait for Hunter. The bartender appears in a black tank top and black jeans. She has a long lavendar hair with short bangs and a large scorpion tattooed on her arm. We order Bloody Marys and I watch her pouring tomato juice and shaking cayenne pepper into our drinks with finesse.

Ava gives us one of her mini history lessons. "This building was built in the 1700's and was known to be a meeting place for Lafitte and other pirates."

"Is it true that Lafitte kept his gold hidden in the fireplace?" I get up and run my hands all over the fireplace, dipping my fingers in the crevices.

The bartender says, "Legend says so, but if I had a quarter for every crackpot who came in here with a metal detector, I'd have my own damn treasure and never have to work again. There is the cigar smoke, though. That's real."

"What about cigar smoke?" Bellamy asks.

"Some people claim they've seen Lafitte's ghost sitting at the piano smoking a cigar with a drink in his hand. I've never seen the ghost, even though I work at a psychic hotline and if anyone was going to see a ghost it would be me, but I've definitely smelled the cigar smoke."

"Hey, what's with ghosts and cigars?" I ask. "The ghost over in the Faulker's House bookshop in Pirate's Alley also smokes cigars. Joe told us he and his wife smells cigar smoke in the house sometimes when no one else is home."

Winston is a devoted Faulkner fan. He nods. "Faulkner loved cigars."

"Who knew cigars were so popular among the undead?" Bellamy says, getting up to come help us investigate the fireplace.

Ava whispers to the bartender but we can all hear her, "Do you have psychic powers? What exactly is a psychic hotline?"

"Oh people call in looking for guidance from the spirits. I help them. I'm like a therapist, but a lot cheaper."

Ava taps the old wooden bar with her finger. "You bartend and you work for a psychic hotline? How perfect."

"I'm also a dancer," she says amused.

"I'm a dancer too." I say, trying to yank my hand out from between two rocks. I look at Winston and whisper, "I'm stuck."

He laughs and gingerly works each of my fingers out from between the rocks while I ask the bartender, "Where do you dance?"

"Bob's Mammary Mondays under the freeway."

"Bob's Mammary Mondays? I've never heard of that." Jimmy Tate says.

"It's not very well-known around here. It's a little rough." She holds up one hand that has wrapped knuckles.

Bellamy's eyes are huge when she asks, "You got in a fight?"

The bartender laughs and slaps the bar. "You could say that. I got in a fight with a wall. DJ fucked up my music again."

Ava raises her eyebrows. "So you punched a wall?"

"I know, I know, not classy. But hey, I never claimed to be classy. How about you, where do you dance?"

"I'm retired. I write now, hence the juicy ass." I point at my behind.

"Well, Bob's is lucrative, if you ever decide to dance again. They let you keep all your tips, unlike the joints around here. Cheetah's down the street takes half your tips."

"Half? That doesn't seem fair." Bellamy is now eating the bar snacks.

"Cheetahs?" I look at Winston. "Haven't we been there before?"

He nods. "Yes, for our anniversary." Everyone looks at him. "We came down here for dinner at Stella's and ended up on Bourbon Street."

Jimmy Tate says, "Boy someone should write a song about that exact scenario. I bet that happens every night to more than one group."

Ava is diving into the bar snacks. "They *have* written a song about it. It's called *Take Your Drunken Ass Home.*

I pipe in. "We had our own fabulous dancer named Aston Martin and I had just gotten this gorgeous new silvery blue lace bra from House of Lounge and when I got up to dance on the table with Aston in the champagne room, the bouncer made me sit down. I think I may be the only woman on Bourbon Street who's ever been asked to put her shirt back on. Isn't that sad?"

The bartender shakes her head. "Well, if you ever decide to come out of retirement, Bob is always looking for more dancers. He likes a variety. We don't have anyone your age."

All four of my peeps burst out laughing.

Jimmy Tate says, "Awww, Ellington, you could be the senior citizen dancer."

Ava adds, "That's a good back-up plan if writing takes a downturn. Bob's Mammary Mondays."

Bellamy agrees. "Sounds right up your alley."

"Are y'all treasure hunters?" the bartender asks.

"No, just curious locals."

"Just last week a guy told me his grandfather had found one of Lafitte's treasure chests out near Lafayette."

"Really?"

She nods. "He was clearing land for a wealthy man out on the Vermilion Bayou when he came upon a large chest of doubloons. He says his great-grandfather was an honest man, but if he had reported it, he would have had to give it to the landowner, so he dug it up and laid low. After a while, he bought an island and moved to the Caribbean. Eventually one of his grandsons moved back here and bought a little plantation. Married a woman named Dream. Honest to god."

Just then, Hunter enters the bar in her vintage black slip and black rainboots. "Hunter!" I say, jumping up to hug her, but she seems a bit prickly so I don't. She nods at us like a cowboy tipping his hat in respect, one outlaw to another. She apparently already knows the bartender. "Hey Mamae." Mamae hands Hunter a shot of bourbon, which Hunter throws back. She wipes her mouth with the back of her hand

and lays down a five-dollar bill. "Thanks."

She really is like an outlaw from the old west.

"So, what's up? I'm dying of intrigue," I say.

"Your little key got me thinking. Did you bring it?" I nod. "An unusual key requires an unusual lock. I have a memory for locks, but this one took a while to come to me. I have only ever seen one lock for that key, and it was here."

My stomach drops. "*Here?*

She nods. "Yup."

Mamae is staring at Hunter, her brown eyes huge, while pointing at me. "You don't mean *she* has the key?"

"I think she might."

Chapter 23

Hot and Dirty Martini

Pepper Vodka, Vermouth, Olive Brine, Jalapeno Brine

Mamae hangs a handwritten "Closed for a few minutes" sign on the front shutters of the bar and leads us up a skinny black iron spiral staircase in the back of the building, the kind you'd find in a lighthouse. She opens the door with a large black skeleton key and we all file into the narrow hallway behind her. The hallway opens up into a few small crooked wooden rooms and it smells like an ancient church. I can feel invisible silken cobwebs tickling me and I brush them off my arms. I hold my breath, not daring to look down at the clicking cockroaches and probable rats running into darkness. "We store stuff up here, but we don't come up here very often," Mamae says, brushing the cobwebs out of her hair. This is where the man who built this tavern lived, Nicholas Touze."

"How did this building survive the fires that burned down most of the Quarter?" Ava asks.

"Slate roof." Mamae says, clicking on a big flashlight and leading us to the second floor fireplace area. The room is small and lit softly through the dirty windows. There are several portraits of all different sizes taking up one entire wall and I spot the most common rendering of Jean Lafitte with the big bushy moustache and black hat. Next to him is a painting of an elegant man in a black coat sitting somber with a straight back. The other paintings and photographs are of various people and buildings around the Quarter. The fireplace is made of a jumble of stones like downstairs, and Mamae walks over and slides one of the stones sideways. Behind it is another skeleton key, which she slides out and into her palm. She takes the large portrait of the stiff-backed man off the wall revealing an iron triangle.

Bellamy says, "A safe shaped like an iron triangle? How unusual."

"Not a triangle," Winston says in awe, "a pyramid. The strongest structure, nearly impossible to topple." He is so intrigued he steps forward without thinking and runs his finger along the outline.

Mamae turns to Hunter, who nods. Then she says, "Everyone who works here knows about this iron triangle, but no one has ever been able to figure out what it is. One drunken night, I showed it to Hunter. She figured out it might be a kind of magnetic safe that opens with no visible lock. Over the next few nights we went over every inch of this place until we found the loose stone in the fireplace. This key is not a key, which Hunter knew immediately. It's a magnet."

Mamae hands it to Hunter who slowly slides it down across the top of the pyramid. We hear a click and the pyramid slowly creaks open.

Winston whispers, "Of course it would open from the top, that's where the pyramids connect to the spiritual realm."

Inside there is a drawing of a skull and crossbones painted in some kind of phosphorescent paint glowing on the back side.

"It's a Jolly Roger," I whisper loudly. "Jean Lafitte's treasure?" My brain is lit up like a christmas tree.

Lying on the bottom, there is a wooden box, a little bigger than a Louboutin shoe box, and it's covered in faded symbols drawn in red paint. One of the symbols looks a lot like the winged Isis from the Rex invitation. "Winston? Look!" Hunter and Mamae gently lift it out of the safe and set it on a round side table with the flashlight shining on it even though we can see it with the light from the windows. I'm beside myself with excitement—I want to draw out the moment.

"Have we really found Lafitte's long lost treasure? Finally at last all the legends end here? Is it full of gold? Rubies and diamonds?" We all look at it in silence, holding our breaths and I dig the key out of my Lux De Ville tote.

Hunter and Mamae point to the lock on the side of the box, and I slide the key in and it nestles snugly. When I turn it, there is a loud click and we let out a collective breath. Mamae slowly lifts the lid, and inside are thirteen velvet pockets filled with small vials of liquid. Have they turned the jewels and gold to liquid? How odd. We shine the flashlight over them to get a closer look and see the liquid is all different colors and some vials are half empty.

"What the hell is this?" Bellamy whispers.

"Voodoo?" Ava says softly.

Hunter reaches down to pick up a vial but Mamae stops her. "Hold up, don't touch."

"Why not?"

"Maybe that's not the Jolly Roger pirate symbol. It's also the symbol for..."

"Poison," I say, and my heart sinks. No pirate's treasure, just poisonous vials. How disheartening.

Bellamy peers at the colored liquid carefully. "It could be strychnine."

"Or arsenic," Jimmy Tate says. When we all glance at him, he says, "What? I read a lot of mysteries with poison in them."

I shudder. "These bottles remind me of mini-versions of those colored bottles in the window the old apothecary over on Chartres, the creepy one with all the glass jars filled with different colored water? In the 1800's, that's how they would tell people what was happening in the city. They used yellow for the plague, blue for smallpox, and so on."

Ava says, "That creepy pharmacy didn't just inform people about diseases. The main pharmacist was actually a serial killer. Women kept disappearing and eventually workers found a bunch of bodies in the wall."

Bellamy is staring at the bottles, "Fuck, what if they are viruses, like someone is preserving extinct illnesses like the plague or smallpox?"

I feel sick and I put my shaking hand on my stomach to steady it. "That would explain why people are getting killed. I mean, if you were preserving this stuff to use as a weapon somehow, you'd probably go pretty far to protect it."

Winston says, "I can take it to a lab. I have a research scientist in Public Health at Tulane who works with exotic diseases. She can test it today."

"What if it breaks on the way over there, Winston?" I ask.

"I'll make sure it doesn't break. If it is something serious, we can turn it over the authorities. It might just be colored water."

There is a loud clatter in another room and we all jump. Mamae looks over our shoulders. "What the fuck was that? We're the only ones here."

"Shhh," Hunter says sharply.

I quickly turn my phone to silent and start snapping photos of the entire scene.

Winston silently gestures for the silk scarf around my neck. I give it to him and he carefully wraps the box up and slides it into my tote. It's larger than my bag, but it's wrapped in my scarf so it's incognito. We all quickly head back downstairs and out into the safety of Bourbon Street.

Chapter 24

Blue Blazer

(A flaming whiskey toddy tossed between two cups creating a rainbow arc of fire)
Scotch, Raw sugar, Lemon Peel, metal cups for tossing the flames

We cross the narrow street and stare up at the top of the building to see if we can discern where the noise was coming from. There is a group of students and a few businesspeople standing outside waiting for the bar to re-open. When Mamae flips the sign they all start ordering and she disappears behind the bar. A horse and carriage is parked out front with two older women in it, getting a tour of the Quarter. Winston is carefully holding my bag, but he hands it back to me, saying, "I look odd carrying this. You hold it right there, don't move, and I'll go get the car. We can take it straight to Holly Lumina in Public Health. I'm texting her now," his fingers are flying over the screen of his phone as he talks. "She'll be able to test it immediately." He pauses a minute, then says, "On second thought, we better stick together. I'm not leaving your side till this thing is over."

Bellamy, Jimmy Tate, Ava and Hunter are standing next to me and no one is talking. I think we're all in a bit of shock. I can hear the carriage tour guide telling his clients about Lafitte, how he and his brother helped make New Orleans into the richest city in the new country with its rum and cotton and pirates. Another horse and carriage pulls up near us pulled by a stunning draft horse. It's extra-large, and dappled gray with fluffy hooves like he's walking on storm clouds. It's unusual because the carriages in the Quarter don't actually use horses, and they never use draft horses. They use large donkeys because they can tolerate the heat.

This carriage is small and driven by a two husky men, one in a black chauffeur cap. They both swing to the ground and get on their knees to fix something on the wheel. As they strain, one calls to Winston in an Irish accent. "Do you mind giving us a hand, Mate?"

"Sure," Winston walks over and before I can say boo they have whisked him into the carriage, covered his head with a sack and are galloping down Bourbon Street.

I am stunned, but I jump in the tour carriage with the donkey. The driver yells, "No way!" But I push him out and grab the reins. Without thinking Bellamy, Hunter, Jimmy Tate, and Ava have jumped into the carriage like hairpins to a magnet, yelling at the women on the tour to get out.

They jump out, thrilled. "Is this part of the tour?" One of them asks in an excited voice as I slap the reins and we take off after Winston.

We are galloping down Bourbon Street, well, the other horse is galloping. Apparently donkeys don't gallop. Which I didn't know until now. This donkey is kind of half-trotting, half-hobbling in a kind of goblin-hop. Cars are slamming on their brakes but it's late in the afternoon so there aren't many of them. The few people on the street hear the commotion and leap out of the way. I have no idea how to drive a carriage although lord knows I've seen so many movies I should be picking it up by osmosis. Luckily, Bellamy has been an equestrian her entire life. She grabs the reins and shakes them hard, spurring the donkey to a near-run but nowhere near fast enough to catch the gray horse.

The gray horse turns a sharp right onto Ursulines Street and we follow. They veer left a block later onto Chartres in front of the Ursuline Convent.

Pedstrians are jumping out of the way when they hear the galloping hooves, and our donkey slows down as we pass Governor Nicholls. No amount of slapping the reins or shouting "Hee-Ya!" is making this donkey move, and I jump out of the carriage and sprint down the street after the first carriage which is long gone. I can't even see it anymore. I fall to the sidewalk sobbing like a child when I feel a gentle hand and turn to see Jimmy Tate. I fall into his arms and he lets me cry as loudly as I want. I feel him smoothing my hair, and Ava puts her arm around me and helps me back to the carriage, which is being held by Bellamy and Hunter. "This... is... all... my... fault," I wail.

"Shhhh," Ava says, rubbing my back. "It's the kidnapper's fault, not yours. And don't you worry, we're going to get him back." I hear the sirens blazing towards us. "I already called the police," Ava says.

Without thinking I hand Jimmy Tate the scarf-wrapped-box and whisper, "Take this to Holly Lumina at Tulane and tell her to test it *now*."

Jimmy Tate says, "On it," and disappears around the corner, taking Ava with him.

The tour driver is running down the street, shouting and shaking his fist.

Hunter has disappeared, so it's me and Bellamy as four police cars pull up, including one with my detectives. I run to Detective Washington and throw my arms around her, sobbing into her uniform.

"W-w-w-w-winston!" I wail. "He's been taken." Bellamy and I both speak at once, giving descriptions of the horse and carriage, the kidnappers and Winston. Detective Boudreau repeats everything we say into a radio. There is a team already looking for the runaway carriage. After the full description, two of the police cars take off in pursuit. Bellamy and I are sitting in the back of a police car, and I'm hoping they aren't going to arrest me, and with every moment I can feel Winston getting further and further away. I'm so frantic with worry I can barely register where I am. Maybe this will be it, the final straw for me. Maybe now my brain really will rewire and I'll end up so crazy they'll have to put me in a straightjacket and lobotomize me like they did Jessica Lange in *Frances*. I'll be the woman in the hospital gown shuffling down the street.

"Ellington?" Detective Washington startles me by snapping my name. She hands me a bottle of water. I look at it like I don't know what to do with it. My eyes are so swollen from crying I can barely see. I am filled with a flush of focused energy. *"We have to find him."*

Detective Washington and Detective Boudreau are standing next to me. "Believe me, we will. We have five units on the case right now as we speak. That carriage can't have gotten far and will be impossible to hide. We will find it and we will find him, but Ellington," she looks at me with serious eyes, "You need to tell us what is going on. The truth now, the *whole* truth. The more you tell us, the more we can help Winston."

I nod. It's time to come clean. Bellamy pats me gently but her eyes grow wider and wider as I tell them everything I've learned from the beginning, including the key, which they take from me. I'm so sick about Winston, that's all I can think about. While I'm talking, Detective Boudreau gets a phone call. His face turns grim and my stomach drops. Please, *oh please* let Winston be all right.

"They found the carriage."

"And Winston?"

"Nothing yet." He shakes his head and I crumple to the ground like an accordion.

Pull it together, Ellington, I say silently to myself. *Winston needs you.* I blow my nose and rise like a phoenix from the ashes, calm and assured. "Where's the carriage?" I ask, tossing my hair.

"Just down the street from the convent. They pulled into a courtyard and shut the door, but a neighbor saw and reported it."

We drive with the sirens on to the courtyard, which has been cordoned off by the other police cars. I can't believe how I'm holding it together. Jackie O. would be so proud. In the courtyard the carriage is there but the horses and the driver and Winston are not. I look around and can't imagine how they got those enormous horses out of here. Detective Washington points to the carriage. Was this the carriage that took Winston?"

"That's the one."

"Positive ID on the kidnapping vehicle," she says into her walkie-talkie.

Several police officers are climbing over the carriage with gloves and plastic bags, looking for evidence I suppose. I stride over and look inside. One of the officers says, "Step back, Miss." But I don't listen. I have to see for myself if there's any clue in there as to where they have taken Winston. The carriage is empty. I guess he didn't have time to scratch a message for me into the wood. The courtyard is slowly coming into focus and I see that it's dilapidated.

The palm fronds are overgrown, the giant stone fountain in the center is broken and tilts in the middle, dirty and overgrown with moss. Moss is growing up the walls and balconies and several of the balcony railings are missing. I can see police walking through the dirty broken plantation shutters on the second floor. They are moving slowly, probably because the second floor ceiling may cave in at any point. I look for some evidence of where they could have exited. I guess they could have rolled him up in a rug and discreetly carried him out like Cleopatra meeting Caesar, but they couldn't have hidden the horses. Horses don't roll up in rugs very well and they're too big to hide. Then I remember the tunnel at Pierre Maspero's.

I turn to my detectives. "Could there be a tunnel here like Maspero's tunnel?"

They look at each other, then march to the police captain who is standing near the carriage. He whistles and the police officers gather to him. He is telling them to look for evidence of a tunnel when there are shouts from the roof. We all look up and see Winston with two police officers flanking him. He is waving at me with his big beautiful smile while shouting "Ellington!"

"Winston!" I'm jumping up and down and wishing I was a cat or a monkey so I could spring high enough to scale the wall and meet him. I see a broken outdoor stairway and race up it, leaping over the broken parts like a gazelle. The police are yelling something at me but I can't hear them because all I can hear is Winston calling my name. The steps don't go all the way to the roof and I run inside to find a way up. I see a stairway and as I rush to it, Winston is rushing down and straight into my arms. My face is a flood of tears of relief. I don't ever want to let him go.

The police officers in the courtyard are right behind me and they all head up onto the roof. I didn't even consider the roof, although horses on the roof? How would that have worked? I don't know and at the moment I don't care. Winston is safe and I never want to be apart from him again. Although I am also enjoying the idea of those gorgeous gray dappled horses leaping from roof to roof across New Orleans, their raincloud hooves and silvery manes flying behind them. But that only adds to my complete and utter joy at finding my beloved safe. When I finally pull away from him to look into his eyes, I see his face is dirty and bruised. His lip is swollen and cracked with dried blood. His shirt is torn and one eye is swollen and turning black and blue. I cup his face in my hands. "That's quite a shiner, Mr. Martini."

The detectives interrupt us, "Sorry Mr. and Mrs. Martini

but we need to know if you got a look at your abductors. Any identifiable mark will help. "How many were there?"

Winston holds me tightly while he answers. "There was one man driving the carriage and two men who grabbed me, threw a bag over my head and tossed me in."

"Can you describe the men?"

He squints his eyes and winces. "I didn't really get a good look at them before they put the bag over my head. It all happened so fast."

"Were they taller or shorter than you?"

"Shorter. That I know because they jumped down but had to reach up to put the bag over my head."

"And you are... what, 6'2?"

"6'4."

"Were they heavier than you?"

"Definitely. Well, the two that jumped down were heavier than me. I weight around 180, but they had a good forty pounds on me at least. The driver was shorter, but more wiry."

"Do you remember what clothing they were wearing?"

"Yes. They were wearing dark colors. I think they were wearing dark pants and gray shirts. The shirts had collars, like golf shirts."

"Were any of them wearing anything on their heads? Like bandannas or baseball hats?"

"Yes. The driver had on one of those, what do they call them, chauffeur caps? Newsboy caps? And both guys who grabbed me had on baseball caps, I think."

The detectives nod, taking notes. "Please stay here for a minute, we'll be right back."

"Can I take him down to the courtyard to sit down?"

"Does he need medical attention?" an officer asks. "We can call an ambulance right now."

I look at Winston and he shakes his head. "No, I'm ok. Just bruised."

The officer steps away and talks into his walkie-talkie. I

lead Winston gently down the stairs, and we find a stone bench to sit on. A gecko skitters across the top and disappears into the thick green vines around it. I straddle the cool bench and scoot as close to Winston as possible, wrapping my arms and legs around him. He winces and adjusts me so I'm not pressing on his bruises. I'm dying to know exactly what happened, but for this moment, all I want to do is hold him in silence, feel his heart beating. I take his hand and press my palm against his; wide, flat, solid. I see angry red marks around his wrists and realize he must have been tied up. I immediately feel my own wrists sting in sympathy as I tenderly lift his wrists to my lips and kiss the marks, never taking my eyes off his.

The detectives return. Detective Boudreau pulls out his cell phone to record. "Can you tell us what happened."

I interject, "No detail is too small. It's often the smallest details that help them catch..." I stop talking.

The detectives are looking at me.

Winston takes a deep breath and tells them about having a drink at the tavern after the funeral. He tells them how two men threw a bag over his head and dragged him into the carriage. When he struggled they punched him, gagged him, and tied his hands behind his back. One sat on his legs so he was pinned down. They went through his pockets. Then the carriage stopped and they threw him out. They dragged him upstairs, and told him to lie on his stomach. I can hardly bear to think of him being hurt, but I won't cry. I squeeze his hand.

Then Winston says, "The next thing I knew, two police officers were pulling the bag off my head and untying me." He smiles and looks at me and my heart melts all over again.

I lean forward and softly kiss his cheek.

"Ellington told us about the key that appeared in her purse the morning after the murder. Do you think these people might have been looking for it?"

"I don't know."

Detective Boudreau turns off the recording device. "I

don't like this. You two are caught up in something. Either you're up to no good yourselves, or someone is out to get you. Care to enlighten us?"

"Detectives," I say, "I can promise you that we've led normal, quiet lives until the night the monk was murdered and fell on me. Ever since then, weird things have been happening. My purse was stolen, Winston was kidnapped, someone is looking for... something from us. It must be the key, what else could it be?"

"The monk also gave you that photo. We recently had the men in it identified. John Wilkes Booth was one of them." Detective Washington thumbs through her notes. "Albert Pike, Judah Benjamin, and G.W. Baird. Do you know who those men are?"

We nod.

"Do you have any idea why this photo might have been so important it was shoved into your hand by a dying man?"

"No." I shake my head. "Well, maybe."

Detective Washington sighs. "You two are coming to the station." She looks at Detective Boudreau. "I'm taking them in. Can you track down the Captain and give him an update and we'll meet you there."

Detective Boudreau hesitates. "Why don't *I* take them in and you find the captain."

Detective Washington folds her arms with steely eyes. Wow, she oozes power and she is not budging. I love her. I want to be her. Maybe it's the power of the uniform? Or the badge? I need a badge. Girl scout badges don't count. A real badge, a shiny one. With silence she got her way. We get into her patrol car and once we turn the corner, I scoot forward in my seat. "Detective Washington, is there any way we can tell you what we know without Detective Boudreau? You'll understand once I tell you. There's a lot of sensitive information and I'm not sure who we can trust right now."

She pulls her car over without hesitation. "Start talking."

I tell her everything we have learned including the box. I

tell her about Pike, Baird, Benjamin and Booth. I tell her about Skull and Bones and their connection to Comus and now Rex. I tell her about the Freemasons and the meaning of the 'killing of the king' and the latin inscription of the key: 'sic volvo iubeo'. The more I talk, the better I feel. "Now you. Can you tell us what you know?"

Her phone rings and she turns it off. "We don't have much time, but in a nutshell, we traced that murder weapon back to the Cushing family."

"Cushing?" I say. "That doesn't sound familiar."

"Caleb Cushing was the partner-founder of Skull and Bones at Yale, of which Duncan Pike was also a member. Cushing later became a congressman. He sent Pike here to establish a southern Freemason group. Cushing's family made their fortune as international drug smugglers. There's also a lot of talk that he was involved with several assassinations. I didn't believe it, but when I checked his records, it turned out he was promoted in some way with each assassination."

I feel prickles rising over my arms and down my back and I'm feeling dizzy. I dig through my purse for my tiny bottle of perfume. I spritz my wrists and neck to lift my spirits and the car fills with the smell of nectarines and honey.

Winston chokes. "What is that?"

"Perfume." I wave my hand in front of his face so the scent dissipates.

Detective Washington rolls down the window and starts the car. As we head out onto the streets of the Quarter, she says, "We better get to the station unless there's something else you need to tell me?"

"I think that's it," I answer.

Winston whispers, "Why do you insist on wearing the perfume of a teeny-bopper?"

I spray his shirt and he groans, trying to wipe it off.

"Stick out your tongue," I say, holding the bottle in front of his mouth with my finger on the mister.

"Noooo!" he laughs. "Are you going to pull root beer lip

gloss out of that purse next?"

I dig in my purse and pull out lip gloss—it's pink glitter, not root beer.

Just then my phone rings. It's Jimmy Tate. "Girl, Holly is a superstar! She knew what that vial was just by looking at it."

"What?"

"Arsenic!"

"Fuck." I shiver as I lean forward and inform Winston and Detective Washington.

I sit back and finally put on my lip gloss. Winston is shaking his head at my fruity smells as I blow him a kiss and a scream erupts from me.

My lips and my chest have erupted in fire. I'm screaming and gasping as I tear at my clothes and wipe my lips. Fire! Fire! Fire! And the world goes black.

Chapter 25

Zombie

*White, Golden, Dark, and 151- Proof Rum, Brandy,
Pineapple juice, Papaya juice, Grenadine*

The air is so thick with fog I can barely see. I see the soft outline of a figure that looks like it's ice skating. "Beau...ti...ful!" I sing softly. I feel a squeeze on my foot, then my leg as the shadow skates closer. I smile as Winston comes into clarity. "Hi, Honey," I sing. It seems appropriate to sing and not talk.

He puts his hand on my forehead and I close my eyes. "Ellington, can you hear me?"

Oh can I ever you hot, hot professor. I smile. "Yyyeeessss."

"Ellington, can you remember anything?" His eyebrows are scrunched together like they do when he worries, and I can think of a few things I could do to make him feel better, but my arms and legs seem to be moving through a giant jar of honey so any romantic plans will have to wait. I see another shadow move toward me and suddenly the room comes into sharp focus. I look around, surprised.

"Is this a hospital room?"

"Ellington, are you okay? Do you remember how you got here?"

I tilt my head. "Nope, can't say that I do." And the room goes black again.

Then the fog is back, and I'm reminded of my year of teaching preschool on Martha's Vineyard in my Tolstoy phase when the fog would roll in suddenly and everything that was clear and sunny a few moments ago turns gray and murky and you hear the deep and mournful foghorn deep and then a sunny spot appears under the mist and there is a mama and baby deer eating grass in a meadow of wildflowers with the ocean rolling in the distance, peeps of blue in between the fog. It makes my heart ache with its beauty.

But this time it's not the sun peeking through the fog but the lights in the hospital room, and now I see Winston looking just like a pirate again with messy hair and a 5 o'clock shadow and rumpled clothing. There are other people too, all in white, and I think how kind they are to be speaking so softly. I wonder if maybe I've died and my parents are right— everyone in the afterlife wears white. Wouldn't that be depressing? I look down at my clothing and find I'm wearing a hospital gown. How hideous. How do they expect anyone to feel better in an outfit like this? They start poking me and talking gently and slowly and the overwhelming smell of rubbing alcohol suddenly slices through the air. Winston takes my hand with a big warm smile.

"What happened?" I ask, as the events of the past week come barreling towards me like a Mack truck with faulty brakes and I remember the murder; the blood; the poison; the box; Winston's kidnapping. I look at him and I am slammed back into fear. I shake my head frantically and cover it with a pillow. "No, no, no."

But when everything turns black again, and then re-emerges again, and I remember everything, I handle it with grace and courage. Calmly, I look at Winston who is now sleeping in a chair next to my bed. The nurses and doctor are gone, and Winston looks so vulnerable sleeping there with his head on the back of the chair and his legs sprawled out, the same way he sleeps on planes.

He wakes up looking around and when he sees my eyes open, he jumps up and takes my hand. "How do you feel?"

"Good." I look into his face in silence for a long time. "I remember everything, and I'm okay."

He sighs with relief and sits on the side of the bed. "Good, do you know how long you've been here?"

I shake my head.

"Four days."

I try to sit up but only make it to my elbows before crashing back down. "Did I miss the ball? What happened? The last thing I remember was sitting in Detective Washington's car."

He squeezes my hand. "You were poisoned. There was poison on your lipstick thing. You went into convulsions and we raced you here. Detective Washington has been amazing, calling to check on you several times a day and stopping by every night after work. Jimmy Tate, Bellamy and Ava have been stopping by and calling every day too. Even Hunter sent flowers."

I look around the room and see it is filled with so many large bouquets of flowers it looks like a solarium. "What happened with the poison box?"

"Holly is testing all of it, so far, every vial has been filled with a different type of poison. Detective Washington is on it. They think it's the House of Rothschild evidence box. Even Fausto has gotten involved."

"You've been talking to Fausto?" For some reason, the image of no-nonsense Winston talking to lot's-of-nonsense-Fausto strikes me as hilarious and I hurt myself laughing. Winston hands me a glass of water and when I catch my breath, I ask him, "Have you learned anything else about Duncan?"

"You need to rest. I'll tell you everything when you get

stronger."

"Winston Martini, don't you dare withhold information from me. I am not a child, nor a swooning maiden, and I need to know right now what is going on. And don't leave anything out."

Winston sighs, but he's smiling when he kisses my hand and starts to talk. "Detective Washington talked to someone she knows at the FBI who handles chthonic groups in our country, aka extremists, and they are thinking Duncan was recruited but wanted out."

"Chthonic?"

"It's a greek word for "under the earth" and it's used for cults that exist in opposition to the rest of the world, the "underground cults." Fausto said bloodlines are very important to many of these groups which is why they really go after the children of the original members. A descendant of Albert Pike, who was one of the original Freemasons here, and a powerful one, would have been a real coup. They have found information on Duncan's computer, messages between his girlfriend and him, about how he wanted out. Just telling his girlfriend, he broke the vow of secrecy so he was already in trouble."

"So he didn't kill his girlfriend?"

"Nope. They poisoned her and him, but he was stronger than they thought and he ran. The stabbing was to take him down before he could talk to anyone, but he ran into you before he took his last breath."

"Do they know who did it?"

"They're working on it. According to this guy, this thirty-third level has always been a kind of 'Brotherhood of Death'. It's actually a rite of passage to participate in an assassination. Then they have you locked in for the rest of your life."

"So in order to be in the thirty-third level you had to participate in a 'killing of the king'?" I ask.

Winston nods. "Something like that."

"So who was Duncan talking about when he whispered to

me?"

"They aren't positive but they think Katharine Sanders, the Vermont Senator. She's the power guest at Rex this year. The public aspect of the assassination is important to the cult as a way to show their power and the consequences of standing in their way. They have beefed up security at the ball."

"But Winston, why would they tell you all this? It seems privileged information."

He looks guilty as the Cheshire cat. "Oh, well, Fausto…"

The nurse enters. "Oh you're awake." She looks at Winston. "You were supposed to ring us when she woke up.

"She just barely woke up."

She takes my vitals and asks how I'm feeling. I tell her I feel fine.

"You look good. Your color has returned. You may be able to go home later tonight. I'll let the doctor know. And your guard."

I look at Winston. "My guard?"

"Detective Washington ordered protection for you," Winston says, affectionately squeezing my hand. "You've been the object of a hit, my love. You have to be protected until we find out who's after you."

"They're after you, too."

"Not me, they only kidnapped me to get the vial back. Whatever that sound was when we were upstairs at Lafitte's, someone was watching us. They must have seen me take the vial and came after me. While we were outside, Mamae headed back upstairs and found someone trying to get into the safe."

My eyes grow huge. "What did he look like?"

"Her description sounded just like the guy we chased when your purse got snatched."

"What did she do?"

"She pulled out her shotgun and the guy ran."

"Oh my god," I say, then put my hand over my mouth.

"I know. Apparently French Quarter bartenders keep shotguns handy."

"I guess if you work at a place called Bob's Mammary Mondays, you'd better be handy with a shotgun."

The doctor comes in and we stop talking. She checks my vital signs. "I think we can send you home tonight, Ms. Martini. You're a very lucky lady, getting to the hospital as fast as you did. All your vitals seem stable. We'll keep an eye on you for a few more hours and send you home." She pats my leg on top of the blanket and leaves the room.

Winston comes over to kiss me on the forehead.

"I want to rewind two weeks ago," I say.

"Me, too."

"I wish none of this had ever happened and that damn Duncan had fallen on someone else."

"Me too," he says, gently brushing my hair off my forehead.

"But we're going to be all right now?"

"Always."

Chapter 26

Lion's Tail

Bourbon, Allspice Dram, Fresh Lime, Gomme Syrup,
Angostura Bitters

Winston can be very rejuvenating and after a wonderful warm cozy night at home where I make three new umbrellas and bake two different kinds of banana bread while he sits at the counter making me laugh, I awaken the next morning feeling strong and ready for anything. But Winston stays home from work anyway to keep an eye on me. He's working in the living room when the doorbell rings and Jimmy Tate saunters in. He throws his arms around me and hugs me tightly. "We were all so worried about you. Bellamy would be here but she's at the office today and Ava is teaching but they'll be over after work. Even Bianca has been calling us to see how you are. And her kids."

I lead him back to the kitchen. "How did Bianca know what was happening?"

He shrugs. "Dish and Swish, Darlin'. You know how word spreads around here, like wildfire. Especially something this juicy." He fills me in on what happened while I was in the hospital, about his new friendship with Holly in Public

Health, who, it turns out, has always wanted to try Pilates. She's still testing all the vials but so far she's found 4 different kinds of poison in them.

As he's talking, his voice fades but I can still see his mouth moving. I feel far away, and when he finally looks into my face, he says, "Darlin', you look greener than a treefrog. Let's get you lying down with a cup of tea."

He helps me to my sunny yellow couch and fluffs a tangerine pillow under my head and covers me with my green velvet blanket, tucking the edges around my body. "You don't worry about a thing, Sugar. I'll go make tea."

He disappears and returns with a tray of tea stuff, but then I remember the story of Buchanan's tea poisoning at his inaugural dinner and I'm can't drink it. I tell Jimmy Tate the story while he sits across from me, one hand across his chest like a shocked matron. "Dear Lord, Darlin', no wonder you look like you're about to crack. This whole thing is just crazy. I didn't know people even killed by poison anymore. I know it was all the rage in the French courts in the 1600's."

"What?"

"Sure. There was the Affair of the Poisons where several people were poisoned and over five years more than four hundred people were arrested and thirty-six were executed— no lie. But who knew it was so popular in our very own country in the 1800's?"

"I guess they skip the poisoning part in high school history class."

"I guess that makes sense. Oh, I almost forgot to tell you, while you were sleeping for four days, we looked further into Caleb Cushing and Judah Benjamin? Here's some of the research."

He hands me a file full of loose papers. I look at the sources. "Wikipedia? You got your information from Wikipedia?"

He shrugs. "That's one of many sources. They were both high up in government, diplomats or congressmen or senators or something like that.

A name catches my eye. "Caleb Cushing's wife was Caroline Elizabeth Archer? I wonder if she's any relation to Father Archer?"

"I don't know, but we did look into any connections between the Freemasons and the Jesuits."

"Who's we?"

"Me, Ava, Bellamy, and Fausto."

"Fausto? That guy is everywhere."

"Well, he is the leading expert. Listen to this." He clears his throat and reads from a paper. "So, Ignatius Loyola, started a group called the Alumbrados in Spain back in the early 1500's. They were essentially the Spanish version of the Illuminati."

"Ignatius Loyola as in the founder of the Jesuits and namesake of Loyola?"

"One and the same. And listen to this little bit:

When a Jesuit of the minor rank is to be elevated to command, he is conducted into the Chapel of the Convent of the Order, where there are only three others present, the principal or Superior standing in front of the altar. On either side stands a monk, one of whom holds a banner of yellow and white, which are the Papal colors, and the other a black banner with a dagger and red cross above a skull and crossbones, with the word inri, and below them the words iustum, necar, reges, impious. The meaning of which is, It is just to exterminate or annihilate impious or heretical Kings, Governments, or Rulers.

I jump up. "Stop the killing of the king. That's it! It's the same thing! Loyola has to be tied up in this. Wait, did you get that off Wikipedia?"

"No," he laughs. "It's from *Congressional Record House Bill 1523* from a 1913 court case."

"Loyola? That makes so much sense. Call Detective Washington."

He hands me my cell phone and takes my tea tray. "You call her. I'll pour us some champagne to celebrate."

By the time Bellamy and Ava arrive we are feeling great, laughing and making plans. I feel so much better it almost seems like old times before the damn monk fell on me. The bell rings again and Detective Washington comes in and I text Winston to come downstairs, too. We waste no time catching up all three of them on our latest discovery.

Winston drops his head in his hands. "I can promise you that Loyola is not involved in any of this. I have worked there for years and never seen anything suspicious or even strange."

"Honey, Caleb Cushing married an Archer. What if Father Archer is related to him? What if he is carrying on the Cushing Brotherhood of Death tradition? And what about your psycho extremists in the faculty, like that guy from The Columns?"

"Gerry Batracho." Jimmy Tate agrees.

"And they always seem to be lurking, following us." Winston seems resolute about Loyola's innocence, which kind of deflates me. I was sure we had cracked the case. I slump over. "You're right Winston, I can't imagine Father Archer doing anything of ill repute. Ever."

Detective Washington stands. "Then he won't mind if we ask him a few questions?"

Winston drops his head in his hands again. "This is my *job*, guys. You can't interfere with my job."

Detective Washington adjusts her holster. "Don't worry Winston. I'll be discreet. I'll question him pertaining to Ellington's safety. He won't object that, and he won't suspect a thing."

"I'm coming," I say, grabbing my hot pink Lux De Ville Bowler bag.

"We're coming too," Bellamy, Ava and Jimmy Tate all say over each other, grabbing their bags.

Detective Washington laughs. "That *will* make him suspicious. Ellington and Winston can come, that won't raise any flags."

Jimmy Tate sighs. "Alright but you have to swear you'll

call as soon as it's all over and let us know what he said."

"Better yet, why don't the three of you make yourselves at home here and wait for us. We won't be long."

Chapter 27

Pepper Smash

Mint, Aquavit, Fresh Lime, Yellow Bell Pepper, Maple Syrup

We walk briskly through the massive oak trees with their branches draped in Spanish moss like ladies at a ball and it smells like a dewy lawn on a summer morning. The grass is moist and squishes under our feet and we can hear children screaming and laughing from the St. Charles playground as we cross the street to Loyola. The campus is lovely, with its stunning cathedral surrounded by a walkway full of gorgeous pointed arches. We walk past the music building and I can smell popcorn and hear the students practicing their opera and I'm even more delighted when I see they are in full costume, walking the non-descript hallways in rich red velvet gowns and capes while singing at full throttle. If we weren't on such a dark mission, I would be feeling quite enchanted.

The Business School is a very different building than the rest of the campus. The outside is some sort of black marble that reflects like a mirror. The air inside the lobby smells like a new car, and I always marvel at the portrait on the wall of a past Dean named Dick because his nose looks exactly like a penis. We ride the pristine elevator up to Father Archer's office and when Detective Washington's phone rings, she says, "I have to get this and ducks into the stairwell to speak privately.

Winston and I look at each other and he sighs. "This is a very bad idea Ell. We're interfering with my livelihood here. There's no way Father Archer is involved."

"Well I'm sure he's not, but I'm also sure he would want to help us in any way he can, right? Maybe he can give us new information without even knowing it."

"What are we going to say to him?"

"Detective Washington won't let you lose your job. Don't worry."

"Ellington, I…"

He is interrupted by a brusque Detective Washington who has barged through the stairwell door, marched to Father Archer's office and entered without knocking.

Man, I love her chutzpah.

When Winston and I follow her in, Father Archer stands up, startled, and says, "Hello? Can I help you?" His demeanor changes when he recognizes us. "Ah Winston and Ellington, welcome. Please come in." He seems a bit confused by the presence of Detective Washington but he doesn't say anything. He just smiles. His office is large and has windows on three sides overlooking the park, the campus, and the cathedral. He has a large glass case against one wall with shelves of antique weapons and a large glass case against the other wall with shelves of religious artifacts. One artifact in particular catches my eye and I can't help but stare at it in horrified fascination. It is a shriveled finger, and I'm reminded of the shrunken head in Madame Banjeau's bedroom. For the life of me I can't figure out why anyone would keep shriveled body parts of dead people anywhere around them. Father Archer sees my horror looking at the finger and he laughs. "It's a relic. It was a gift to me from the Cardinal in Siena. I was his apprentice. How can I help you today?"

Detective Washington is all business. She cuts to the bone immediately. Folding her arms across her chest, she says, "As you know, Ellington just got out of the hospital after being poisoned."

He turns to me and solemnly says, "I heard. I'm so sorry, Ellington. I hope everything is all right now."

I'm about to tell him I'm okay, but Detective Washington interjects, "She's fine now, but she nearly died. And you keep turning up at the most unusual times. So why don't you tell us what's going on?"

Father Archer scrunches his eyebrows together and says in a calm clear voice, "Sounds like you know everything I know."

Just then the door slams open and Gerry Batracho enters. "I heard..." He stops when he sees us.

"Oh," Gerry says, "I didn't know you had people in here. I'll come back." He starts to leave but Detective Washington stops him by shutting the door and standing in front of it with her arms folded so he can't leave.

With words like ice picks, she says, "Mr. Batracho, you were also at The Columns the night Ms. Martini's bag was stolen? Yes?"

He nods.

I watch her put her hands over the weapons on her belt and see her discreetly push a button. "I need both you and Father Archer to come to the station. New evidence has come to our attention regarding your relationship with Mr. Duncan Pike."

I'm wondering what the hell she is doing and Gerry is staring at her with the cold ruthless eyes of an alligator who has spotted his dinner. He slowly shakes his head side-to-side.

Father Archer seems confused. "What relationship? Gerry, what is she talking about?"

Gerry seems to be short-circuiting. If he was a robot he would be turning in circles. He grabs a sharp letter opener off the desk and wields it at all of us like a knife. "Not a chance. I am not going with you anywhere." His hands are shaking a little, but he's remarkably calm. "Do you know who I am? I *run* this city. I was *chosen* to run this city. And that little shit Duncan Pike will not take us down. True bloodline?" He scoffs, spit flying from his mouth. "There's no way that sniveling coward is true blood. Generation after generation of Pikes saved this city, saved this entire country. And he falls in love with some girl and wants to quit? *You don't quit.* You can't quit once you're in. He throws away his future, his family, the greater good of our city for his own selfish whims. What a waste of a human being. I had no choice but to silence him, but he was stronger than I predicted and talked to the snoop over there before I could stop him. I won't be that careless again."

Detective Washington is holding her gun pointed straight at him. "Gerry, put down your weapon."

He lunges at her and manages to knock the gun to the ground. The entire room swoops down on him but he manages to duck away and out the door.

Detective Washington grabs her gun off the ground and takes off after him and on instinct, Father Archer, Winston and I follow. We chase him down the hallway and he turns into a doorway, throws it open and half-tumbles half-runs down the stairwell. He gets back up, his nose bleeding, and continues running out the door into the common area. People are jumping out of the way and police cars are pulling onto the lawn as Gerry makes a sharp turn to run through the Music Building. The opera singers are still floating through the hallways in full costume, singing, as we all come barreling through. They stop singing and jump out of the way, and I can't help but quickly admire one diva's red tiered opera gown. We follow Gerry out into the music courtyard and he tries to climb the steps that will take him to the Gothic arches, but he's slowing down, huffing and puffing.

I stop running because the police have moved over to the top of the music amphitheater and there's a group at the arches too. All have their weapons drawn and they move slowly towards him, yelling at him to raise his hands. He slowly raises his hands above his head, but in a weirdly calm way, like he's making a Y out of his body. They finally grab him and handcuff him.

I stand panting, my hands on my hips, Winston beside me. We look at each other. "I have no idea what just happened," I say.

He laughs, "Me neither. But I think it's good." We wrap our arms around each other's waists and watch Detective Washington get into a patrol car and drive away.

"I think we may have done it, Watson. I think we cracked the case."

We slowly walk home through the park with its pink magnolia flowers lightly bouncing up and down like can-can girls lifting their skirts to reveal their ruffles. I take off my shoes and ground myself by walking barefoot on the damp earth while the turtles silently sun themselves and the smell of honeysuckle and camellias wafts around me. I feel rooted here among these oaks, and the world seems mud luscious, as my old Huckleberry friend ee Cummings would say. Someone has turned on Sidney Bechet's "Preachin' the Blues". I can hear the scratchy, catchy melody in the distance drifting out someone's window. I watch a crane shaking out her white wings, then gracefully folding them while nestling into its large nest, almost in time to the music. "Can we sit down a minute?" I say softly to Winston, not wanting to disturb this moment of peace. I make my way over to a magnificent oak tree with roots big enough to be a kitchen chair. I sit among the roots and Winston sits down next to me. I nestle myself into him, heave a big sigh, and we sit quietly in each other's' arms.

Chapter 28

Singapore Sling

*Gin, Cherry Heering, Benedictine, Cointreau, Orange
and Pineapple Juice, Soda Water*

Detective Washington swings by the next day to fill us in on
the details of the Loyola Crackdown. I serve her a mocktail of
pineapple-cranberry juice in a martini glass with a little
umbrella while she fills us in. Apparently she knew more than
she was telling. She and Detective Boudreau had been
cracking the case all along. They had been watching the
Loyola Business School for some time, suspecting it of shady
work. That's why the FBI had been called in.

Gerry Batracho wasn't working alone. He had enlisted
another professor and even one of his students into his little
crime club. The student was the one who had snatched my
purse and that had sent me the message at Fifi Mahoney's.
Gerry planned to assassinate Senator Sanders at the Rex Ball
in full sight of security and hundreds of people to establish his
power.

"Gerry found a direct descendant of the original secret
society in Duncan Pike. After Pike worked his way up to the
highest level in Skull and Bones at Yale, he returned to New

Orleans for medical school."

I turn to Winston. "There's always a doctor. Remember what Fausto said?"

Winston lets out a long breath.

Detective Washington continues, "Batracho enlisted him into his secret club. At first Pike went along with it, but when he found out that he would have to assassinate someone as his inititation, he tried to get out. Batracho was down in the Quarter that night dressed as a monk passing out wooden medieval coins. He had the colichemarde with him and after a meeting with Pike went south, it appears one of Batracho's accomplices poisoned Pike, but instead of dying, he ran out into the parade. Batracho stabbed him, but Pike still managed to stay alive long enough to talk to you. We don't know if he saw you at the Napolean and followed you down the street or if he spotted you in Jackson Square and recognized you as a friend of his cousin, or if he just stumbled towards a familiar face. In any case, you two are finally safe."

I'd like to believe that.

Chapter 29

Glass Slipper

Vanilla Vodka, Godiva Chocolate Liqueur, Kiss

The next few days are a blur of delirious joy for me as I get primped for the ball. I have moments of sadness over the crazy events of the past few weeks, but I joyously push them away to focus on important stuff like painting my nails. On the big night, I am playing Bessie Smith as I slowly slide black silk stockings from Paris up my legs. I love silk stockings. Winston and I bought them at a divine pink shop near the Louvre called Chantelle. Even the name is glamorous. I had a woman come to my house earlier to curl my hair into Veronica Lake waves. As I fasten my unruly belly into a black corset, I curse Bianca, but when I see how adorable my waist looks two inches smaller, I praise her. I had planned not to wear a corset at all, but my dress has gotten tighter over the past few weeks due to all the banana bread and chocolate croissants I've been eating, so I'm forced to have a little extra help. The dress slides on easily over the corset, and I'm pretty sure I'm going to regret wearing a tight corset for so many hours, but after a few drinks no one will notice if I ditch it. I fluff out my gown, the crimson satin drapes beautifully out from my waist, making it look even smaller. Oh how I do love illusions. I fasten my dripping diamond drop earrings and necklace, pull on my long evening gloves, and spritz my neck with nectarine and honey blossom perfume. I whisk into the room and Winston stops what he's doing and stares at me, exactly the effect a woman wants after dressing for a ball. I twirl for him so he can revel in my beauty, and lift one side of my gown to show off the true show-stopper, my shoes.

I have a rainy day fund for shoes, and I had finally treated myself to a pair of Louboutin Lady Peeptoes with hand-placed crystals and they are truly a work of art. When I lift my dress to unveil one glittering shoe, Winston applauds. I'll be sitting down most of the night with my shoes peeking out, catching the light, and it's a good thing because I can barely walk in them... I have to tiptoe. So in another moment of ballgirl savvy, I slipped a little pair of black ballet flats into my purse for the dancing portion of the evening.

Winston has pulled out our beautiful antique convertible to drive us to the ball. It's a Sunbeam Alpine in bright blue just like the car Grace Kelly drove in *To Catch a Thief*. We pull up to the Rex Ball and the valets say they will keep it out front and keep an eye on it. Winston and I walk up the red carpet, up the grand staircase, and into the opulent ballroom. Golden silk and velvet are draped luxuriously over the walls and ceiling. Triple tiered chandeliers hang down from the fabric and the enormous Rex throne area sits waiting for its royalty. Enormous candelabras are scattered around the ballroom, and Winston and I are seated underneath the most massive glittering chandelier I have ever seen in real life. I feel like I'm sitting under a spectacular sky of stars every time I look up.

The ball begins with the Marine Corps band and then the Rex king and queen are brought in dressed in pure gold with enormous crowns. There are small children wearing golden tunics and capes trimmed in white fur and golden hats with fluffy white plumes standing at least a foot above their heads. They are holding trays with the Rex medallions on them, like ring bearers at a wedding.

After Rex royalty parades around, they present the special guests with the Rex medallions. It's all very formal and posh and sumptuous, but I find my eyes getting heavy and when a yawn escapes, Winston catches me and laughs. He leans over "Do you want my phone to play Solitaire?"

I whisper, "When does Senator Sanders make her entrance?" Winston shrugs, but another guest at the table leans over and says, "Senator Sanders is running late."

People are shooting me dirty looks for whispering so I nod in reply. Aside from all the drama, and me basically saving her life, I'm really excited to see Senator Sanders in person. I've been a fan of hers for years.

I watch a masked Rex man walking with a group of people for the Grand March and first dance. I do love to watch people dance, but I'm pretty sure my lipstick is fading, so before I head to the dance floor myself, I excuse myself and head to the powder room. When I open my purse to get my lipstick, I notice my phone has vibrated. Phones aren't allowed out in the ballroom since there are no photos allowed, but I've noticed more than a few people discreetly checking the insides of their pockets or purses and tapping away. I read a text while applying my Ruby Slipper lipstick. It's one of my few talents—applying lipstick without looking in the mirror. *It's Detective Washington. Meet me upstairs right away.*

Upstairs? I didn't know this place had an upstairs. Perplexing. Why would Detective Washington be texting me *here*? Unless, *unless* there was some sort of emergency and she didn't want to make a scene by pulling me out. If Detective Washington needs me, then Senator Sanders probably needs me, and that's the same as my country needing me, and when duty calls, Ellington Martini answers.

I consider walking back to the table to tell Winston to come with me, but my dogs are barking already, even though we've been sitting all night, and the thought of traipsing all the way to the table and back upstairs deters me. I'll just pop up there quickly.

I find the door leading to the stairs and I can hear music and distant applause, and I'm thinking they keep these stairways awfully dirty for a hotel. I finally realize while most of the hotel is new, the ballroom section is the historical part and the upstairs really is an attic of sorts where they store things. It's dimly lit by the streetlights outside and I can see the outline of large covered pieces of furniture like hulking ghosts all around me.

How odd that Detective Washington would want to meet here. I can't wait till we're really good friends and I can call her by her first name, Tula. I love that name. I think that's a perfect name for my next kitten or puppy or horse…

Just then I feel a hand cover my mouth and something hard presses into my back. Before I can even think, my Bartitsu training from the other night comes into play and I stomp one sharp heel into the attacker's toe while elbowing him hard in the gut. I hear a grunt and a yelp and I run behind a large white ghost as far from my attacker as possible.

Everything is silent for what seems like a long time and the more I try to breathe silently, the louder I seem to get. Whoever is in here is either holding still as a statue or moving silent as a cat. I can't see a way out except the door I came in which is blocked by whomever attacked me. I don't even know if it's more than one person. I see the outline of a square in the floor beside me and I'm thinking it might lead to an air conditioning duct or could be a laundry chute or an old dumbwaiter… I'm just hoping it's something, anything, to get me out of here. It has an iron handle on top and I pry it open with a loud thunk. Shit. I look down it and see it's actually a trap door into the ceiling right above the ballroom. It's connected to the huge chandelier above our table. I hear the procession music. Oh no, if they are bringing out Senator Sanders right now, she could really be in trouble.

Something smashes to the floor and I hear a skitter. *Please don't let that be a rodent.* Please oh please! If a rat comes near me I will not be able to stay in hiding, I don't care how many murderers there are running around this attic. Fucking footsteps! And not just regular footsteps but the scariest kind: limp-drag footsteps. Maybe I injured him with my stomp.

I realize the sharp heels of my Louboutins make an excellent weapon and I silently slide them off. They catch a moonbeam and sparkle, like the most beautiful north star. I make a quick silent wish: please let me get out of here alive. I readjust them in both hands for full-force. Wouldn't that be cool if there were little daggers in these heels? Or tiny derringers in the heels? And everyone said I was a fool for buying $5,000 shoes! Ha! My heart is pounding right out of my ribcage, no easy feat in this tight-ass corset. Breathe, Ellington.

These bastards have no idea who they are dealing with. They think I'm some soft cream puff they can easily squash but they have another thing coming. I hear footsteps getting closer and closer. I take a deep breath. OK I admit it, I'm scared. But no fear! I feel my strength gathering as I picture me stepping out from behind this cabinet in full sparkling-nunchuck glory. My spinning shoes would blind the villains with their dazzle. I'm like that crouched golden panther from Cartier stalking its prey.

Damn I wish I had a swirling cape I could disappear into right now. But I don't. So here goes. I jump out from my hiding place with my shoes in my hands yelling, "Bring it on!" But all I see is Uncle Beau. Now I'm really confused. "Uncle Beau?" I whisper. "You need to hide. There's a killer in this attic."

He says, "I know," and I see he's holding a gun.

I'm so relieved. "Oh good! You're armed. I'll get behind you." I'm about to run over and hide behind him, but he seems to be pointing the weapon at me. Now I'm really confused. He steps and I see he's limping. "Uncle Beau? How? What? I don't believe it. You're not a villain."

He smiles at me. "Of course I'm not, Ellington, I'm one of the good guys. And that's the problem, here. I have an ethical conundrum. I don't want to hurt anyone, but people keep getting in the way and have to be removed. Take you, for example. You just wouldn't quit poking your nose where it didn't belong. And worst of all, you're a writer, and I can't have you rewriting our history. It's too important. Your writing would blow the lid off everything I've built, everything my ancestors built."

In a moment of inspiration, I hurl my shoe at him as hard as possible. He tries to block it, but the heel hits him in the face. Bullseye! My little league pitching skills rock! The only way out that I can see is the trapdoor. I'm going to have go for it and hope I land somewhere soft.

I don't even hesitate as I lower myself through the trapdoor and slide down the chandelier just like I did when I played Peasblossom. People scream as the chandelier swings dangerously back and forth across the ballroom. It's a long drop and going to cause some serious damage if the chain breaks. I hang on for dear life. Damn I have always dreamed of coming out of the ceiling on a swing, surrounded by bubbles, but this is not what I had in mind! "Stop!" I scream. I'm barely heard among the screams and shouts of the people below me who don't know whether to run to safety from the heavy chandelier or stay where they are to catch me should I fall.

"Stop the procession!" I scream again, but no one can hear me, and it doesn't matter anyway. There will be no procession as long as there's a woman dangling dangerously on a chandelier in the middle of the room. I look for our table and spot Winston staring at me dumbfounded. He jumps to his feet, rushing to save me. I hear sirens as security rushes forward and they all stare up at me, trying to figure out how to safely get me down. Maybe handsome firefighters will bring a trampoline for me to jump on and I'll do a triple back flip from my circus days and everyone will applaud. Except I could never even do one back flip.

I can't think anymore because the molding of the ceiling

holding the chandelier is starting to crack.

Oh shitake mushrooms.

It can handle the weight but not the swinging. I cling to the chain as it drops dangerously and then stops, causing me to spin. I look for Winston to yell my last words to him. I know this is the end. But several men have joined forces to form four makeshift catchers for me, holding onto each other's forearms just like cheerleaders when they throw up the top of the pyramid and catch them over and over. Winston's group has my massive velvet cape between them, forming a nice little basket for me to fall into. They all start yelling for me to jump before the chandelier falls. They can't catch me if the chandelier falls under me, plus survival is unlikely.

I can think of nothing better at this moment than sinking into velvet, so I lean with my weight to make the chandelier swing where I want it to go. I lower myself quickly to a metal arm as the chandelier drops another few feet. Now everyone is frantically screaming and I see the firefighters and police officers swarming the ballroom as I swing backward one last time, swing forward and catapult my body towards my velvet cape and the strong loving arms of Winston. I know it should feel scary, but it feels wonderful to fly through the air and Ha! I *knew* those trapeze lessons would come in handy one day. The men catch me in my cape, although I do hear Winston grunt with the effort. I am so happy I am safe I erupt into tears as they gently lay me down. My leap and the change in weight has caused the chandelier to swing the other direction and lose its attachment to the ceiling. It crashes to the floor in a glorious smashing explosion of shattering crystal turning rainbow colors under the lights. It's beautiful and sad and dangerous, kind of like my life at the moment.

Winston kneels and puts his hands on my face. "Are you all right?"

I nod as I say, "Call Tula! Uncle Beau is upstairs in the attic and he's the killer."

"She already knows. The police are up there right now."

"She's incredible. You're my hero. I love you." I wrap my arms around him, but when I hug him every bone in my body hurts. Maybe dropping from a chandelier wasn't the best idea. I lay back on my cape, bury my head in its softness, and the next time I open my eyes I'm on a bed in an ambulance wrapped in a blanket.

Winston squeezes my hand. "The paramedics did a check and gave you thumbs up. You'll be sore for a few days, but I think it really *is* over now." He helps me out of the ambulance and we sit down on the steps for a few minutes. People in black tie are milling around everywhere.

Jimmy Tate, Bellamy, and Ava come galloping up. "We came as soon as we heard. My god, Ellington, this is all crazy." They sit down next to us on the steps.

The police captain saunters over to me. "Well if it isn't Ellington Martini again. We have to stop meeting like this, My Dear. I'm going to have to start carrying your books around with me for an autograph for our next run-in."

Detective Washington is right behind him. "All clear, Ms. Martini. Beauregard Pike is in custody now, and hopefully that's the end of the all this business." She sits down by me. "I'm impressed by you," she says, tipping her hat before she walks back to her patrol car.

I sigh happily.

I see Grandpa Boogie with his walking stick talking to a group of formally dressed ladies. He's making them laugh, and then he starts circling his hips, which makes them laugh even harder. He turns to look at me and winks and waves.

"What's Ed doing here?"

Winston says, "He was out here when we came out."

I lay my head on Winston's shoulder. "Take me home and to bed?"

"There nothing I'd rather do more."

Acknowledgements

Gratitude List:

Annabelle and Henry – my deepest truest every moment miracles.

George for being the Nick to my Nora.

Marlise and Maria for being the hoes in my Garden Club, the lanterns in the dark forest, forever lighting my way.

My Martini Club for all our Hot and Dirty nights of laughter and hot pink martini socks.

For Mom and Dad for being my lighthouses (even though I asked you how you liked my book and you said "what book?" and I reminded you of the manuscript I had sent you and you said "Oh yeah, we started it, it's here somewhere.") (It's ok, you're 80.)

To the rest of my enormous family (all 55 of you and counting!) thank you for the endless laughter and rocking dance parties—I cherish every moment.

Monk, Bootsy, Ella, and Dizzy for keeping my feet and heart warm.

My New Orleans Peeps Flora, Ashley, and Grandpa Boogie for all the adventures.

New Orleans Cathy Weeks—your eye for beauty inspired so much of this book.

Chuck E. Weiss for being the best goddam liar I ever had the good fortune to meet.

Sharon—my insanely glamorous partner-in-crime who lifted the veil of New Orleans and took me to all the insider spots, many of which appear here.

Greg Sarris for the enthusiastic encouragement of my writing all those years ago.

Stanford OWC—especially Joshua Mohr and Aldebaran for guiding me and cheering me through every chapter.

Cuchi Cuchi for so many fabulous vintage cocktail recipes.

Rik Hall and Wild Seas Formatting for making the mundane magical.

Rocket Sapphire my soul sister for believing in me always.

Michelle Finamore: you are the bees knees.

Jimmy Raye, Coco, Tristan and Cathryn for wrapping me in Boston glamour and laughter so I didn't die when I left NOLA.

Courtney Nelson and Mary Ellen Courtney: you are the cats pajamas.

The magical ones who lit my path: you know who you are.

And my beloved New Orleans.

About the Author

Marci Darling is a sassy bon vivant whose previous careers include: belly dancer, showgirl, circus acrobat, burlesque dancer, and preschool teacher. She has performed around the world and lived in Paris, Florence, Hollywood, New Orleans and Boston. She has written for multiple publications and holds degrees from UCLA and Harvard. She lives in a cottage by the sea with her magical family: two kids, two cats, two dogs, and one husband.

Made in the USA
Middletown, DE
13 November 2016